The truth is like surgery: it hurts but cures.
Lies are like painkillers: they give you
instant relief but have many side effects.

—Based on a quote by Han Suyin

The Hidden Gate
A Fallen Petal
Double Trouble
Whispering Bells
Where Time Stood Still
The Weight of Years

Savannah Secrets

The Weight of Years

DeAnna Julie Dodson

Guideposts
Danbury, Connecticut

Published by Guideposts Books & Inspirational Media
100 Reserve Road, Suite E200
Danbury, CT 06810
Guideposts.org

Cover and interior design by Müllerhaus
Cover illustration by Pierre Droal, represented by Deborah Wolfe, LTD.
Typeset by Aptara, Inc.

Printed and bound in the United States of America
10 9 8 7 6 5 4 3 2 1

Chapter One

"We're pretty full this afternoon," Julia Foley said, surveying the graceful elegance of the Savannah Historical Society's meeting room. With its lush draperies and tall white columns, intricately carved crown molding and gleaming parquet floor, it made her feel as if she were in the ballroom of a grand estate house before the Civil War. Her reflection in one of the pier glass mirrors made her almost wish that she had her silver hair swept up into a chignon and was wearing a dove-colored gown that would make her gray eyes sparkle—instead of her practical pink knit top, linen jacket, and black slacks.

Her friend and business partner, Meredith Bellefontaine, looked the room over too and nodded her curly blond head. "It's not every month the society gets to hear Miss Charlotte Lockwood speak."

"It's not every month *anybody* gets to hear Miss Charlotte Lockwood speak. Beatrice really outdid herself getting her to come."

"She did. And she won't hesitate to tell us about it either."

"Anyway, I don't blame Miss Charlotte for not getting out much anymore. If I were nearly ninety, I wouldn't do anything but exactly what I felt like doing."

"We've got another twenty-five years before we have to worry about that," Meredith said. "Who knows what we'll be up to by then?"

Julia started to answer and then turned her attention to the podium as Beatrice Enterline, the head of the historical society, began to speak.

"Good afternoon, ladies and gentlemen," she said, her hazel eyes bright with triumph. "I am sure that all of you have heard about the Alice Delorme Lockwood Foundation for Children, a foundation that has done so much to bring hope and happiness to Savannah's children since 1905. This afternoon, I am delighted to present to you one of Savannah's most celebrated citizens, the owner of the historic Delorme Estate and director for the past seventy years of the Lockwood Foundation, Miss Charlotte Delorme Lockwood."

As the applause sounded, Beatrice stepped away from the podium, and Miss Charlotte stepped forward, leaning on an ebony walking stick and on the arm of a stout, middle-aged black woman. Miss Charlotte was small and elegant, her back as straight as her cane, her carriage as regal as any queen. Despite her years, her face was nearly unlined and her skin was luminous over the fine bones of her face and the blue veins of her hands. Her hair was white as snow and lay in a coiled braid on top of her head. It must have gone quite past her waist when it was down. It looked all the whiter set off by the pure black of the simple, full-skirted dress she wore. A string of large, but not too large, pearls with matching earrings completed the picture, gracious, exquisite, and unyielding.

She stood with a slight smile on her face, waiting for the applause to die down, and then she stepped closer to the microphone.

"Thank you very much," she said, her voice stronger than Julia would have expected, marked with the soft edges of a Southern accent and with only the slightest quaver of age in it. "And my thanks to Mrs. Enterline for her kind invitation to speak to you all today. If you have been in Savannah long, you have most likely heard of the Lockwood Foundation. We are quite proud of our accomplishments for over a century in finding homes for children who have none. We have a long history of making resources available for those who are looking into the possibility of adoption or who have already opened their homes and hearts to these precious little ones. When we help bring a child into a family, that is only the beginning of the foundation's work. From that first moment, the Lockwood Foundation is there to see that the newly blended family grows stronger with each passing year."

Julia looked over at Meredith. So far this sounded like the beginning of an appeal for donations.

"But, as generous as Savannah has been in supporting our work," Miss Charlotte continued, "I am reminded that I am here this afternoon to talk not about the present or the future but the past. My great-grandmother, Alice Delorme Lockwood, was born on the Delorme Estate in 1859." She smiled mischievously. "That was a very long time ago, even for me. She was raised in the war, as she liked to say, and lived all her life in a struggle of one kind or other. She outlived her family, her husband, her son, and her grandson, my father. My parents died when I was very young and my grandparents well before then, but Grandmama brought me up in the great tradition of the Delormes, teaching me what it meant to bear the name and the duties that came with it. I remember her in the days before she died. She was ninety years old then, a milestone I will soon reach, and still running the estate and the foundation to suit herself."

For the next twenty minutes, Miss Charlotte spoke of the things her great-grandmother had told her about Savannah of the 1860s and '70s, of the Civil War and of Reconstruction, of how society changed, sometimes painfully, over time, of innovations and setbacks, bitter conflicts and eventual understanding. Her voice grew stronger as she went on, and the light in her pale blue eyes seemed to intensify as she told Alice's story, much of it Savannah's story, to her rapt audience.

"Then," she said at last, "the summer I turned eighteen, she sat me down and told me she was placing the estate, the foundation, and the honor of the name into my hands. How she knew it was time, I don't know, but it was only six hours later that she went to sleep in the sun on the back veranda and never woke up." She glanced back at the black woman who was sitting behind her, who had watched her protectively, almost anxiously, the whole while she spoke. "My dear Brenda is here. It was her grandmother, Hannah, who found Grandmama and came to tell me she was gone. And when I went to her, she looked sweetly at rest, and I knew she had made her peace."

By then, Julia felt a pang of loss. It was not only for Alice Lockwood, but for all she had known and done in her long life. For all those things that people now could read about and have told to them but would never really know, not in the same way Alice had known them. Or the same way Miss Charlotte knew them now. Before long, even her memories would be buried under the weight of years.

"One day soon, I will also have to pass on the estate and the foundation," Miss Charlotte said in closing, "but they will both continue on in memory of, and in the tradition of, Alice Delorme Lockwood, for the love of Savannah and its children."

She stood there for a moment, nodding in gracious acknowledgment of the audience's applause, but she seemed to wilt a little, sinking into herself, the animation of her storytelling gone. Brenda, her assistant, came up beside her and took her arm, helping her to a chair as Beatrice came back to the podium.

"Thank you so much, Miss Charlotte, for that wonderful talk. Did y'all enjoy that?"

The applause swelled, and Miss Charlotte nodded her appreciation, looking too spent to do more.

"Would you like Miss Charlotte to come back?" Beatrice asked, and again there was applause.

"How amazing that must have been," Meredith told Julia quietly. "Actually talking to someone who lived through the Civil War and everything that came afterward."

"Miss Charlotte is quite a speaker," Julia whispered back as Beatrice thanked her guest, reminded everyone to give generously to the Lockwood Foundation, and then moved on to the business portion of the meeting. "She must really rake in the donations for her charity."

"I bet."

"I don't know if she'll remember me from the fundraiser she spoke at last year, but I'd love to say hello to her again."

"Do you know Miss Lockwood?" an unfamiliar voice asked.

Julia and Meredith both turned to the young woman sitting behind them.

"I really enjoyed her talk," the woman continued, a light in her golden-brown eyes. "Do you think they'd let me meet her? I wouldn't keep her long, but I'd love to say hello to her."

Julia smiled. "If she stays after the meeting," she said, keeping her voice low, "I'm going to say hello. Would you like to come with me?"

The woman's blond spiral curls bounced with the enthusiastic nodding of her head.

Fortunately for everyone, Beatrice kept the boring parts of the meeting short and to the point, and soon it was dismissed. Several people made a beeline toward Miss Charlotte.

"We'd better hurry if we're going to get a chance to talk to her," Julia said. "She already looks worn out."

"Thanks for letting me go with you," the young woman said, getting to her feet. She couldn't have been more than two or three inches over five feet tall. "My name's Jaden Browning."

Julia shook her hand. "I'm Julia Foley. This is my friend and business partner, Meredith Bellefontaine."

"Good to meet you," Meredith said, shaking Jaden's hand too. "Do you live in Savannah?"

They walked toward where Miss Charlotte was sitting. Beatrice was standing over her, chattering away, no doubt gushing over how lovely it was to have the head of the Lockwood Foundation speak at her own little old historical society.

"Dallas, actually," Jaden said. "I'm getting my degree in journalism at UTD."

"UTD?" Meredith asked.

"The University of Texas at Dallas. I still have a semester to go, but I heard about Miss Lockwood speaking here today, and I thought I'd take a chance and come hear her."

Julia raised her eyebrows. "That's a long way to come only for a twenty-minute talk, isn't it?"

"Well, yes and no." Jaden's grin wrinkled the dusting of freckles on her nose. "I was assigned to do a paper on her foundation in one of my classes a little while back, and I've been interested in her ever since. She'd know better than anybody what Alice Lockwood was like, and not trying to be grim or anything, but she's nearly ninety. She's not going to be around forever. If anybody's going to write a real book about Alice Lockwood and the foundation, it's got to be done pretty soon."

"So you came not for the talk but for the introduction."

Jaden nodded. "But it was a wonderful talk, wasn't it? Maddening though. Just enough to whet my appetite. There's so much I'd like to know. I mean, she's actually spoken to somebody who lived back then."

The corners of Meredith's mouth turned up. Julia knew they both understood Jaden's excitement and her desire to salvage whatever was left of Alice Lockwood's tales and Miss Charlotte's memories of them.

They had to wait only a few more minutes for their turn to talk to Miss Charlotte, thanks to a minor crisis on the other side of the room that demanded Beatrice's attention. Beatrice excused herself, but by then Miss Charlotte looked exhausted. Still, she smiled serenely and welcomed Julia, Meredith, and Jaden to sit by her.

"Of course I remember you, Mrs. Foley. You helped raise a good deal of money for the foundation, and I am very grateful."

"I was happy to help. And, please, do call me Julia. This is my friend, Meredith Bellefontaine."

"Mrs. Bellefontaine," Miss Charlotte said with a nod. "I met your husband several years ago. Please accept my condolences on his passing."

Meredith looked surprised and touched. "Thank you. I didn't realize you knew him. I miss him very much, but my memories are happy."

Jaden looked at Julia expectantly.

"And this is Jaden Browning," Julia told Miss Charlotte. "We just met her, but she enjoyed your talk so much, she was hoping you wouldn't mind if we introduced her to you."

"I didn't like to barge up here and start talking," Jaden said.

"Very polite of you, Miss Browning." Miss Charlotte wasn't quite smiling, but she looked indulgent. "So many these days, young and old, never take thought for the niceties."

"No, ma'am," Jaden said. "I guess they don't much anymore. But I think it's only right to show respect."

Miss Charlotte seemed pleased with that.

"And did you enjoy our little talk, Miss Browning?" she asked, and then her assistant came up beside her and touched her forearm lightly.

"We don't want to overdo, Miss Charlotte, I'm sure."

Miss Charlotte patted her hand fondly. "No, Brenda, I suppose we don't. I hope you ladies will excuse us."

Brenda helped her to her feet and gave her her cane.

"Oh," Jaden breathed.

Miss Charlotte turned back to her, one silvery eyebrow raised.

"Oh, no, I'm sorry, ma'am," Jaden said, her face turning a little pink. "I know you must be tired, but I had really hoped I could talk to you for a few minutes. After coming all this way, I mean."

"From where did you come?" Miss Charlotte asked.

"From Dallas. I'm in school there. Journalism. I was really hoping…" She trailed off under Brenda's disapproving stare. "I know you're tired. I'm so glad to have met you anyway. Thank you. I really enjoyed your talk."

"Thank you. It means a great deal to me to hear that. Was there something specific you wished to talk about, Miss Browning?"

Jaden glanced at Julia, and then turned again to Miss Charlotte. "I want to write a book."

The almost-breathless admission brought a twinkle to the older woman's eye.

"Do you now? What sort of a book?"

"About Alice Lockwood and her foundation. I mean I want to write about you both, since she raised you and you took over her work after she died." Jaden managed a tremulous smile. "You know so much about her, I was hoping you would let me write it all down before it's too late." She caught a quick breath and put one hand over her mouth. "I mean, uh, before I have to go back home and—"

"You mean while I'm still around to tell you about her."

That twinkle was still in Miss Charlotte's eye.

"Oh, ma'am—"

"No need to get all flustered. Truth is truth. I know how old I am, and I know I'm on the wrong end of a long life." Miss Charlotte put one finger under Jaden's chin and tilted up her face. "I think a book would be a fine idea. What I remember of Grandmama should not be lost once I'm gone. What do you expect to make from writing this sort of book? Or maybe it's the fame you're after."

Jaden's blush deepened. "Oh, no, ma'am. I know historical biographies usually aren't bestsellers. I don't mind that. But everything your great-grandmother told you firsthand about her life, I would hate for that all to be lost."

"So you're going to write it just because of that?"

Jaden nodded.

"And you don't expect any money from it?"

"Not in particular, no."

"And what if I said I would grant you whatever interviews you'd like, as they fit into my schedule, of course, on the condition that you would donate the proceeds to my foundation?"

Again Jaden nodded, this time with a touch of a smile on her face. "I'd like that."

Julia glanced over at Meredith, sure her partner was as surprised by the exchange as she was.

Miss Charlotte looked the young woman over coolly. "And you get nothing out of it but the satisfaction of having done it?"

"Well, there is one thing," Jaden admitted.

Again, Miss Charlotte raised one fine brow.

"I was hoping to use it for my master's thesis too. I mean if you wouldn't mind." Jaden's expression was touched with a sudden bit of mischief. "I'm not sure if I want to be a novelist or work for one of the big papers when I'm through with school, but having my name on a book cover sure wouldn't hurt either way."

Miss Charlotte laughed softly. "I think that would be the least you should get from it." She patted Jaden's shoulder. "Well, not to worry. If I were to guess, I'd say we could work out between us more equitable terms than that. Brenda, would you please give Miss Browning one of my cards? And if she will be kind enough to call sometime tomorrow afternoon, I'm sure you will be able to find a time that would be mutually convenient for both of us to have a pleasant talk about Grandmama."

"Yes, Miss Charlotte," Brenda said, "as soon as you sit back down here and rest yourself."

She helped the older lady get comfortable once more and then dug in her purse for a business card.

"If you'd call sometime tomorrow afternoon, Miss Browning," Brenda said, handing Jaden the card, "I'll be able to check Miss Charlotte's schedule for you."

"Oh, thank you," Jaden said, clutching the card against her heart.

"If either of you would like to join us, Mrs. Bellefontaine, Mrs. Foley," Miss Charlotte said, "you're both very welcome. I understand you both were born and raised here in Savannah. Maybe you can help me keep my facts in order when I have to answer the young lady's questions and not just rattle off what I memorized for my speech."

"Oh, we'd love to," Julia said. "We stay pretty busy of course, but we have room in our schedule, don't we?" She looked at Meredith questioningly.

"We can certainly check. I know I'd love to come."

"Before the meeting began, Meredith and I were saying how wonderful it would be to know more of what your great-grandmother's life was like."

"I know you have a lot more you could tell about her than you could in only the few minutes they gave you here at the meeting," Meredith added.

"We're agreed then," Miss Charlotte said, and she laid her hand on Brenda's sturdy arm. "Please give each of these ladies my card."

"Yes, Miss Charlotte."

"I'm thinking now that a nice luncheon at home would be agreeable to all of us," Miss Charlotte said as Brenda handed out two more of her cards. "Would all of you enjoy that?"

"Oh, yes, please," Jaden said, clasping her hands together.

"Very well then. If you will each give your telephone number to Brenda, we'll be able to settle things easily."

Brenda took down their numbers and put the slip of paper into the small planning journal she carried with her.

"Now," Miss Charlotte said, "I will discuss the matter with Brenda this afternoon, and she will call each of you tomorrow to see if the time we choose will serve. Good afternoon."

With her ebony cane and Brenda's assistance, Miss Charlotte stood and made her way out of the room.

"Wow," Jaden said, her hands still clasped together with the business card between them. "Oh wow. It's almost like talking to Alice Lockwood herself."

"It is a little, isn't it?" Julia said. "She does have that effect on people."

"Thank you so much," Jaden gushed. "I would never have gotten to talk to her, and I especially wouldn't have gotten invited to lunch at the Delorme Estate, if you hadn't introduced us."

"I didn't expect we'd be invited too," Meredith said. "I've visited the estate before, only the places that are open to the public, of course, and I've seen the grape arbors and the fields of vegetables and soybeans, but I never thought I'd actually be invited for lunch there."

"I didn't know Miss Charlotte knew Ron before he died," Julia said. "Or that she knew he died."

She looked at the card Brenda had given her. It was as elegant as the woman whose name it bore, black raised script on slightly off-white linen cardstock with Miss Charlotte's contact information and, in the lower left corner, a faint etching of the front of the Delorme Estate, Corinthian columns and all.

"Miss Charlotte may not get out much," Meredith said, "but it sounds to me like she keeps track of everything that happens in Savannah. I hadn't thought about it for years, but now I remember Ron did do some work for her. Background check on someone she wanted to hire, if I remember right."

"Oh really? Hire to do what?"

Meredith frowned. "I can't remember now. There's probably some record in the office. We'll check it out."

"I want to thank you both again," Jaden said. "This is *so* exciting, I can hardly stand it. I've got to go find something to wear when we have lunch at the Delorme Estate."

With a soft little shriek, Jaden hurried away.

Meredith smiled and shook her head. "At least we've made somebody ecstatically happy today."

"She's cute, isn't she, with that curly hair and turned-up nose? I was a kind of surprised, though, when she agreed to Miss Charlotte's terms about the book. She'll be doing all that work writing it and get nothing for it."

Meredith shrugged. "Well, if she can use it for her thesis as well as a start in the writing business, that might not be such a bad deal in the long run."

"Yeah, that would be okay, if that's all she's after."

"Oh, don't be so suspicious of everybody. She's interested in history, and Miss Charlotte is certainly worth talking to about it, especially about Savannah history. Besides, without her, we wouldn't be having lunch at the Delorme Estate."

Meredith imitated Jaden's soft little squeal, and Julia laughed.

"I suppose not, but if we weren't—"

"Who's having lunch at the Delorme Estate?" Beatrice asked as she rushed over to them, her penciled brows almost lost in her short black hair. "Meredith, dear, you really must tell me." She heaved a dramatic sigh. "I see Miss Charlotte is gone now, and I didn't get a chance to give her a proper thank-you. Maybe I should call her."

"I wouldn't," Meredith said. "Not today anyway. I think she was really tired out."

"Maybe so," Beatrice said, chewing her lip. "Maybe so. If I hadn't had to settle an argument about the Historical Society Christmas party—"

"Was it that important?"

Beatrice put her hands on her hips. "Meredith Bellefontaine, you were the president of the society only last year. You know we nearly disbanded over whether we were having a live tree or an artificial one!"

Julia stifled a giggle.

Meredith rolled her eyes. "One of the reasons I'm very glad that, this year, you are president of the Savannah Historical Society and I'm not."

Beatrice pursed her lips. "So who's lunching at the Delorme Estate? That girl you were talking to?"

"She and Miss Charlotte talked about it," Julia said, leaving out that she and Meredith had also been invited. "But they didn't set an actual date or anything. It's something about a paper she wants to write for a class she's taking."

"I ought to give her a call," Beatrice said, taking a pen and paper from her purse. "If she's writing about dear Savannah, there's no better place for her to start than with Savannah's own historical society. Did you get her number?"

"I'm afraid not. Miss Charlotte's assistant took her number and is supposed to call her later."

"I suppose I'll just have to speak to Brenda tomorrow and find out what she knows. I need to talk to her anyway about when Miss Charlotte can come speak here again. Everyone loved her, didn't you think?" Beatrice patted Julia's and Meredith's shoulders. "Now you both excuse me, please. I have got to go talk to Marilyn Simmons before she leaves about the hors d'oeuvres she's got planned for next month's meeting."

With a little flutter of her fingers, she hurried away.

Julia and Meredith shook their heads at each other and then walked out to Julia's car.

"Back to the office?" Meredith asked as they got in.

"I thought we could see what we can find about the work Ron did for Miss Charlotte. I'm curious."

"Sure. I'm curious too. It was probably something that was settled years ago one way or another."

"Yeah, probably."

They buckled up and headed toward the yellow Victorian that housed Magnolia Investigations, the private investigation agency that had been run by Meredith's husband until his death two years ago.

"I hope Brenda doesn't say anything to Beatrice about us being invited to that lunch too," Julia said as she turned on to Whitaker Street, and she glanced over at Meredith. "Beatrice would only try to—"

"Look out!" Meredith cried.

Julia slammed on her brakes.

Chapter Two

Julia exhaled heavily as the long-legged tabby cat blinked at her and then darted across the street.

"I didn't see it. Oh man. I guess I'm awake now."

"And everything in my purse is on the floorboard," Meredith said.

"Oh, I'm sorry. I should have been watching the road instead of looking over at you."

Meredith sighed. "I don't think it would have made any difference in this case. It just ran out from between those two cars."

Julia started down the street once more. "I'm glad I didn't hit it. That would be too awful."

"Be careful," Meredith said, trying to scoop up the lipstick that had rolled under her seat. "Sometimes they run right back out—"

With a gasp, Julia jammed her foot down on the brake again. This time there was the squeal of brakes and a decided thump.

"Oh no." She squeezed her eyes shut, trying not to cry. "I didn't want that to happen."

She and Meredith both threw off their seat belts and got out of the car. The cat was lying on its side, open-mouthed and panting.

"At least it's not dead," Meredith said. "And I don't see any blood."

"It might have some internal injuries." Julia looked up and down the street. "Do you suppose it belongs to someone who lives here?"

"I don't see a collar. It might be microchipped though."

"We've got to get it to the vet." Julia reached toward the cat, and it hissed at her in return and then growled low in its throat. "Maybe I'd better not try to pick it up."

"We need to get a box or something," Meredith said, "so we can move it without hurting it. And so it'll feel more secure."

"There's a box in my back seat with some sweaters I was going to donate. Why don't you get it, and we can try to make the cat a place it'll feel safe in."

The cat tried to get up when Meredith came toward it with the box, but its back legs wouldn't cooperate. All it could do was hiss and growl warnings as Julia and Meredith managed to put it into the sweater-padded box and close the lid.

"If you can keep it in there till we can get to the vet," Julia said, "I think we'll be okay."

Meredith carried the box to the car, and then Julia held it while Meredith got in and buckled up. Then she settled the box in Meredith's lap. The cat let out a mournful howl.

"We're hurrying," Julia promised, and she hurried around to the driver's side of the car and drove away.

There was a veterinary hospital a few buildings away from the office, and it took her only a minute or two to get there. The cat wailed the whole way.

"It sounds awful," Julia said, not taking her eyes off what she was doing as she pulled into a parking place. "It must really be hurt."

"I don't know," Meredith said. "It could be it's just upset to be riding in a car. I know my cat doesn't like it."

Julia turned off the engine and hurried over to take the box from Meredith.

"You go on inside," Meredith said. "I have to pick up the things from my purse, but I'll be right in."

The hospital was in a peach-colored two-story antebellum home with a curved front and tall white columns and didn't look hospital-like at all, but the inside was full of a variety of animal patients who, along with their owners, stared at the howling box Julia carried.

"I accidentally hit this cat with my car," she told the girl at the front desk. "Somebody needs to help it right away."

"Is the cat a patient here?"

"I don't know. It's not my cat, but it needs help."

The girl picked up the phone and punched an inside line. "Is there a doctor available for an emergency?" She paused and then said, "I'll bring it back."

She hung up and then stood to take the box from Julia, offering her a clipboard in exchange.

"I'll take the cat back. You'll need to fill out this paperwork."

"But—"

The girl vanished through the door behind her desk, and with a sigh, Julia sank into a chair.

"What did they say?" Meredith asked, looking over Julia's shoulder at the clipboard when she came into the waiting room.

"Nothing yet. They just took the cat back. I told her it wasn't my cat. I don't know if they'll refuse to treat it or what. I guess they'll tell us. Maybe they'll tell us if it's a boy or a girl too. I hate calling it an it."

"I'm sure they will," Meredith said, still looking at the clipboard. "Looks like part of that form says you'll accept financial responsibility."

Julia scanned it quickly. "Exactly. Maybe I'd better see what they say first."

"They're not going to throw it back into the street, you know."

"No, I suppose not, but I'm sure they can't afford to treat animals for free either. I guess they'll make sure it's not in pain, but I wouldn't want them to put it down simply because it's hurt and nobody will pay to get it taken care of." Julia's throat tightened. "It was my fault in the first place."

"No it wasn't. I don't know why some animals do that, run in front of a car and then run right back the other way." Meredith squeezed her hand. "Anyway, it's not your fault. Maybe it'll be all right anyway."

"It can't walk. Maybe its back is broken. Oh, I hate this."

"Now, don't start assuming things you don't know. Cats are pretty resilient. Let's wait till the doctor has had a chance to look at it."

Julia went ahead and filled out the form, financial responsibility and all. Then she and Meredith waited. The next few minutes seemed like hours, but the girl finally came back to the waiting area.

"The doctor would like to see you." She took the clipboard and led Julia and Meredith to an examination room. "If you'll wait here, he'll be right with you."

The doctor was a tall, thin man, younger than Julia expected. He was carrying an X-ray.

"I'm Dr. Preston," he said, shaking hands with both women and then looking at them expectantly.

"I'm Julia Foley, and this is Meredith Bellefontaine. We have an office down the street, Magnolia Investigations."

"Ah. I've seen the sign."

"Anyway, we were heading back to the office when the cat ran out in front of me. I stopped in time, but then, when the car was moving again, it ran right back."

"Yes, they do that sometimes," the doctor said sympathetically. "Sounds like she got scared and confused."

"So it's a girl."

The doctor nodded. "And the good news is that she doesn't seem to have any severe injuries. I show no indication of internal injuries or nerve damage."

Julia let out a relieved sigh. "Oh good. But she couldn't walk."

"I'm afraid both of her back legs are broken, the left one is more serious than the right, which is really not much more than a hairline fracture."

He clipped the X-ray to the light box fastened to the wall and flipped the switch. The box lit, showing them the cat's skeleton from the midway point of the back to the tip of her tail.

"As you can see," he said, pointing with a pen from the breast pocket of his lab coat, "here's the left one. It's got a fairly significant break. And then there's the right, that line right there near the joint."

Julia nodded. "Is she in much pain?"

"We've given her something to take care of that and calm her down. I understand she doesn't belong to you, is that right?"

"Neither of us had ever seen her before today, but I want to make sure she has what she needs to get well. Do you have any way of tracking down her owner?"

"We did scan her for a microchip," the doctor said, "but we're not finding one. So, at least for now, she's yours."

"All right. How long will she need to be here?"

"I'd like to keep her overnight. As I said, the fractures don't seem too severe, but she's not a young cat. I'd guess she's between ten and twelve years old. She's in relatively good shape for a cat of that age living on the street, so I'd guess somebody's been helping her out with food and shelter at times. Or she might have had a home until recently. Sometimes an owner passes away and the family doesn't want to be bothered with finding a once-loved pet a new home."

"That's sad," Julia said.

The vet nodded. "For now, I want to make sure she can get around at least a little bit in her casts before I release her to you. She's already been spayed, but she'll need to be cleaned up and vaccinated. And, if you don't have cats already, you'll need to get some things—cat food, a litter box, and so on—before you'll be ready to take her home."

"I hadn't thought of all that." Julia turned to Meredith. "Beau isn't going to be happy."

The doctor raised his dark brows. "Is there a problem?"

"Beau's my husband," Julia told him. "I'm not sure what he's going to think about us suddenly having a cat."

The doctor chuckled. "We can always keep the cat here until she's healed up. But we'd have to charge for boarding. That's at least four to six weeks, maybe more for an older cat."

"Beau won't like that either," Meredith murmured.

"We'll deal with it," Julia said, and then she smiled at the doctor. "Thank you, Dr. Preston. I'll come back tomorrow to pick her up."

"All right. And don't worry. We'll take good care of her."

Julia paid for the cat's treatment, and then she and Meredith went back to the car.

"Maybe you'd better call home," Meredith suggested. "I'd offer to take her, but GK would never forgive me."

Julia snickered at the thought of Meredith's purebred Russian Blue setting eyes on a feline intruder, a street cat at that. "I can't imagine him putting up with any competition."

"He's definitely an only cat."

Julia sighed. "Yeah, I'd better give Beau a call. Then by the time I pick up the supplies I need from the pet store and we get some things done at the office, maybe Beau won't still want to kill me when I get home."

"Now, you know Beau isn't going to turn away anyone in need," Meredith said. "And it's only temporary, right?"

"Definitely."

Julia called Beau before they left the parking lot, got a reluctant-but-understanding okay to bring the cat home for the time being, and promised she'd make one of his favorites for dinner. Then she and Meredith drove to the pet supply store on Victory Drive. It was pretty late in the afternoon before they got to the office.

Their receptionist, Carmen Lopez, looked up with concern in her dark eyes. "I thought I was going to have to hire a private investigator to track you down. Your meeting must have lasted a long time."

"Actually, it was a fairly short one," Julia said, "but we had a little bit of an accident on the way home."

"Are you all right?"

"Oh, we're fine. But a cat ran in front of my car—"

"Ay, no!"

"She's going to be all right," Meredith assured her. "The vet says she'll be fine. Just a couple of broken bones. One just a hairline fracture."

"*Pobrecita*. Poor little thing. What will they do with her? Did you find her owner?"

"We ought to be able to," Meredith said. "We are investigators, after all."

"Right now she's spending the night at the vet's," Julia said. "She's comfortable and getting the treatment she needs. We'll see what we can do about finding out who she belongs to, if anyone, starting tomorrow. If we don't find anybody, she'll come home with me until she's well."

"And then what?" Carmen asked, her hands on the hips of her stylish leopard-print skirt.

"I don't know. Would you like a cat?"

Carmen's eyebrows went up. "Would you like to give me a raise to cover the pet deposit?"

Meredith cleared her throat. "How about you do us a favor and search the records for anything Ron might have done for Miss Charlotte Lockwood?"

"Okay," Carmen said with a cheeky grin, "but I'd rather have the raise."

Julia and Meredith helped themselves to coffee and went into Julia's office to confer.

"All right," Julia said, sinking down into her chair. "What were we supposed to have been doing for the past couple of hours instead of being at the animal hospital?"

Meredith sighed and started reading the list.

***

Despite the notices Julia put out around the neighborhood and on the social media sites, no one claimed the long-legged tabby that had run in front of her car the day before. And, despite Carmen's search of Ron's old records, they still had very little information about his work for Miss Charlotte Lockwood.

"It doesn't tell much about her family," Meredith said as they reviewed the information again that morning. "Although I thought her cousin-of-some-variety, Richard Sheldon, ran the estate when Ron was working for Miss Charlotte and still runs it now."

Julia nodded. "What I've always heard is that before the Civil War, an Englishwoman, some kind of minor aristocrat, came here to marry Miss Charlotte's great-great-grandfather, James Delorme, and that his brother or cousin or something was overseer of the estate." She glanced again at the notes she'd taken. "Okay, it was his nephew. And Richard Sheldon is his some-number-of-great-grandson, and his family has always managed the property. That's why it's a little odd that Miss Charlotte was having Ron background check other property managers."

"Whatever he found out must have made Miss Charlotte reconsider changing overseers. How long ago was that again?"

"Four years ago last July," Carmen said, coming in to lay a related file folder on the desk. "Mr. Bellefontaine did background checks on three different applicants, and Miss Charlotte didn't hire any of them."

"Well, Richard Sheldon is still in charge of the estate," Julia said, "so that must be the case. Did you find anything that says why?"

"One of those men was very bad. He'd been in trouble in two different states out west for embezzlement. From some ranches he managed. But the other two checked out all right from what it says in the notes. Guess Miss Charlotte changed her mind about getting a new overseer."

"Thanks for finding this for us."

The phone rang, and Carmen picked up the one on Julia's desk. "Magnolia Investigations. May I help you?"

There was the garbled sound of a voice on the other end of the line, and then Carmen nodded. "Yes, she is. One moment please."

She put the call on hold. "It's a Brenda James calling from Miss Charlotte's."

Julia glanced at Meredith and then held out her hand for the phone. "Thank you. I'll take it."

She pushed the button. "Hello, Brenda. How nice to hear from you."

"Good afternoon," Brenda said. "Miss Charlotte wanted me to ask you if you and Mrs. Bellefontaine could come to lunch at the estate tomorrow at one."

"Let me check to be sure," Julia said, "but I think tomorrow would probably be fine. Have you already spoken to Jaden?"

"Yes, I have. Miss Browning said that would be a good time for her as well."

"Wonderful. If you'll hold on for a minute, let me make sure my schedule is clear and that Meredith's is too."

"I'll hold. Thank you."

"Tomorrow at one," Julia told Meredith. "Will that work?"

Meredith already had her calendar pulled up on her phone. "That ought to be fine. I have a hair appointment, but I can move that. I don't want to miss having a real chat with Miss Charlotte."

Julia checked her own schedule. "I don't have anything that has to be done tomorrow. I'll be picking up the cat from the vet sometime today. Brenda said she already confirmed things with Jaden, so I guess we're set." She pushed the button to take her call off hold. "Brenda? Yes, please tell Miss Charlotte that Meredith and I would be delighted to come tomorrow at one. And please thank her for us."

"I'll do that. If you would, please come to the west entrance, that's the main one at the front of the house. Miss Charlotte's driver will be there to take your car and show you inside."

"That sounds perfect. Thank you, Brenda."

"You're very welcome. Good afternoon."

Julia hung up the phone. "Well, we're all set. Tomorrow at one. Why do I feel like it's 1930-something?"

"Good," Meredith said, chuckling. "We ought to bring flowers or some kind of hostess gift."

"Good idea." Julia bit her lip. "I wish I'd thought to ask Brenda what Miss Charlotte likes."

"Call her back," Meredith suggested. "She'd tell you."

"No, that's all right. We'll get some roses. They're never a bad choice. Maybe some cheerful yellow ones."

"That sounds nice."

"I'll order them for tomorrow," Carmen said. "You want one dozen or two?"

Meredith shrugged. "What do you think?"

"Better make it two," Julia said.

"Got it," Carmen walked to the door. "I'll call that flower shop around the corner."

"That's taken care of," Meredith told Julia when Carmen was gone. "I guess it would be rude of me to take a list of questions along with us. You know, things we always wanted to know."

"Yes, it would be rude," Julia said with an amused shake of her head. "But there's no reason we can't figure out what we'd like to talk about ahead of time and write down some specific things and then look at it right before we go into the house."

Meredith chuckled again. "That ought to work, though I'd be surprised if Jaden didn't have a whole notebook full of things she'd like to ask Miss Charlotte."

"She sure is interested. That's kind of funny for someone from Dallas, isn't it? To be that interested in the Delorme place? I mean, it's a beautifully preserved historic home, but it's not particularly well known, and it wasn't the site of any famous historic event."

"I think it's Miss Charlotte herself that interests her," Meredith said. "The idea that Miss Charlotte actually knew Alice Lockwood, lived with her and heard her stories, is pretty fascinating. I know it makes me want to soak up everything Miss Charlotte remembers. Of course, I'm from Savannah, and that makes it special to me."

"I'm sure that's part of it," Julia said. "We don't know that much about Jaden though. Just because she lives in Dallas right now, that doesn't mean she was born there. Maybe she's from Savannah. We'll have to find out more about her during lunch too. I'm interested in the kinds of questions she's going to ask. I'd expect her to have thought this all out in detail."

"Yeah, I'd think so. This is her big chance, right? I mean, not to sound morbid or anything, but none of us is guaranteed tomorrow. Who knows how much longer Miss Charlotte will be around? If Jaden wants to find out more about Alice and her family and the estate, she needs to *carpe diem*, right?"

"Definitely. So, what is it we want to find out tomorrow?" Julia got out a legal pad and a pencil, prepared to brainstorm, and then she stopped and rummaged in her purse. "While I'm thinking about it, I'd better check on the cat and see if anybody's claimed her. If I'm going to take her home with me tonight, I ought to remind Beau she's coming. Not that all the cat paraphernalia I brought home isn't a pretty big clue, but still."

She found the phone number on the receipt she'd gotten yesterday and quickly dialed. A few seconds later, a perky voice came on the line.

"Whitaker Street Animal Hospital. This is Jen. Can I help you?"

"Hello, Jen," Julia said. "This is Julia Foley. I brought a cat in there yesterday. She has two broken legs. Can you tell me how she's doing?"

"If you'll give me a minute, I'll go back and find out. Could you hold, please?"

"That would be great," Julia said. "Thank you."

Three or four minutes later, Jen came back to the phone. "Mrs. Foley? Yes, I spoke to the doctor about the cat. He says you can take her home today, if you'd like. She's doing very well. She's got a cast on her left leg, that's the one with the major break. The right is only splinted. We'll have a detailed printout of care instructions for you when you get here. Mostly you need to keep her confined so she doesn't do any jumping or running."

"I thought I'd put her in my guest bathroom," Julia said. "It's not big, but she'd be comfortable and protected in there. Would that do?"

"Actually, it would be better if you could keep her from getting up on the toilet or the sink. She could hurt herself jumping down. Is it possible for you to get a small dog crate to keep her in temporarily?"

"If that's what you'd recommend, sure. I can stop by the pet supply store and pick one up."

"That would be perfect. So we can expect you today? We close at six."

"Right. I should be there before then with no problems. I'm just down the street."

"That's good. Oh, and I see that we didn't get this yesterday, but I need a name for the cat."

"A name for the cat?"

"For our records, yes."

Julia looked over at Meredith who shrugged at her.

"I once had a friend with a cat called Bunny. I thought it was cute."

Julia giggled. "Bunny would be perfect." She spoke into the phone again. "How about Bunny?"

"That's fine," Jen said. "We'll put that on her record."

"Great. I'll see you and Bunny before six." Julia hung up the phone. "A cat called Bunny. Beau isn't going to know what to think of her."

"Well, he won't have to put up with her for long," Meredith said.

"I feel bad for the poor thing though. Older cats like her, especially if she ends up having some permanent problems getting around, don't usually get adopted very quickly if at all. I feel so terrible about this."

"It wasn't your fault," Meredith said. "Really. Animals can be unpredictable sometimes."

"But I should have been watching the road instead of talking to you."

"But you stopped without hitting her the first time. You *were* watching the road when she darted back out again and got hit. There wasn't anything you could have done. Besides, she'll be fine. If you'd hit her in the first place, she probably wouldn't have made it at all. So be thankful that she wasn't hurt too badly and try not to beat yourself up about it anymore." Meredith looked Julia straight in the eye. "She's going to be okay. Understand? Cats are pretty resilient. They don't say they have nine lives for nothing."

Julia smiled a little. "I understand. Thanks."

"Okay. Now what are we going to talk about with Miss Charlotte tomorrow?"

Julia opened her mouth to answer and then closed it when the front door opened.

"For Mrs. Foley and Mrs. Bellefontaine," a man's low voice said.

Carmen thanked him, and the door closed.

Julia and Meredith both looked toward the doorway, and as expected, Carmen immediately came in.

"*Tan elegante*," she said with a click of her tongue as she handed Julia and Meredith each a wax-sealed envelope.

The envelopes didn't have any return address on them or any address at all, actually. The fronts bore only their names in an exquisite copperplate hand on expensive linen paper. The seal, a tasteful blush pink, had been impressed with a letter *L* that ended with a five-loop flourish underneath. They were indeed very elegant as Carmen had said.

"*L* for Lockwood," Meredith said as she opened hers.

"I expect."

Julia broke the seal on her envelope. Inside was an invitation with the same line drawing of the Delorme Estate from Miss Charlotte's card printed lightly in the background. Over it, in the same perfect copperplate hand as her name on the front, was written,

My dear Mrs. Foley,

It was such a pleasure to speak with you at the Savannah Historical Society meeting yesterday. As you discussed with Brenda, I would be very happy to have you come to lunch at

the Delorme Estate at one o'clock tomorrow. I am delighted at the prospect of becoming better acquainted with you and Mrs. Bellefontaine. And, of course, Miss Browning will also be joining us to discuss the biography she is proposing of my great-grandmother.

I am very much looking forward to seeing all of you then.

Charlotte Delorme Lockwood

Meredith looked up from her own invitation. "Handwritten and hand delivered too. Very elegant, as Carmen said."

"And we'll have to send her handwritten thank-yous afterward too," Julia said. "It's only proper."

"You could send an email," Carmen said with a shrug.

Julia and Meredith both looked at her in horror, and Carmen gave them a sly grin.

"Very funny," Meredith said, grinning too. "Don't you have something to file?"

"Oh," Julia said suddenly. "Could I ask you to run an errand for me, Carmen?"

"Sure."

"Would you go to the pet store and get me a small dog crate? I already bought everything else I thought I'd need, but I didn't think of a crate."

"Okay, sure," Carmen said. "Anything else while I'm out?"

Julia and Meredith both shook their heads, and Carmen gave them a little wave and hurried out.

"Maybe we should have had her get some appropriate kind of stationery," Meredith said when Carmen was gone. "I really never have much use for it anymore, but it's kind of nice to get a real invitation."

"It is. I know everybody's busy these days, and email and texts are so much easier than letters, but it is a lovely thing to get, isn't it? Of course, I can't imagine Miss Charlotte doing anything less. I have a feeling that her great-grandmother made sure she was always a proper lady no matter what anyone else did."

"Evidently." Meredith looked down at the empty page on the desk in front of her. "Now what are we going to talk to her about?"

Carmen wasn't gone long, and with her help, they filled up the top page of the legal pad and were well into the next when Julia looked at her watch.

"Oh man, I've got to get out of here. It's after five already."

"We're only down the street from the animal hospital," Meredith reminded her. "You can be there in five minutes."

"You can be there in five minutes if there's no traffic," Carmen said.

Julia stood up and grabbed her purse. "I'd better go now just to be sure. We'll have plenty to talk about tomorrow anyway. If either of us thinks of anything else, Mere, we can always write it down and talk about it on the way to lunch."

"That's fine. Do we want to meet here and then drive together?"

"That would be perfect," Julia said. "We'll need to come back here anyway after lunch. What do you think? Twelve? Would that be time enough to get out there by one?"

Meredith considered for a minute. "Maybe we should make it eleven thirty. It's kind of out of the way, and I'd hate for us to be late.

If we get there too early, we can always sit in the car out of sight and go over all the things we want to talk about."

"Eleven thirty then. I'll meet you here. I'm going to try to get a little work done tonight and maybe in the morning too before I come in." Julia gathered up some files she had been working on and headed for the door, glad the fall weather was warm enough still for her not to need a jacket. "I'll be in about eleven thirty."

"Take care of Bunny," Carmen said, "And make sure you bring back those files, *entiendes*?"

Julia nodded. "Yes, I understand."

"Otherwise, don't ask me later where they are."

Julia shook her head, smiling too. "I wouldn't dream of it."

Chapter Three

"How did it go last night with Bunny?" Meredith asked when Julia came into the office about a quarter after eleven the next day. "Crazy?"

"Not too bad. After she cried the whole way home and then for over an hour in her crate, I was afraid we were going to have to board her after all until she's well. But she settled down nicely after that. Slept a lot. I did notice she ate a little. Not much, but some. She hasn't used the litter box yet, or at least she hadn't by the time I left, but she might have a little trouble getting in and out of it at first. But it has very low sides, the kind the vet recommended, so I think she'll be fine."

Meredith nodded. "She's probably a little groggy and disoriented still, poor little thing."

"She is on pain medication, so you're probably right."

"And what did Beau say?"

"Right when I thought the cat crying was going to drive us both crazy, he just smiled and put in his earbuds." Julia grinned. "Fortunately, things settled down after that."

"You're lucky you have such a sweetheart of a husband."

They settled down in Meredith's office with some coffee and the legal pad from the afternoon before.

"Did you think of anything we ought to add?" Julia asked, looking it over.

There was a sudden eagerness in Meredith's eyes. "One thing I did consider is that we're asking Miss Charlotte about her great-grandmother. It would be interesting to find out if Alice Lockwood ever told Miss Charlotte about her own grandparents or great-grandparents. If any of them lived as long as Alice or Miss Charlotte, the stories they could have told would go back pretty far, maybe back into the seventeen hundreds. I'd love to ask Miss Charlotte about any stories like that."

"Definitely." Julia glanced toward the door. "Did the flowers come yet?"

She and Meredith looked at each other knowingly when Carmen stuck her head in the door.

"Do you want the flowers in here? I put them in some water when they came first thing this morning."

"No, they're fine where they are," Julia said. "Thanks for putting them in water. How do they look?"

"Oh, very nice," Carmen said. "Two dozen perfect yellow roses with little ferns and *flor de nube*. Baby's breath. It's very pretty."

"Perfect." Meredith stood up and smoothed the skirt of her calf-length powder-blue dress. "What do you think? Is this suitable for a luncheon at the Delorme Estate with Miss Charlotte herself?"

"Wonderful. How did you find earrings that match so perfectly?"

"Aren't they great?" Meredith smiled as she touched one finger to her ear. "The dress had a little baggie with two spare buttons in it stapled to one of the inside seams. Since they're the nice fabric-covered kind, all I had to do was glue earring backs to them, and there you go."

"Great idea. And that color is perfect for your eyes." Julia stood too. "Do you think I'll pass?"

Meredith looked her over critically and then nodded. "You can never go wrong with a slim black skirt and floral silk blouse."

"Not too business-y?"

"Oh, no. With that little string of pearls, you look like you stepped right off the society page. I'm sure Miss Charlotte will approve of your presence at her table."

"You're both *tan bonita*," Carmen said. "You'll have to tell me all about it when you get back."

"We will," Julia assured her. "Would you please get the roses so we can get going?"

It was a minute or two before Carmen came back.

"I put them back in," she explained, handing Meredith the long box with the name of the florist printed in script along its side. "They'll be easier to carry that way, and then somebody can put them in water later."

"Thanks. We'll see you in a little while."

"We might be late getting back," Julia said. "It's a long drive and, if things go well, there's a lot we'll be talking about while we're there."

"And Jaden will want to get a question or two in there too," Meredith reminded her. "So you can go ahead and lock up and go home if we're not back by quitting time."

"You don't have to tell me twice," Carmen said, and with a little wave, she saw them out the door.

***

It was about ten minutes till one when Julia and Meredith turned down the long drive lined with Spanish moss–draped oak trees that would eventually take them up to the Delorme mansion.

"The first time I came here," Julia said, "I thought I had made a wrong turn. It took so long to get to where I could see the house."

"I've always heard that Alice Lockwood liked her privacy. Miss Charlotte certainly does. I'm a little bit surprised that she invited us to come."

"She has always been a bit of a recluse, true, but she was very nice the two times I met her. She's probably a little bit lonely too. And I know she'll enjoy talking about her family and the estate again. Maybe she wasn't sure what she'd do with someone Jaden's age, you know, in case they didn't end up having much in common."

Meredith snickered. "Looked to me like Jaden is fascinated with Miss Charlotte's family history. She'd probably be happy just to sit for hours and listen to her talk about Alice Lockwood and the estate."

"I'm sure Miss Charlotte has a lot of stories to tell. And probably some nobody knows about."

Julia slowed to a stop when the house came into view, taking a moment to admire the sight at the end of the archway of trees that shaded the road. There was a stone-and-ironwork gate with DELORME carved into it in weather-softened block letters. From there, beyond the front lawn that stretched wide and long and blemish free, the paved drive curved up alongside the steps that were, like the columned porch, as wide as the whole front of the house. There was a veranda the length of the second floor and then a wide balcony in front of French doors coming from the third. As promised, there was a man in a sedate black suit waiting for them on the bottom step. He was tall and fit, not young, judging by the gray at his temples, but not old either, and his eyes were a soft green in his latte-brown face.

He came to the passenger side of the car and opened the door. "Good afternoon, ladies. Mrs. Foley? Mrs. Bellefontaine? Miss Charlotte is expecting you." He helped Meredith and Julia out of the car and then held out his gloved palm. "May I take your keys, ma'am?"

"Thank you." Julia gave him her key ring, slightly embarrassed by the little plastic bar-code tags hanging from it that identified her as a frequent shopper at three local grocery stores.

He escorted them to the door, left them with Miss Charlotte's personal assistant, and went to park the car.

"Good afternoon, Mrs. Foley. Mrs. Bellefontaine."

"Brenda," Julia said, almost relieved to see a familiar face. "How are you?"

Brenda's expression was serene and professional, but her eyes were warm and welcoming. "Very well, thank you, Mrs. Foley."

"We brought these for Miss Charlotte," Meredith said, handing her the box of roses. "And please, Brenda, call us Meredith and Julia."

"I would love to." Brenda smiled and lowered her voice conspiratorially. "But only out of earshot of Miss Charlotte." She opened the box. "Oh, she will enjoy these. I'll put them in a vase for the table. Will you come with me? Miss Charlotte and Miss Browning are in the small dining room."

"The small dining room" was a mere thirty feet long and twenty wide. The windows were draped in tasseled antique-gold velvet, and every bit of the polished cherrywood furniture, from the long, glossy table to the inlaid sideboard, looked as if it had been there since before the war. If only all of it could talk, it would no doubt have stories to tell well worth the hearing.

"Mrs. Foley and Mrs. Bellefontaine, ma'am," Brenda said.

At the head of the table, Miss Charlotte, regal in a high-collared white dress with long sleeves and an impressive number of buttons down the front and securing her six-inch cuffs, gave a gracious nod of her head. "Thank you, Brenda. Please have Ellen begin serving."

There were already platters of fresh fruit and fresh vegetable sticks on the table, all artfully sliced and displayed to be as beautiful as they were delicious. Beside them was a three-tiered crystal serving tray, crustless finger sandwiches filled with tuna or chicken salad, maybe some of each, and egg salad on the bottom, a selection of cheeses and crackers in the middle, and an array of dips for the vegetables on top. Julia couldn't imagine what else Ellen would have to serve.

"Welcome, ladies," Miss Charlotte said. "Do sit down. Miss Browning and I were just discussing how my great-grandmother came to be mistress of the Delorme Estate."

"It's so tragic," Jaden said, pity in her golden-brown eyes as she made notes in a spiral notebook. "I mean, I already knew that's what happened, but I didn't know *how* it happened."

Julia sat down on the left of Miss Charlotte, across from Jaden, and Meredith sat next to her. A woman in a neat black dress with a white apron and a cap covering her graying blond hair, presumably Ellen, came in with a crystal pitcher of iced tea and four tall crystal glasses. Behind her, Brenda brought in a crystal vase filled with the yellow roses.

"Mrs. Foley and Mrs. Bellefontaine brought you these, Miss Charlotte. Aren't they pretty?"

"Just lovely," Miss Charlotte said, leaning close to breathe in their scent. "And they smell delightful. Thank you both so much. You needn't have gone to the trouble."

"It was no trouble," Meredith said. "We hoped you might enjoy them."

"I do and I will. Thank you."

"Now, what did we miss?" Julia asked.

They had arrived on time, but evidently Jaden had been eagerly early.

"Miss Browning was just telling us about herself," Miss Charlotte said. "She has two older brothers in Wyoming, her parents live in Atlanta, and she has a cat called Packard."

Julia couldn't help smiling at the succinct summation. "Is your family from Atlanta, Jaden?"

"They were originally from Savannah, actually. At least my grandmother was. Did you ever know Ruby Davis, Miss Charlotte?"

Miss Charlotte considered for a moment, studying Jaden's face. "I knew a Genevieve Davis who married a man named Robbins Whitson. They both passed some time back, but their daughter, Jeanette, still lives here in the city. I don't believe she ever married."

"My grandmother was Ruby Davis. My mother moved to Atlanta to go to school there, and that's where she met Daddy. She said it was a good thing to go away from home, at least for a while, before you settle down, so I went to the University of Texas in Austin and ended up getting a job in Dallas after I got my bachelor's degree."

"Do you work for the newspaper there?" Meredith asked.

Jaden gave her a rueful smile. "Actually, I'm doing office work for one of the big companies there. I hope having a master's degree makes it easier to get the kind of work I'm looking for. That's why I'm hoping you'll let me write about your great-grandmother, ma'am. I don't know how my professors could resist that story."

"That would depend on how well you write it," Miss Charlotte said severely. "But I will leave that in your no-doubt-capable hands. Now, I find it most helpful to begin at the beginning. Grandmama was born in this house two years before the war started. Her mother was the Honorable Catherine Beaufort, youngest daughter of Baron Romily. Catherine came from England to Savannah in 1851 to marry James Delorme."

"Miss Alice's grandfather was a baron?" Jaden asked. "I didn't know that part."

Ellen brought in a tray with four bowls of soup and set one down before each of the ladies.

"Thank you, Ellen," Miss Charlotte said, and then she nodded at Jaden. "Oh yes. Grandmama said her mother was a quiet, very proper gentlewoman, very strict on what was and was not correct behavior for a young lady even in the wilds of America."

Jaden giggled.

"Was she the Delormes' only child?" Julia asked.

"No, Grandmama had two brothers. Nathan was six years older, and Evan was three years younger. She wasn't yet seventeen when they died."

"It must have been unusual for a girl that young to come into that kind of property," Julia said.

"It was, indeed. But those were unusual and difficult times." Miss Charlotte shook her head. "It was very common in those days for families to go visiting for extended periods. The Delormes, with a few servants, went into the city to visit the family of Elias and Adella Whitman, old friends of theirs. Grandmama said there was a company of actors performing Shakespeare in repertory, and they all wanted to go, even though it was the hottest time of the year when most folks stayed in the country if they could." She leaned a little closer to Jaden, a twinkle in her eye. "She never said anything about it, but Grandmama kept a photograph of one of the actors, a gorgeous young man with wavy black hair, light-colored eyes, and the longest lashes you ever saw. It could be he was why she was so insistent on going to the plays."

Jaden grinned. "I'd like to see that picture."

"Remind me to show it to you. I still have it put away." Miss Charlotte's expression grew pensive. "But, as it happened, only one of the plays was ever performed before the company and everyone else who could manage it left the city."

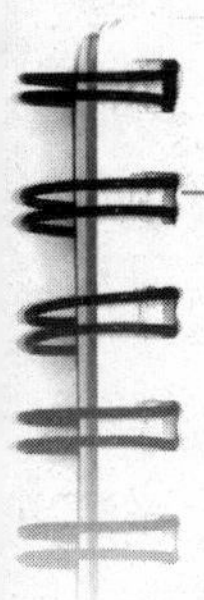

Savannah
August 1876

"Miss Alice? Miss Alice, are you awake? The doctor is here."

I struggled to open my eyes, to lift my head, to even breathe without pain. Still, I was alive. And, as it seemed, I was going to stay alive.

"Are you the young lady's maid?" the doctor asked, no doubt surprised by the heavy English accent in her voice, the voice I'd known all my life.

"Yes, Doctor. My name is Beryl Watson. I've looked after her since she was born and poor Mrs. Delorme too from when she was a girl back in England. Now they're all gone, the whole family, and my own girl, along with them, all but Miss Alice here. But where's Dr. Golding? He was to come back and tend to everyone. I must know if Miss Alice is well enough to be taken away from this terrible place."

"I'm afraid Dr. Golding has taken sick too," the doctor said, and his voice seemed very high above me. "I am Dr. Price. Who else is in the house besides this young lady? I thought this place belonged to Mr. Whitman and his family."

"Yes, sir. We come to visit the Whitmans. Miss Alice and the Whitman girl, Miss Eva, they most wanted to see the actors that was here, but then the fever spread over the city, and when Miss Alice took sick, Mr. Whitman took his family, servants and all, and went to their house in Macon. Miss Alice couldn't be moved, and then Mrs. Delorme took ill and the

young gentlemen too and then Mr. Delorme last of all. That left me to look after all of them. That flighty Ezekiel, Mr. Delorme's valet, he and the other servants we brought with us disappeared when the family came down with the fever. Never so much as a by-your-leave."

"I was told to tend to Mr. and Mrs. Delorme as well as young Mr. Nathan and Mr. Evan. Are you saying they're dead now, Beryl?"

"Oh, Doctor."

It was too hard for me to turn my head to look at her, but I was sure she was dabbing her eyes with that voluminous handkerchief she always carried. I didn't want to think about the whole family being gone. If I did, I couldn't bear it. I couldn't carry on, no matter what Mother had told me.

"All but my boy, Teddy," she sobbed. "How he and I were spared and my poor daughter was taken..."

"There, there," the doctor said wearily. "When did it happen?"

"Mr. Delorme, yesterday afternoon. The young masters and Mrs. Delorme in the night. My daughter this morning, right at dawn."

"And Miss Delorme is recovering?"

"That's what Dr. Golding said. She was took first, poor lamb. Maybe she'd fought it off enough by the time the rest were struck down that it couldn't get hold of her again."

"That could be," the doctor said. "I'd better examine her."

He lifted my wrist, pressing it with his fingers, and even that gentle touch, even the slight movement of my arm, made me whimper with pain. I was too weak to do more.

"Miss Delorme?" He laid his hand on my forehead, the light touch sending waves of pain through my skull. "Miss Alice?"

Alice. Yes, I was Alice. Mother had told me so.

I managed to open my eyes. "Yes."

"I'm Dr. Price, Miss Alice. I understand you've been very ill the past few days."

I nodded vaguely. Wasn't that what...Beryl, yes, Beryl, had just told him?

"Where are you hurting today?"

"Everywhere," I murmured. "Head. Back. Everywhere."

He asked me a few more questions about my symptoms. I told him what little I remembered. Beryl filled in the rest. I was merely thankful they had mostly subsided, for they were horrible to consider, more horrible to endure.

"Can she be moved, Doctor?" Beryl asked after the doctor examined me more thoroughly. "Out of the city, I mean. Somewhere far from this terrible yellow fever. The sickness comes up from the drains and from the gutters here. I fear Miss Alice isn't strong enough yet to go, but I'm afraid for her to stay. For any of us to stay."

"Most of those who could leave the city have already gone," the doctor said. "That leaves only the poor and those who are already sick. But you needn't worry about Miss Alice. She seems to be improving. Not yet, but soon she ought to

be able to be driven by carriage back home. That is, if you are very careful. You say your son is here with you?"

"Yes, Doctor. My Teddy. He drove us into Savannah and has been looking after Mr. Delorme's horses. I thought he could arrange for us to be leaving here now."

"Not now," the doctor told Beryl again. "But I will be back in another day or two to check on you, Miss Alice." His voice was distinct and hearty and made my head pound afresh. "You lie still till then and let your maid see to you." He turned again to Beryl. "A word with you, if I may."

Beryl walked to the bedroom door with him, but I could still hear what he was saying.

"There will be someone by here sometime this morning to see to the remains. For now, it's best if no one moves them or touches them."

"But I'm sure Mr. Delorme would want—"

"We can't worry about that now," the doctor said sharply. "The bodies must be buried quickly if there's to be any hope of stopping the spread of the fever. Good heavens, woman, this is an epidemic. Hundreds have already died. We can't worry about the niceties of the burials."

I couldn't think about it either. About "the niceties." Beryl hadn't told me, but I knew. I knew there were five bodies in the house. One of them was about my age. I'd grown up with her, and we'd been friends despite the differences in our social positions. A lady's maid's daughter and the daughter of a wealthy estate owner, weren't they still only young girls, the same but for the names they carried?

Weren't they both the same when standing face-to-face with death?

Now one was gone and one was left. I was left. I had only Beryl and Teddy to look after me. Beryl would make me well. Teddy would take me somewhere safe. They would know what to do.

Beryl looked from the doctor over to me, her pale face sallow and her blue eyes heavy with worry, and I wondered how her once-fair hair had suddenly grown so gray.

"Doctor," she said, her hands clasped together against her heart, "I'm worried about the poor lamb. I know she's like to get well again, but it can't be good for her to go back to that estate all alone. It would only remind her that her dear mother and father and her poor brothers will never come back there again. When she's ready to leave here, do you think it might be better to take her somewhere else? Somewhere new that won't remind her of all this?"

"Certainly," the doctor said, coming back to the bedside to study my face.

A tear slipped from the corner of my eye, and I looked away.

He patted my hand. "There now, my dear. I know it is a heavy burden to bear, but you mustn't give way. Time will bring healing, body, mind, and spirit." He turned to Beryl. "Is there family she could go to? Somewhere she would be welcomed and cared for?"

"No, I'm sorry to say, Doctor. There is her mother's family back in Hampshire, but I don't know as a long voyage like that would be best for her, weak as she is."

"No, no. I couldn't recommend it. Perhaps in time but not yet." The doctor thought for a moment. "Perhaps your son, Teddy, is it? Perhaps Teddy could find a place for you, somewhere out of the city, where the young lady could recover for a few days, and then you could decide what to do."

"I could do that."

I looked toward the voice and saw Teddy leaning his lanky frame against the door. The doctor was a little more subtle than most people when they first saw his eyes, one pale blue, the other deep brown, but I could tell he had noticed. I could tell he was interested. I suppose any medical man would be curious about so rare a condition when he chanced on it.

"Uh, yes," the doctor said, clearing his throat. "Very good then. It seems Miss Delorme is in capable hands. I will return as soon as I'm able, to make certain her recovery is going well. Get her to drink all the fresh water you can, Mrs. Watson. Boil it first. And try to keep her as comfortable as possible."

"Of course, Doctor," Beryl said. "Of course."

"Oh, and you might want to look for someplace to stay that's well away from the city, Teddy. I don't believe Miss Delorme is contagious any longer, but you may have trouble finding anyone who will rent to you if you tell them you've come from here."

"I'll see to it, Doctor. Now that Mr. and Mrs. Delorme are gone, we'll see to it Miss Alice is well looked after."

Teddy fixed his eyes on me, and I swiftly turned away. I was used to the way he looked, having seen him most every day since I could remember, but his expression now, mild as it was, sent a shiver through me.

"Doctor," I breathed.

Dr. Pierce leaned down to me and took my hand. "What is it, child?"

"The—the others, will they—?"

"Don't let it trouble you, Miss Delorme. Your parents and brothers will be seen to with as much care as can be afforded them during this crisis."

"But I—"

"Our duty now is to the living, however much we would wish to honor the dead."

"But I'm not—"

"Shh, shh, now, sweetheart." Beryl came over to me, laying a gentle hand on my lips. "Your mama and papa and brothers have gone on to their reward along with my sweet girl. What remains behind here is nothing more than dust." She stroked my hair back, smiling into my eyes. "You go to sleep now, Miss Alice. It will all look better in the morning, and you'll see we've only done what's best for everyone."

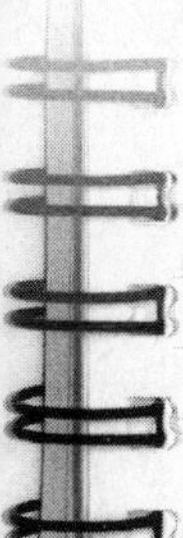

I closed my eyes, too tired to resist. Maybe it truly was for the best. For everyone.

Chapter Four

"THAT HAD TO BE so awful for Alice," Julia said after Miss Charlotte had told them about the loss of her great-grandmother's family. "I'm glad she had her maid and the maid's son to take care of her then. It was terrible that the family they were staying with abandoned them like that."

"They must have been terrified of catching the yellow fever," Meredith said. "They knew so little about it back then, and with so many people dying all around them and nothing they could do for Alice and her family, it would have been very hard for them to stay. Miss Charlotte, do you know how many people died in that epidemic?"

"The records aren't very helpful in many cases," Miss Charlotte said, pushing away her half-eaten food. "Some of the doctors refused to list yellow fever as the cause of death on death certificates, listing the symptoms that led to the death instead, so there isn't an accurate death count. But they say somewhere between nine hundred and fifteen hundred people died in the epidemic. And that was only one of the many they had throughout the eighteenth and nineteenth centuries."

"I understand the rains were particularly heavy that year," Meredith said, "and the weather was hot. And, of course, the drains and sanitation were poor. No wonder people used to leave the city during the summer."

"And they didn't know mosquitoes carried the disease," Jaden said.

"I didn't know that," Julia said. "Do they teach that in journalism classes these days?"

Jaden colored a little and shook her head. "You know how it is in journalism. You read a lot, all kinds of useless facts."

Miss Charlotte's eyes narrowed. "I trust you don't find the history of Savannah useless," she said, and then her severity was tempered by a slight smile.

"Oh, no, ma'am. All of this is fascinating. I could listen for hours."

"Not," Miss Charlotte said, "without dessert."

Ellen was either very perceptive about the timing of the Lockwood meals or she'd been listening in. Either way, she came in at that moment bringing four tall fluted sundae glasses filled with strawberry mousse topped with sliced fresh strawberries and a swirl of whipped cream on top. She cleared away the luncheon plates, replacing each one with a glass of the frothy pink dessert.

Julia tasted hers with the long-handled spoon Ellen had brought with it and then squeezed her eyes closed. "Oh, that's heavenly."

"Ellen will get you the recipe, if you'd like," Miss Charlotte said serenely. "Our cook has been with us since after the war."

Jaden's eyes widened, and there was a touch of mischievousness on their hostess's face.

"The war in Afghanistan, of course."

"I'll have to watch out for you, Miss Charlotte," Jaden said, fighting a smile. "I won't know what to believe and what not to believe."

Miss Charlotte took a prim sip of her tea.

"But what happened after the epidemic?" Jaden asked as the others enjoyed their mousse. "Obviously, Alice got well and came back here to live."

"Oh, no," Miss Charlotte said. "She did get well, of course, but she didn't come back here. Not for a very long time."

"I always heard she loved this house," Meredith said. "I've read what she wrote when she set up the foundation, and she mentioned that she could live nowhere but Savannah and that only if she was here at the estate."

"You're very right," Miss Charlotte told her. "But that was many years later. Right after the epidemic, she stayed in a cottage Teddy Watson found for them to rent. It was in a little town well out of the city that hadn't been touched by the fever. But when Grandmama was well enough to really travel, she went all the way to Chicago. She wrote to the estate overseer to let him know that she wanted him to continue doing so on her behalf until she returned." She took a dainty bite of her dessert and then touched her linen napkin to the corners of her mouth. "It was a year later that one of her father's nephews, hearing of Grandmama's loss, came from Tennessee to see her in Chicago. His name was Conrad Dumont, and he agreed to take over managing the estate for her."

"It's his family that's looked after the estate all these years, isn't it?" Meredith asked.

"It is. Richard, Richard Sheldon, is his great-great-great-grandson. He was brought up here, and his grandfather taught him all about running the place. His boy, Tony, and grandson, Jeff, are learning from him." Miss Charlotte nodded with satisfaction. "I believe in continuity and consistency just as Grandmama did. She always set great store in finding loyal and trustworthy people and treating them well."

"I suppose that came from when her maid and her maid's son took care of her when everyone else left them during the epidemic," Jaden said, looking up from her notebook. "It sounds like they treated her almost like family."

"And that's why Grandmama was always good to her people and taught me the same," Miss Charlotte said stiffly. "Things certainly would have turned out differently for her if they hadn't been there."

Julia let the last bite of her mousse melt on her tongue and then put down her spoon. "Everything was so delicious, Miss Charlotte. I think you've spoiled me for life."

"You must come again," Miss Charlotte said. "All of you. I've enjoyed talking to you. You know, Brenda has been trying to get me to get out more. Grandmama was not one to do very much socializing, and the estate never did host the grand balls it had when her parents were alive. I fear I am like her in that. But perhaps Brenda is right." She leaned a little closer to Jaden. "I think, Miss Browning, that I am going to enjoy telling you my stories for your book."

"Oh, you don't know how much I want to hear, ma'am," Jaden gushed. "Not just for my thesis either. It's like you bring the whole history of this place and your family to life. But you've made me curious now to know why Alice didn't come back here for so many years. Was it that hard for her?"

"It wasn't that it was hard," Miss Charlotte told her. "When she went to Chicago, she engaged an attorney to see to her business matters for her. Now the attorney was an old friend of her father's and very experienced in those sorts of things, but he had a young clerk only five years older than Alice."

Jaden's eyes lit. "You mean she stayed up there to marry him?"

Before Miss Charlotte could answer her, there was a discreet cough from the doorway that led to the back of the house.

"Excuse me, Miss Charlotte," Brenda said, "but you wanted to be reminded of your appointment."

"Yes, thank you, Brenda." Miss Charlotte glanced at the delicate gold and diamond brooch watch pinned to the front of her dress. "I hope you ladies will excuse me. I've chatted on far too long."

"We've taken too much of your time," Julia said, standing.

Meredith and Jaden followed suit.

"Thank you so much for having us, Miss Charlotte," Meredith said. "Everything was lovely."

"I trust dear Brenda to arrange these things for me," Miss Charlotte said. "I don't know what I would do without her here."

"It's my pleasure, Miss Charlotte," Brenda said.

"Thank you for letting me come," Jaden said. "I really appreciate it, but the story was just getting interesting. What about Alice and the lawyer? You can't leave it like this."

Miss Charlotte gave her a long, appraising look and then turned to Brenda. "Perhaps, Brenda, you could find another afternoon convenient for these ladies to come back and hear more about Grandmama."

"Yes, ma'am. I can certainly do that."

"Excellent. Thank you."

"Thank you, Miss Charlotte," Jaden said. "I hope we can talk again soon. There's so much I want to know." She walked over to the grouping of pictures on the dining room wall, one of them the portrait of Miss Alice that was featured in all the foundation literature. "I still want to know about all of these people. And I still would like to see a picture of Miss Alice's son or grandson."

"We can discuss that when you come back. Brenda will be in contact with you."

Then Brenda led them all back to the front porch, where the dark-suited man had Julia's car and a little black Honda waiting for them.

"Wasn't that great?" Jaden asked Julia. "I'm glad you got to hear too. That way if I forget something or write it down wrong, I can call you and find out what you remember. Would that be okay?"

Julia and Meredith glanced at each other and nodded. It seemed odd that someone Jaden's age didn't simply ask to use her phone to record the conversations with Miss Charlotte. Very odd.

"I don't see why not," Meredith said, handing her a business card. "Here's the information for our agency. Our numbers are on there."

"Agency?" Jaden asked, looking the card over. "You're private investigators?" She grinned at them. "No way."

"Plenty of way," Julia told her. "Even if we are old ladies."

Jaden laughed. "No, it's just I've never met private investigators before. Do you ever do any genealogical research for people?"

Julia and Meredith looked at each other again.

"There are services that specialize in that," Meredith said. "We've never done it. Not for our clients anyway."

"I guess we could give it a shot," Julia added, "but you'd probably do better with an expert."

"You're probably right." Jaden stuck the card in her purse. "But that's still pretty cool."

"We can talk about it more when we get to talk to Miss Charlotte again," Julia said. "We'll look forward to hearing from you, Brenda."

"I'll be in touch as soon as Miss Charlotte decides what she'd like to do," Brenda replied. "Thank you all for coming."

At Brenda's nod, the man escorted Jaden to her car and opened the door for her, closing it again once she was inside.

Julia expected him to do the same for her and Meredith after that, but Brenda put one hand on her arm.

"Will you both wait for a moment? Miss Charlotte would like to see you again."

"All right."

Julia smiled and nodded as if she and Brenda were just casually chatting, and she and Meredith waved as Jaden drove away.

"I'm sorry," Brenda said as she and Julia and Meredith went back into the house. "Since Jaden got here before you, Miss Charlotte didn't have a chance to talk to you first. But she told me if that happened that I wasn't to let you leave until she asked you something."

Julia glanced at Meredith and then back at Brenda. "All right."

Miss Charlotte was waiting for them in the dining room.

"I'm glad you could come back in," she said. "Will you be good enough to sit down for a moment?"

Meredith nodded. "Of course."

She and Julia both sat.

"Would either of you like anything?" Miss Charlotte asked. "Some coffee perhaps?"

"I don't think I could hold another sip or another bite of anything," Julia said.

Meredith nodded. "Me neither. But thank you all the same."

"Very well." Miss Charlotte turned to Brenda. "Will you sit with us too? If I'm being overly suspicious, I want you to tell me so."

"We already discussed it, Miss Charlotte." Brenda took a seat at Miss Charlotte's side. "I think you're doing the only smart thing."

Looking reassured, Miss Charlotte turned to Julia and Meredith. "I want to know, and tell me honestly now, your opinion of Miss Browning."

"We don't know much about her," Meredith said. "She seems very eager to find out more about you and your family and to write her book."

"Very eager," Julia said, wondering if maybe she was too eager. "Is there something about her that bothers you, Miss Charlotte?"

"I'm not entirely sure. She seems very sweet and intelligent. Very interested in the history of Savannah and of my family. You saw how interested she was in these photographs." Miss Charlotte indicated the collection on the dining room wall. "Before you came, she asked me all about them. She wanted to know everything I remember."

"She is writing a book," Meredith said.

"Not about them though," Julia told her. "Was there something unusual about what she asked, Miss Charlotte?"

"No, I can't actually say that. And I can't think of a reason she'd have to deceive me about any of this except there are times when she seems very determined. Almost too enthused. I actually like her a great deal. But I've lived a long time, and I've seen how people act when they know someone has money. They aren't always up-front about their motives."

"I'm sure anyone in your position has to be careful," Julia said. "But Jaden's interest seems genuine."

"Seems," Miss Charlotte said sharply. "Mrs. Foley, I would like to hire you and Mrs. Bellefontaine to do a job for me."

"Yes?" Julia prompted, sure she knew exactly why Miss Charlotte wanted to hire her and Meredith.

"I would like you to do a background check on Miss Browning." Miss Charlotte gave her a regal nod. "She has presented herself in a certain way. If all she has told us is true, then well and good. If not, I would like to know what *is* true and why she is really here."

Julia glanced over at Meredith, eyebrows raised.

"We can do that, Miss Charlotte," Meredith said quickly. "If that would put your mind at ease."

"And you mustn't let the girl know about this."

"Of course not."

"Is there something in particular that bothers you about her?" Julia asked, hoping to have something specific to base her uncertainty on. "Has she said or done anything that makes you think she's not what she says she is?"

"No." Miss Charlotte looked down at the handkerchief still clutched in her hand. "No, of course not. I-I'm afraid I've grown fretful in my old age and suspicious of nearly everyone."

"We can certainly check her out," Meredith said.

"I haven't mentioned this before," Miss Charlotte said, "but when she was here before the two of you arrived, she was full of questions."

"She was full of questions after we arrived," Julia said.

"True. Very true. But she's asked me quite a few things that have nothing to do with the estate or with the foundation. Not impertinently personal questions, but things that have no connection as far as I can tell with the book she's planning."

Julia frowned. "Like what?"

"She was asking about family history. Not merely what Grandmama had done or anyone else in the family, but whether we had any kind of unusual medical history. Of course, I told her we hadn't any such thing."

"Anything else unusual?"

Miss Charlotte thought for a moment. "I'm just not sure what I ought to be concerned about. She's almost too absorbed in this project. I understand her reasons for wanting to write the book, but it's almost like she has a personal stake in it."

"A lot of people get emotionally involved in their work," Meredith said. "Or they get caught up in the mythology of a certain time or place and just have to know every detail about it. Some are just naturally excited about everything they're involved in. It's hard to say about Jaden. We don't really know that much about her yet. But we can sure find out more."

"She does seem very, very attached to this place and to your family's history," Julia added. "Has she talked about that at all? I mean, about why she's focused on your family in particular?"

"Only what she said before," Miss Charlotte said, "that she was assigned to do a report on us for her class and that she's been interested ever since. She's certainly an engaging young woman. I just don't quite know what to make of her."

"Let us see what we can find out for you. If nothing else, we should be able to rule out anything shady in her background."

"And if there is something to be concerned about," Meredith said, "at least you'll know."

Miss Charlotte gave a solemn nod. "Yes, I definitely want you to find out what you can. Even if she didn't make me wonder sometimes, I think it would be a wise thing to do before I give her my permission to present the history of my family and of this place to the general public. I know that because Brenda told me so."

Brenda gave her a look, and they both laughed softly.

"So, will you do that for me?" Miss Charlotte asked, sobering. "I would very much appreciate it, and I'm sure whatever your fee is will be entirely worth it."

"For your peace of mind, Miss Charlotte," Brenda said.

Miss Charlotte nodded. "Thank you, ladies. I have enjoyed having you visit me. I hope you can both come back soon."

Julia and Meredith thanked her, and Brenda took them back out to the front porch where the man in the black suit was waiting for them. He opened Julia's passenger door and helped Meredith inside and then walked around to do the same for Julia and handed her her keys. Then he and Brenda stood on the porch watching until they drove away.

"I'm glad Miss Charlotte decided to let us find out more about Jaden," Julia said.

"I am too. Just because it's a good idea, whether or not Jaden is up to something."

"Miss Charlotte is a very well-off old lady. And I think she's lonely too. Someone like Jaden, who's young and lively and interested in what she has to say, might be very attractive to her. And Miss Charlotte's money might be very attractive to someone whose conscience wouldn't be bothered by fleecing an old lady."

"Do you think that's what Jaden is up to? I didn't get that impression at all."

Julia sighed. "I'm not sure what I think. She just seems so eager to be around Miss Charlotte. Too eager. A girl like that, with school and work and, I suppose, socializing, wouldn't be trying to spend all her free time with an elderly lady she doesn't even know, would she? I mean, without a motive?"

"But we know her motive," Meredith said. "She wants to write Alice's story for her thesis, and Miss Charlotte's too. That seems pretty straightforward. And maybe she's excited about it because, well, because she's just excited. We should all be that interested in our work, right? We'd all be a lot happier if we were. And I can't blame her in this case. I could listen to Miss Charlotte talk all day long."

"I know. She makes you feel like you were right there when those things were happening."

"Do you suppose all of that is what Alice told her happened? Or do you think she's embellished it over the years?"

"It's been nearly a hundred and fifty years since that particular epidemic," Julia said. "And it has to be seventy or eighty years since Alice told Miss Charlotte about it. I have to wonder how much Alice embellished it by that time. Still, it's as close as we're ever going to get to talking to Alice face-to-face."

"Fascinating stuff anyway," Meredith said with a contented sigh. "Beatrice is going to want to know all the details."

Julia grinned. "She can always read Jaden's book when it comes out."

"Boy, Jaden's got it bad, doesn't she? I mean, I love history, especially our history, but I never saw anyone quite so determined. She really wants to spend time with Miss Charlotte."

"Yeah, maybe. Maybe I'm too suspicious, but I know there are people who prey on the elderly, rich or poor. If you think about it, Jaden just showed up out of the blue and got us to introduce her to Miss Charlotte. I'd feel really awful if something bad happened because of it."

"Oh, don't be such a cynic. Sometimes people are just interested in learning things. I feel that way about a lot of historical people and places. Miss Charlotte is a direct connection to Alice Lockwood, who by all accounts was a remarkable woman. It doesn't have to be anything more than that."

Julia shrugged and turned onto the road that would take them back to the office. "You're probably right," she said, "but I'm glad we're going to be checking her out all the same."

Chapter Five

THEY WENT BACK TO THE office and spent most of the rest of the afternoon and the next day tackling the mountain of background checks they'd been hired to do.

"The divorce cases are more interesting," Julia said as they took a break over a cup of coffee, "but they're usually pretty sad. It's hard to tell a husband or wife that, yes, your spouse has been seeing someone else and lying to you about it and this is what happened to your investment account and most of your savings."

"At least we have the green light to check up on Jaden now."

Meredith chuckled. "I knew you'd be happy about that."

"Not happy exactly," Julia admitted. "But I'd feel better knowing more. Miss Charlotte really likes her, and I don't want her to be disappointed. I wonder if she's noticed something that makes her uncertain about Jaden or if it's only that feeling that if something—or somebody, in our case—seems too good to be true, it, or she, probably is. Anyway, it should be interesting."

"I wish we had some insurance fraud investigations. Those are usually interesting. Some people get pretty clever when they think they can get some money for nothing."

"True. Most of them don't really think it all the way through and leave something that gives them away. Though I wonder if there are some we've missed because they did outsmart us."

Meredith snickered. "They are more interesting than background checks, but at least we've got plenty to do. Nearly everybody wants one of those before they'll hire anybody," Meredith said. "Especially schools."

"I'm glad they do," Julia said, "and I'm happy to have the work, but couldn't we track down somebody who embezzled several million dollars and faked his own death? Or how about finding out who's depositing money into a woman's checking account and why?"

"That would be something different at least."

"Different from what?" a low baritone voice asked.

Julia and Meredith both turned.

"Quin," Meredith said, looking equal parts delighted and mortified to see the trim, silver-haired man standing in the doorway. "What brings you here?"

A smile in his eyes, one of them copper brown and the other tropical-ocean blue, Quin came into Julia's office and took a seat across from her at the desk, the one that was closest to Meredith's.

Carmen came in right behind him and handed him a cup of coffee. "Different from doing background checks all day. But, *puedo dicirte*, that's better than hunting down a lot of records all the time and then having to file them right back." She tilted her head from side to side, making her dangly gold earrings dance. "Back and forth, back and forth. I like it better when we have a real mystery. Then it gets exciting."

"How about this exciting job?" Meredith asked, handing her a stack of file folders to return to their places.

"*Ay de mi,*" Carmen sighed as she went back to her desk. "I haven't had this much excitement since I had to wait for the plumber to come unclog my sink."

Quin chuckled. "I guess the job I have for you won't help things much."

"What is it?" Julia asked.

"One of my clients is considering going into partnership with another man in order to develop an invention."

"What kind of invention?" Julia asked.

He tapped the side of his nose. "I am not yet at liberty to say."

Meredith rolled her eyes. "Then what do you want us to do?"

"Well, this particular client gets excited pretty easily. I'm a little surprised that he asked me to check over their agreement instead of just going ahead and signing it. But I'm really not so sure about the guy he wants to go into business with. I haven't found out anything really troubling about him, but I keep thinking there's something not right about him either. So I was hoping—"

"You were hoping we'd do a background check on him for you," Julia said.

Meredith sighed. "Wouldn't you know it."

"There's nobody I'd trust more," Quin said. "I mean, if it's not putting you out too much."

"Of course not," Meredith said, with a grin. "It's our bread and butter."

"Even if you'd like a crêpe suzette or two once in a while. I can understand that."

"Oh, you know how it is. Now, if I could make a living just listening to Miss Charlotte Lockwood talking about family and local history, I'd be the happiest woman in Savannah."

Quin gave her an enigmatic smile. "Ah, the elusive Miss Charlotte. She's a throwback even for her age. I think she'd be perfectly at home in Governor Cobb's mansion in 1854."

"She's certainly the epitome of the gracious southern lady," Julia said. "I didn't know you knew her."

"We haven't been introduced, no," Quin said, "but I have heard her speak. I was mesmerized."

"She spoke at the historical society meeting this week," Julia told him. "It was so interesting. She certainly knows how to tell a story."

"And we had lunch with her yesterday," Meredith added with a smile. "At the Delorme Estate no less."

"Now I am impressed," Quin said. "I didn't think Miss Charlotte received visitors very often."

"That's what I've always heard too," Meredith said. "But lunch was her idea. There was a young woman at the meeting who wants to write a book about the Lockwood Foundation and about Alice Lockwood. She asked us to introduce her to Miss Charlotte, and the two of them evidently hit it off. We're all supposed to go back when Miss Charlotte has time. She's going to tell us more about Alice and all that happened to her."

"That sounds fascinating," Quin said. "I wouldn't mind listening in on that conversation."

Meredith patted his arm. "You can always get a copy of Jaden's book when it comes out. She seems very determined to get all the details."

"I'd at least like to hear about it from you two, whatever you find out. But back to my background-checking case. Are we on?"

"Sure," Julia said. "Let me just get the information from you, and we'll see what we can find out."

"Thanks." Quin glanced at Meredith, his expression nonchalant. "Did you know the Savannah Philharmonic will be playing for free in Forsyth Park on Saturday?"

"Oh, Beau and I are going to that," Julia said. "And taking a picnic and everything. Are you planning on going?"

"I was considering it," Quin admitted. "Only I hate going alone."

Meredith kept her eyes on her lap, but there was a telltale twitch in her lips.

"You could always come with us," Julia said innocently. "I'm sure we'll pack plenty to eat and drink."

"That would be great," Quin said, "but I hate to be a third wheel. If I could only find someone else who'd like to listen to the music and enjoy the park. I hear the weather is supposed to be especially fine that day, warm and sunny."

Meredith looked up at him contemplatively, still trying not to smile. "I don't know. I've got some leftover meatloaf I was planning to heat up on Saturday."

"Well, bring it along," Quin said. "We'll be eating our lobster and caviar or whatever Julia serves, so I don't know why you shouldn't have your meatloaf if you're set on it."

Julia chuckled. "You're both crazy. And Beau and I would love for you both to come. Nothing fancy. I haven't decided on a menu yet, just something tasty and portable. What do you think?"

"It'd be great to see Beau," Quin said. "We need to play a round of golf again sometime soon. And, yes, I'd love to go to the concert, if you're sure you don't mind me coming along. And, of course, if Meredith will bring her meatloaf."

"Okay, it sounds fun," Meredith said. "And I guess the meatloaf can wait. Is there anything I can bring, Jules?"

"I'll let you know when I decide what I'm making. Maybe we can talk about it today sometime."

"Is Bunny going to be okay by herself while you and Beau are gone?"

"Oh sure," Julia said. "She's mostly been sleeping anyway."

"Bunny?" Quin asked.

Julia sighed. "It's a long story. I accidentally hit a cat a couple of days ago, and now she's at my house recovering from two broken legs."

"Oh, I'm sorry to hear that. That's hard on her and on you."

"I feel so guilty still," Julia admitted, swirling the little bit of coffee left in the bottom of her cup as she looked down into it.

"It really wasn't Julia's fault," Meredith put in. "The cat ran in front of us. There was just no way to avoid it."

"I realize that," Julia said. "That doesn't mean I don't still feel bad about it happening. But the vet says she'll be fine. She just has to heal somewhere. I didn't want her to have to go to a shelter, and I sure wasn't paying to have her boarded for six weeks. Not on top of the vet bills I already had."

"That's very kind of you, taking her in," Quin said. "That must have come as a surprise to Beau."

"He's been pretty funny about it. He'd been talking about getting a small dog someday, but we decided they can be a lot of trouble. One of us would always have to be at home to let it out several times a day. Not that he wanted a cat at all, and not that we're keeping this one, but I did catch him checking on Bunny several times since she's been staying with us. I guess since he used to be an anesthesiologist, he worries about reactions to medications and recovery and all that. He was afraid she was being too quiet during the first night, because for about an hour after I brought her home, she wailed nonstop, but then she just stopped. He went to check on her and found that she was just asleep...until his coming in woke her up."

Quin chuckled.

"She actually seems to be pretty content to just relax in her crate," Julia said. "Somehow she manages to hobble around with a cast on one back leg and a splint on the other and get to her food and water and to her box. I'm a little surprised at how little we actually need to do for her even while she's recovering."

"They're pretty low maintenance, aren't they? Of course, when she gets well, that may be a whole other story."

"I don't know. She's an older cat, so she might be pretty calm at this point. That's another reason I didn't want to take her to the shelter. It's so hard to find homes for any of the rescues, but the older ones have an especially hard time. Everybody wants a kitten, but they don't realize that the older ones have a lot of advantages. You already know how big they're going to get and what their personalities are like. They're usually already vaccinated and have been spayed or neutered. And they have longer attention spans than kittens, so it's easier to teach them what you expect from them."

"I didn't know you knew so much about cats," Meredith said. "I'm impressed."

"Actually, unlike you, I didn't know that until last night. I happened to see an article that said that next month is 'Adopt a Senior Pet' month, and it gave some reasons why that's a good idea. I thought it was interesting. Not that we're keeping Bunny." She gave Meredith a stern look. "I mean it."

"Whatever you say."

Julia turned deliberately to Quin, waiting until the look of amusement on his face turned into earnest innocence. "I'll give you a call to let you know what our plans are for the concert and picnic."

"I'll be happy to bring something too. Dessert? Lemonade? Whatever you say."

"That would be great. We'll let you know as soon as we know what we need."

"And my background check?"

"Oh yeah."

Julia got a notepad and a pen and took down the basic information about the subject and exactly what Quin was concerned about.

"We'll get back to you as soon as we know something."

"Don't forget you're supposed to have tea with Miss Charlotte too," Carmen called from the hallway.

"Okay," she called back. "Thanks."

Meredith stifled a giggle.

"Sounds like you need an intercom," Quin observed.

Julia gestured toward the box on the desk. "We've got one."

"Ah. Well, it sounds as if you have everything in hand here. I'd better be going. Let me hear from you about Saturday."

"I will."

"I'll see you both then," Quin said.

Meredith smiled. "See you soon."

Julia waited until she heard Quin say goodbye to Carmen and the front door open and close before she said anything.

"I hope you don't mind my asking him to come with us."

Meredith shrugged. "That's fine. He didn't have to agree to go. And I didn't have to agree to go either."

"I'm glad you did anyway. It'll be fun. And you and he can go just as friends. It doesn't have to be a big deal."

"I know. I'm just not sure how big of a deal I want it to be."

"And you don't have to be," Julia assured her. "Just go and have a good time. He's a nice guy. That's good enough for a Saturday afternoon."

"Yeah. I think it will be. Now what about his background check?" Meredith looked over the list Julia had taken down regarding Quin's concerns about his client's potential partner. "There's not much to go on, is there?"

Before they got very far into planning how they were going to investigate the case, Julia's cell phone rang. The display showed the name Brenda James. Julia answered it at once.

"Brenda. Hi. How are you?"

"Very well, thank you," Brenda said. "I'm calling for Miss Charlotte regarding having tea with her and Jaden. She's available Saturday afternoon, if you and Meredith would care to come."

"Saturday afternoon?"

Julia looked at Meredith. They had just made plans for Saturday, but how could they refuse Miss Charlotte, especially when she had gone out of her way to invite them for a second time? If they turned her down at this point, it was quite possible she would never ask them back. One simply did not ask Miss Charlotte Lockwood to rearrange her schedule.

Still.

"Oh dear," Julia said. "That's almost the only time we can't make it. Is it possible for us to come another time?"

"Let me see," Brenda said, and Julia heard the crackle of a page being turned. "We could try for Friday afternoon, but I would have to call Jaden to see if she would be available then too. What do you think?"

"Hold on just a second." Julia pressed the MUTE button on her phone. "Can you do Friday afternoon?"

Meredith nodded enthusiastically.

"I think Friday would work great," Julia told Brenda.

"All right," Brenda said. "I will speak to Jaden and see if she's available then. If so, you would need to come about three since Miss Charlotte has a brunch she has to go to that morning. That would give all of you a chance to talk for a while before tea at four and after, if you'd like. Would that work for you and Meredith?"

"That sounds perfect. We'll be there."

"All right. And I know it hasn't been long, but is there anything I can tell Miss Charlotte about your investigation?"

"No," Julia said. "We haven't really gotten started yet, but we'll find out what we can as soon as we can, all right?"

"I'll let Miss Charlotte know. And if for some reason Jaden has a conflict for Friday, I'll call you right back."

"Thanks. We'll plan on Friday at three unless we hear from you." Julia ended the call and put her phone back into her purse. "I hope Jaden can do Friday. I really don't want to miss the concert or have to put Miss Charlotte off."

Meredith shrugged. "The concert isn't a big deal. We could always do something Sunday afternoon with the guys, or even Saturday night."

"But I'd hate to feel rushed at Miss Charlotte's if we plan something for after we meet with her. I'd like to feel like we can stay as long as she feels like putting up with us."

Meredith was silent for a moment. "Do you really think she had another appointment she had to go to when we were there? Or was that Brenda's tactful way of telling Miss Charlotte she needed to rest for a while?"

"I was wondering about that myself. We need to make sure we're not tiring her out while we're there. Maybe we should say something to Jaden before we go too. She's so excited about talking to Miss Charlotte, I don't know if she'd notice."

"We can just keep our eyes open and, if it looks like Miss Charlotte needs a rest, we can suggest that it's time to go. I'm sure Jaden would get the hint."

Julia nodded. "That would work. Of course, Miss Charlotte's the one who initiated the whole thing. She seems awfully eager to have us."

"Like you said before, she's probably lonely. And it's got to be hard to say no to someone like Jaden who hangs on every word she says, especially someone so charming."

"She is that," Julia admitted. "I hope that's all she is."

"Me too," Meredith said. "I guess we'd better get to work finding out."

Chapter Six

"We don't have a lot to go on in checking on Jaden," Meredith said, starting a list. "Went to UTD. Working on her master's. Lives in Dallas. Works for a large company."

"Maybe. I guess we'll get a chance to get to know her better on Friday." Julia shrugged. "I would love for her to be just what she says she is. I think it would be good for Miss Charlotte and for Jaden too if they could actually be friends. To tell the truth, I'm surprised someone like Miss Charlotte never married and had children. You'd think that someone as traditional as she is would have, that she'd want to leave her foundation and the estate to her own flesh and blood."

"Maybe it's as simple as her never having met the right man. Or maybe the man she loved married someone else or died young. Who knows?" There was a sudden gleam in Meredith's blue eyes. "Maybe we could find out. I'd like to know anyway."

"Learning these things is what we do," Julia said. "Maybe we can bring the conversation around to Miss Charlotte's life, subtly of course, when we go on Friday. She might volunteer the information when she's talking about her family. If it's something too painful for her, she probably won't say anything, and we won't ask directly."

"I guess we could look to see if she was ever married. She's been more or less a recluse since her great-grandmother died. It's possible she was married and then lost her husband."

"He might have died, true," Julia said. "And if they were divorced, it would have still been fairly scandalous back then, especially for a woman of Miss Charlotte's standing. Either way, Miss Charlotte being such a private person, maybe the marriage and what happened to the husband never became public knowledge."

"If there was a marriage," Meredith reminded her.

"That's something we ought to be able to find out fairly easily, especially if they were married in Savannah. I'll see what I can find out in the Chatham County records."

"We need more information on Jaden before we start on her, so I guess that leaves me to work on Quin's background check."

Julia gave her a sympathetic look. "Would you rather switch?"

"No, that's okay. It's got to be done sometime." Meredith got up and went to the door. "Better sooner than later, I guess."

"True," Julia said. "I'll let you know if I learn anything interesting."

"Yeah, me too."

Once Meredith was gone, Julia turned to her computer and started searching the county marriage records. She found nothing on any Charlotte Lockwood from the year she would have turned sixteen through the present. Curious, she looked further back and found the record showing the marriage of Miss Charlotte's father, Marcus Breyden Lockwood, to a Gladys Conway, and before that, the marriage of Miss Charlotte's grandfather, Matthew Lockwood to Amelia Jane Collins.

Feeling smugly proud of such success in a relatively short time, she looked for something under the name Alice Delorme, but came up empty. Miss Charlotte had told them that Alice had stayed up north for a while after the epidemic. Girls back then were often married at fifteen or sixteen, and she would have been quite an eligible bride too, having inherited her father's land and fortune, but it seemed more likely that she would have waited a while before even considering marriage, especially after all she had been through. But then there was that young law clerk Miss Charlotte had mentioned. There was a possibility there.

Julia checked the records for Cook County, Illinois. It took her some time, but she finally tracked down a marriage between Alice Delorme and Calvin Morton Lockwood on December 14, 1878. By then, she decided she might as well try to track down the birth and death dates of Miss Charlotte's father and grandfather, and Alice's too. She was just roughing out a Lockwood family tree when the front door opened.

She recognized the low, masculine voice this time, and looked out to see the man who had parked her car at the Delorme estate. He had two more crisp white envelopes in his hand. Before Carmen could take them from him, Julia went out to meet him.

"Hello again," she said.

"Good afternoon, ma'am." The man touched his cap. "I have letters to you and Mrs. Bellefontaine from Miss Charlotte."

She took them. "Thank you. I suppose we'll be seeing you on Friday."

"Yes, ma'am. Mrs. James said you would be coming. It will be a pleasure to see you again."

"Thank you," she said, knowing he was referring to Brenda. "We're looking forward to coming."

"Thank you, ma'am."

He turned to go, but Julia stopped him.

"I hope you don't mind," she said, "but could I ask your name?"

"Charles, ma'am."

"Have you worked for Miss Charlotte very long?"

His expression warmed with his smile. "Yes, ma'am. Since I got out of the service. I was a mechanic in the army, and when my grandmother told Miss Charlotte about me, she hired me on to drive her and to look after her cars and whatever else needed doing."

"It sounds like you enjoy your job."

He nodded. "Yes, ma'am, I do. I enjoy driving. I always liked tinkering with cars. Nowadays, with all the computers they keep putting in, there's some things I can't work on myself. But most of it I can see to. I pretty much do whatever Miss Charlotte needs done. I'm pretty handy with anything mechanical or electrical. Even plumbing, if it's not too big a job."

"Miss Charlotte must appreciate having you around."

"She tells me so, ma'am, but then she always was a gracious lady, and a fine lady to work for. Always treated me more than fair."

"She seems to have a lot of people working for her that have been there a long time."

"Oh, yes, ma'am. I don't know if there's a lady in Georgia who treats her people better. If there is, I haven't had the pleasure of meeting her."

"That's good to know. Thank you, Charles."

"You're welcome, ma'am. We'll be looking for you on Friday."

He touched his cap again and hurried away.

Carmen got up from her desk and came over to Julia. "Do you think those are more invitations?"

"I guess so. Miss Charlotte would make Emily Post look gauche."

Carmen frowned at her. "What is that?"

"What's what? Gauche? It means kind of awkward socially. Not very graceful or well mannered. Emily Post used to be considered the ultimate expert on good manners."

"Okay. Your Miss Charlotte must be *muy exigente*. Very demanding."

"I don't know if she's demanding as much as just very old-fashioned. She definitely wants things done a certain way, but as far as I can tell, she likes things to go on the way they always have as much as they can. She seems to like to keep the same people and even their families working for her. I think her great-grandmother Alice had a particular way of doing things, and Miss Charlotte has carried on that way ever since. People don't have much time for formal manners anymore. I know I don't. But it's nice to take that time once in a while. It's almost like going back before the Civil War."

"*Tradiciones*, traditions, they are very important to her."

Julia nodded. "I suppose, since she doesn't have any family, they're really all she's got, the family name, the history, the reputation. It's everything to her."

Carmen wrinkled her nose. "I'm sure she's a nice lady, but I would rather not have that kind of name. It must be very hard to be so perfect all the time."

"I don't think I'd like to feel like I had to be," Julia admitted. "But she really is a very nice lady. And I think she has more of a sly sense of humor than people give her credit for."

"I don't think I'd know what to do around her. I might not use the right fork at dinner."

"I don't think she'd ever make you feel uncomfortable. I was a little bit nervous when I went to her house, but she was so nice. I've always heard that good manners are mostly intended to make the other person feel comfortable, and she certainly does that."

"Does what?" Meredith asked, coming from her office. "I was on the phone talking to Quin's guy's apartment manager, who had absolutely nothing interesting or informative to say. What did I miss?"

"Miss Charlotte sent over a couple of notes," Julia said, handing her the envelope with her name on it. "Probably invitations for Friday."

Meredith looked it over and then broke the seal. "I'll be expecting one from you for the Philharmonic on Saturday."

"I'll send one right out," Julia said, opening her own envelope. "Make sure to hold your breath until you get it. Would you like to come hear the Savannah Philharmonic at Forsyth Park on Saturday, Carmen? We're going, and so are my husband and Quin. We'll have a picnic lunch. You're more than welcome to come with us if you'd like."

"Thanks anyway, but I promised Harmony I'd take her to have pizza on Saturday and then to the mall to pick out a costume. There's supposed to be a party at her school on Halloween, and I want her to have something she really likes."

"I think that's much more important than what we're doing," Julia said. "Harmony's a lucky little girl to have a mentor like you."

Carmen beamed at her. "I didn't think I'd like hanging around with a kid this much, especially volunteering with the Boys and Girls Club. It's like something a suburban housewife would do, you know? But it's been fun."

"I'm sure you make it fun for her too," Meredith said.

"Sure. When we're together, I have an excuse to act like I'm six too."

Julia laughed and shook her head and finally read the note Miss Charlotte had sent her.

My dear Mrs. Foley,

It was such a pleasure to have your company at lunch yesterday. I'm so glad to know you'll be coming back to the estate this coming Friday at three o'clock so we can continue our discussion with Miss Browning and Mrs. Bellefontaine. A modest tea will be served at four o'clock.

Charlotte Delorme Lockwood

"Three o'clock on Friday, as planned, with tea at four. Maybe I should wear gloves and a little pillbox hat."

"I'm sure you'd be charming," Meredith said. "And wouldn't it be fun? Did you learn anything that would indicate that Miss Charlotte was ever married?"

"No," Julia admitted, "but I did get some information about her parents and grandparents and great-grandparents. Come see the family tree I made."

***

By the time she got home that evening, Julia was worn out. The idea of cooking something hadn't appealed to her, so she'd picked up some Chinese food and brought it home. She found her husband asleep in his recliner with an open bottle of Cheerwine on the end table beside him and a lapful of cat.

Bunny, who had evidently been asleep, immediately lifted her head, trying to decide if she was going to stay put or run, but as best Julia could tell, her cast and splint made it easier for her to stay put. She was a little surprised that Beau didn't wake up too, but then she noticed he had his earbuds in and probably couldn't hear her enough to disturb his sleep.

She picked up the Cheerwine, not wanting to take the chance of having the cat accidentally knock it over and spill the cherry soft drink onto the carpet. They'd have to make a few adjustments while Bunny was with them. She hadn't thought about it much, but it was more or less like baby-proofing the house. She'd have to ask Meredith about safety risks for cats. She knew sometimes they liked to eat thread or yarn and that, if they did, it could prove fatal to them. She'd have to put up, and make sure Beau put up, anything that could be a danger. Bunny hadn't been here long, but she was already learning to move around despite the bandages. Julia would have to remind Beau to keep her in her crate when she wasn't in his lap.

"In his lap," she whispered, smiling and shaking her head.

She never would have believed it if she hadn't seen it, but then again, why not? Beau was a kindhearted, gentle man. He had spent his whole career caring for people. Why should a cat, especially one that was recovering from an accident, be that much different? Still, it wouldn't do for him to get too attached to her. She'd be well before long and going to a new home.

Bunny blinked at her, looking not quite sure about the intruder who had interrupted her nap, but then she laid her head back on Beau's stomach and closed her eyes.

"You're certainly making yourself at home," Julia said softly. "Just remember that's my husband and not a cat sofa."

Bunny only sighed contentedly and didn't look up.

Julia dished up the moo goo gai pan and poured Beau's Cheerwine over ice before waking him.

He started and then smiled as he took out his earbuds. "Hey there, Julie-bean."

"Hey there yourself," she said, leaning down to plant a kiss on his lips. "Hungry?"

"Yeah. And something smells good. What'd you make?"

"A trip over to the Chinese drive-through."

Beau chuckled and stroked one hand down Bunny's back before carefully gathering her into his arms. "Come on, Jack. Time for you to take a little nap so I can eat dinner with my sweetheart."

Bunny meowed in complaint.

Julia frowned at them. "Jack? You know she's a girl, right?"

"Yeah," Beau said, standing, "but look at those long legs, especially in the back. She looks more like a jackrabbit than a bunny."

Julia laughed softly. "All right. Well, whatever she is, put her in her crate and come eat while it's hot."

Beau went to settle the cat in bed and then came to the table.

"I invited Meredith and Quin to the concert on Saturday," Julia said. "Is that okay with you?"

Beau took a sip of his Cheerwine. "Great. I need to get in touch with him about playing a few holes of golf anyway."

"He said the same thing earlier today. He's a nice guy."

"He is. So does this mean Meredith thinks so too?"

Julia shrugged and took a bite of chicken and rice. "I think she's always thought that. Whether or not she thinks anything more, I don't know. I don't know if she knows yet. But they can enjoy hanging out with us anyway."

"And you didn't encourage this little rendezvous?"

"That was all Quin's idea. No way I'm getting involved in their relationship, no matter what it is."

Beau raised an eyebrow at her.

"Or isn't," she added.

He chuckled and took a sip of his drink.

"Oh, and Miss Charlotte invited Meredith and me back to the estate for tea on Friday."

"Very nice," Beau said. "Will the writer be joining you too?"

"Jaden? Oh, definitely. She and Miss Charlotte have definitely hit it off."

"That ought to be good for both of them."

"Yeah."

Beau looked up from his plate. "You don't sound too sure. What's wrong?"

"Oh, nothing. Really. Meredith thinks I'm being cynical about young people, and she's probably right."

"But?"

"Jaden's just so incredibly interested in Miss Charlotte and her family. It strikes me as a bit much. Especially without a real reason."

"I thought she was doing her master's thesis on the Lockwood Foundation and all that."

Julia speared another piece of chicken with her fork. "True. But there was that recent case where that ninety-two-year-old lady was ripped off by a young couple pretending to be her great-grandchildren"

"That was bad," he said, "but they weren't pretending to be her great-grandchildren. They *were* her great-grandchildren. My point is that I'm sure that thesis is pretty important to Jaden. I don't think it's not a *real reason*."

"I'm sure." She poked around her plate until she found a particularly plump mushroom to corner. "But Miss Charlotte hired us to check Jaden out, so at least we'll know if there's anything to worry about."

"You know what I always say. Listen to your gut and keep your eyes and your mind open."

"Do you always say that?" she asked, fighting a smile.

"Well, I think it a lot, so I guess that counts."

"It's good advice anyway," she said, leaning over to kiss his cheek. "I think I'll take it."

Chapter Seven

FRIDAY'S "MODEST" TEA AT THE Delorme Estate was as lovely and sumptuous as lunch had been. The three-tiered serving plate was full again. The bottom layer held heart-shaped crustless sandwiches filled with a delicate crab salad. The second was filled with lighter-than-air ladyfingers. And crowning it all was the top layer of plump, perfect strawberries surrounding a ramekin of cream cheese to dip them in. Julia was pleased that, as they ate and chatted, she and Meredith managed to delicately and casually find out more about Jaden, the area of Dallas she lived in, the company she worked for, other things about her that could be so telling in an investigation.

"Now I've been meaning to tell you about Grandmama and her law clerk," Miss Charlotte said as Ellen poured her more tea.

"Oh, I've been dying to hear," Jaden said, taking two of the little crab salad sandwiches and a few more strawberries. "Did he end up being your great-grandfather?"

She opened her notebook and looked at their hostess expectantly.

Miss Charlotte smiled enigmatically. "I told you Grandmama and her maid and groom went to Chicago after the epidemic. She left the estate in the hands of her father's old overseer, not wanting to go home only to see how empty it was for her with all her family gone. Chicago was a different world for her, she always said, a place where she knew no one and need not suffer the sympathy of her friends and neighbors."

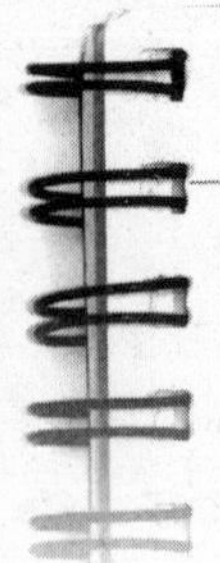

Chicago
October 1876

"I do beg your pardon, Miss Delorme," Mr. Lockwood said as he stood before the fire in the parlor of my townhouse, his tall hat in one hand and his brown sack coat pushed back on one side so he could put his hand in his pocket. He did look genuinely aggrieved and, truly, rather young for someone charged with such weighty matters.

I looked up at Beryl to see what I ought to say to him.

"You must forgive Miss Alice, Mr. Lockwood," Beryl said with a slight curtsy. "The poor child has been very ill until just recently and, I must say, prostrate with grief. It is difficult for her to be without Mr. Parkison's guidance in such a matter."

"I quite understand," Mr. Lockwood said, and his dark eyes were kind. "And, truly, Miss Delorme, Mr. Parkison is devastated that he was unable to meet with you today, but he is involved in a trial of some import, and matters have taken a turn that could prove disastrous not only to his client but to the client's family and business interests. I'm certain you understand the urgency...."

I nodded slightly. "I am certain he would not send you, Mr. Lockwood, if he did not feel you were competent to take his place in my trifling affairs."

Beryl beamed at me.

"Believe me, Miss Delorme, Mr. Parkison places great importance on your affairs and is most eager to assist you in any way possible. But the urgency of this other matter forces him to send me in his stead. But I assure you I am well acquainted with your interests and prepared to see to anything and everything you need."

I nodded again, calm and gracious in my mourning black as Beryl had said I ought to be.

"I spoke to Mr. Parkison about this matter previously, but when he told me all that would be expected of me, in the state I was in at that time—"

"And her being so young yet," Beryl added.

Mr. Lockwood smiled encouragingly at me. "I assure you, he understands, and I understand. And now that you are recovered, now that you are more yourself, you will want to settle the estates of your parents and your brothers and see that everything is in order and that you have clear title to all their holdings." He picked up the portfolio that lay in the chair beside him. "I have prepared, under Mr. Parkison's direction, of course, all the documents you will be required to sign in order to begin the process. He's asked that I review them with you, answer any questions you may have, and then leave them here for your review. He assures me he will be at liberty tomorrow afternoon, and at that time, if it is convenient for you, he will return here with me to answer any further questions you may have and then have you sign them. Would that be agreeable?"

"Yes," I said. "Of course."

"Now," Mr. Lockwood said, offering me his hand. "If you will, might we sit at this table so we will have a place to review these papers?"

I went with him to the settee and we took our places there with the low round mahogany table before us. One by one, he reviewed the papers that would legally acknowledge my interest in all the Delorme holdings.

"Naturally," he said, once we had reviewed the last of them, "these will all have to be approved by your cousin, Mr. Conrad Dumont."

"Oh." I chewed my lower lip. "Oh, yes, of course. I—I haven't seen him in a very long time. Not since I was a child. Will he be coming soon?"

"He responded to Mr. Parkison's letter with a telegram, saying he would be here at his earliest opportunity. I expect it will be sometime within the week. As you are not yet of age, his approval will be required, and as he is your nearest relation now living, it is only natural—"

"I am sure," I said quickly, and I looked over at Beryl. She was immediately beside me as always.

"Now, Miss Alice, you remember Mr. Conrad, I'm sure you do. And he will remember you. Your father always said he was a good boy, a responsible boy, one he'd trust with any of his business. That's why he's been in Tennessee all this

time, seeing to some of your family's business. He'll know what to do, you needn't fear for that, love."

There was a quick knock on the parlor door and then it opened.

"There's a gentleman to see Miss Alice," Teddy said, his one blue and one brown eye fixed mildly on me. "Mr. Dumont."

"Give me a moment," I told him.

Beryl brought my veil and arranged it over my face. It was a very light one, and I would be able to see him quite well through it.

"She is in mourning after all," Beryl said apologetically.

Mr. Lockwood nodded. "Quite right."

Beryl turned to the parlor door. "Teddy, you may bring the gentleman in now."

"Yes, Mum," Teddy said. "This way, Mr. Dumont."

Conrad Dumont was a tall, blond man, rather stolid as I remembered him to be, but kind enough for that. He studied me for a moment and then came to me, both hands outstretched.

"Cousin Alice."

I clasped hands with him, and he took the seat beside me, which Mr. Lockwood had kindly vacated. From my childhood, I remembered Conrad being very businesslike and grown up, but now I realized he was not so much older than I. Perhaps ten years. Perhaps not so much as that.

"I know you have had my letters," he said. "I wish there was no need of this between us, cousin, and that my uncle and aunt and my other cousins were alive yet, but please do not concern yourself over any of these business matters. I very

often spoke to your father about his holdings, and I would be happy to see to them for you as long as you like."

"Thank you," I said, lowering my eyes. "That is most comforting. I-I'm afraid it may be some while before I will be prepared to face returning to the estate. Without Mama and Papa there—" I squeezed his hands. "I'm sure you understand."

"I do. I thought, if you would like, that I could bring Effie and the baby with me there so I could watch over everything for you until you're ready to come back home. Your father was more like a father than an uncle to me when I was young. He taught me everything I know about being a man of business, and I wouldn't think of failing him now."

"You're very kind," I whispered, a sudden catch in my throat.

"There now, Miss Alice," Beryl said. "Perhaps you ought to come lie down and let the gentlemen discuss what needs to be done."

"Yes," I said, standing. "Yes, I will. Forgive me, cousin, but may I introduce Mr. Calvin Lockwood. He is Mr. Parkison's clerk and has been tasked with seeing to all these matters I've been left with."

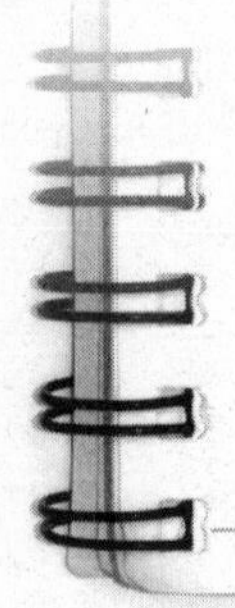

"Mr. Dumont," Mr. Lockwood said, shaking hands. "It is, of course, a great pleasure to meet you. And it is no task, Miss Delorme, but my honor to give you any assistance I may."

"Thank you," I said, and I let Beryl guide me from the room.

"But what happened after that?" Jaden asked. There was only half of a ladyfinger left on her once-full plate, and she was still furiously scribbling notes in her notebook. "I guess she signed all the papers, and since she was a Lockwood, she must have married the lawyer."

"Clerk," Miss Charlotte said, "but he did indeed become a lawyer not so very long afterward."

"And they got married? I guess girls married very young back then."

"Not quite that young," Miss Charlotte said firmly. "Not Grandmama." There was the tiniest curve in her withered lips. "She told me she was rather smitten from the very first, but there was so much else she had to contend with, she really never thought it could become more than a passing fancy. After all, he was 'so very much older' than she. Five years does make a tremendous difference at that age."

"I suppose it wasn't uncommon for girls her age to be married to older men," Meredith said, "especially when they were wealthy and well connected. I'm glad it wasn't the case with her."

"Did she talk much about him?" Jaden asked.

Miss Charlotte paused for a thoughtful moment. "Not a great deal. Not to me. I think, even after so many years, it still pained her. I never saw her but that she wore her brooch with his picture in it."

"Do you have that still?" Jaden glanced at Julia, almost as if she thought she had asked too much too soon, but Miss Charlotte only smiled.

"Brenda," she called, hardly raising her voice.

Brenda came to the dining room door. "Yes, Miss Charlotte?"

"Would you bring me Grandmama's things?"

"Right away, ma'am."

"I have many of her possessions stored away of course," Miss Charlotte told her guests, "but there are several that I prize the most. I like to keep them where I can look at them now and again and remember all she told me."

"Do you have any of her clothes still?" Julia asked, caught up in Jaden's fascination with the woman's history. "Or shoes? I would love to see her shoes."

"Some. Carefully packed away." Miss Charlotte put one delicate hand on Jaden's arm. "One of my treasures, Miss Browning, is Grandmama's wedding dress, along with her veil, gloves, and shoes and even the dainty white Bible she carried with her that day."

"I'd really love to see your family pictures," Jaden pressed. "I've noticed the ones you have hanging here, but I was hoping there'd be more. You know, from Miss Alice's day. Maybe her children and grandchildren."

Miss Charlotte's indulgent smile cooled slightly at the mention of the pictures. "I'm sure we could arrange that."

"Oh," Jaden breathed. "Could we— Do you think we could see them? And everything else?"

"I will ask Brenda to have some of the things brought out and aired so you can look at them the next time you come. We try to keep them from being exposed too much to the light or anything else that might make them deteriorate more quickly."

Jaden beamed at her, and Julia was pleased to know that Miss Charlotte was planning on a next time. For them all, Julia hoped. She was enjoying herself immensely and, now that she and

Meredith were working for Miss Charlotte too, this would give her another opportunity to find out more about Jaden.

"Here it is, Miss Charlotte," Brenda announced as she came back into the dining room. "And I found that picture you were telling them about too."

She was carrying a carved wooden box with drawers and a hinged lid and gold fittings, probably a jewelry box of some kind. It was made of cherrywood so polished that the dining room lights gleamed off it.

Miss Charlotte put on her gold-framed glasses as Brenda set the box down before her. "Excellent. Thank you. And would you be so kind as to see Grandmama's wedding things are brought out and aired for the next time these ladies come to call?"

"I'll see to it, Miss Charlotte. And please don't forget that appointment you have in a little while."

There was a touch of mischief in Miss Charlotte's eyes as she glanced at the brooch watch pinned to her pale blue silk blouse. "I still have a little time before then, but thank you for reminding me."

Brenda pressed her lips together. Not out of displeasure, Julia thought, but to keep herself from any telltale hint of a smile. "Just as you say, Miss Charlotte."

Meredith gave Julia a questioning glance. "Maybe we should save the rest of the story for another time."

Jaden caught a quick breath as if she were going to protest, but then she looked down at her notebook and didn't say anything.

Julia gave Meredith a subtle nod. If Miss Charlotte was getting tired, they certainly didn't want to keep her from her rest. "We don't want to wear out our welcome."

"My schedule can wait a bit longer," Miss Charlotte said, her hands resting on the top of the cherrywood box filled with her great-grandmother's things. "It would hardly be fair to Miss Browning here to bring this out and not give her even a glimpse of what's inside."

Jaden's face lit. "I'd sure love to see even a little bit."

"Don't worry yourself, Miss Browning," Miss Charlotte said. "We will have time to see it all even if that time is not now."

"Yes, ma'am," Jaden said, leaning forward a little, her eyes on the box.

Miss Charlotte lifted the lid and then adjusted her glasses on her nose. "I see you don't need glasses yet, Miss Browning. They are such a nuisance. Or perhaps you've had that procedure I've heard about."

"Lasik?" Jaden asked, blinking her eyes. "Oh, no, ma'am. I'm glad to say my vision is very good so far. Twenty-twenty."

Meredith frowned just slightly, but she didn't comment, and Julia's attention was drawn back to the box sitting in front of their hostess.

Miss Charlotte's eyes warmed as she took out the picture on top. "Mr. Alexander Lawton Harper, the actor Grandmama so admired."

The photograph showed nothing of the man but his face in profile. His eyes were cast down slightly, fringed by long dark lashes as he stared contemplatively past the camera, and there was a touch of a wistful smile on his handsome lips.

"Ooh," Jaden said, when Miss Charlotte handed her the picture. "Too bad he wasn't around for motion pictures. I'd be a fan."

She passed the photograph to Julia.

"No wonder Alice was smitten with him," Meredith said, looking over her shoulder. "Pity she never got to see him perform."

Julia shook her head. "It's a shame. She was such a young thing to suddenly lose her whole family like that. I wonder if she held on to this picture as a remembrance of the happier time before." She smiled wistfully. "I used to hang posters of my favorites on my bedroom walls. I think I still have some of them rolled up somewhere. It's funny to think of someone back then being no different."

Miss Charlotte nodded. "And I used to collect movie magazines. Errol Flynn was so terribly handsome, though Grandmama would never let me read the scandalous stories about him." She opened the box again. "And this was the brooch she always wore. The one with my great-grandfather's picture in it."

She carefully opened the finely etched golden brooch and showed them a picture of Calvin Lockwood. Like the actor, Lockwood had loosely curled dark hair and long lashes. His features weren't quite as perfect, but he was a fine-looking man with both kindness and strength in his expression.

"When did they marry, Miss Charlotte?" Julia asked.

"Grandmama turned nineteen in 1878. They were married that December. Wait a moment." Miss Charlotte opened one of the drawers in the box, shuffled through it and then opened the other. Then she took out another photograph. This one was of a young woman in a sumptuous white silk gown decked with pearls and lace, her fair hair in a chignon low on her graceful neck and crowned by a wreath of orange blossoms. Her eyes were wide, tilted up slightly at the corners, and Julia realized they were much like Miss Charlotte's.

She was on the arm of the young man from the picture in the brooch. He stood tall beside her, making her look almost waifish next to him, though he wasn't heavily built. There was something very sweet and protective in the way his hand caressed hers as it rested on his sleeve.

"That's lovely," Meredith said. "And look how tiny her waist is."

"Grandmama wore a corset every day until well into the First World War," Miss Charlotte said. "She said she felt almost scandalized to give them up, but every nonessential piece of metal was wanted for the war effort, so no more stays."

Jaden giggled.

"She would never admit it," Miss Charlotte told her confidingly, "but I think she was secretly glad."

"I would be too," Julia said. "I don't know how anybody even breathed in one of those things."

"And this," Miss Charlotte said, "was her engagement ring."

She took from the box a gold ring set with a gorgeous oval-cut garnet surrounded by diamonds. Next to it, she set a plain gold band, not wide but still with substance to it. Something lasting.

"That was her wedding ring. I never saw her without them. Not until that last talk we had when she gave them to me."

Before anyone could say anything else, Brenda came back into the room.

"Excuse me, Miss Charlotte, but Mr. Richard would like to speak to you."

Miss Charlotte looked mildly surprised. "You told him I had callers, didn't you?"

"Yes, ma'am, but he said you'd want to know right away. Says it's important."

"Maybe we should go," Meredith said. "We've probably stayed too long."

"Nonsense," Miss Charlotte said, putting the rings back into the box along with the photographs and the brooch. "If he thinks it's that urgent, Brenda, tell him to come in."

"Yes, ma'am."

Brenda left the room and returned with a tall, stocky man about sixty with a toothpick in one corner of his mouth and a small book in both hands. With him was a very young man, probably still in his teens. He too was tall and stocky, and there was a definite resemblance between him and the older man.

"I'm sorry to interrupt, Miss Charlotte," the older man said, "but I think you're going to be very interested in what we just found."

Miss Charlotte gave him a reproving glance and then turned to her guests. "Ladies, this is Mr. Richard Sheldon. He is my fourth cousin once removed and the manager of the Delorme Estate. And this is Jeff Sheldon, his grandson. Richard, this is Mrs. Julia Foley, Mrs. Meredith Bellefontaine, and Miss Jaden Browning."

"Excuse me," Richard said with a quick duck of his head, and he self-consciously left the toothpick on one of the dirty plates on the table. "Good afternoon, ladies. Miss Charlotte, you know that fireplace we're working on in the blue room?"

"Yes?"

"Well, we had to pull some of it down because it was coming down anyway. Steve and Amos Johns had it about half done and Jeff was helping them when they found this in a little cubbyhole in the wall. I never knew that place was even there. I sure didn't know this was there."

With a puzzled frown, Miss Charlotte took the little book from him and opened it. Then her face paled. "Richard, this—"

"Yes, ma'am," Richard said.

Miss Charlotte's fine-boned hands tightened on the book. "This is Grandmama's diary."

Julia leaned a little closer to Miss Charlotte to get a look at the writing on the yellowed page she had opened to. *He accused her of terrible things, and now I can never explain—*

Miss Charlotte snapped the little book shut.

Chapter Eight

"I'M SORRY, BUT I DON'T quite know what to say." Miss Charlotte forced a smile. "Forgive me, but I didn't think that Grandmama left a diary. I remember her mentioning that she kept one, but since it's been so many years now and we never found one after she went on, I thought maybe she'd destroyed it. I can't quite believe it's still around now. Is this all you found, Richard?"

"Yes, ma'am, but I thought you'd want it."

"Granddad wouldn't let us look at it, Miss Charlotte," Jeff said eagerly. "He said it wasn't our place."

"Quite right, Jeff. Thank you."

"Miss Charlotte," Brenda said, coming up to her when the two men had left them, "you look like a ghost. Maybe you ought to take a minute to just sit still."

Miss Charlotte patted her hand. "No, I'm all right now. I only had a bit of a surprise." Again she forced a smile. "Well, ladies, this is very exciting, isn't it? Especially with us talking about Grandmama as we have been."

"Very exciting," Julia said finally. "I'm sure you must be eager to see what's in there."

Jaden leaned closer, her lips parted in anticipation, but then she clasped her hands in front of her and settled back into her chair, her lips now pressed tightly together. Finally, she said, "I can't say I wouldn't love to read that myself, but I'm sure you'll want to do that first before you decide what you want made public."

"Grandmama was always discreet," Miss Charlotte said serenely. "And I will, of course, respect her privacy even now. But I'm sure there is a wealth of information in here that will add depth and authenticity to your book, Miss Browning, and I will be happy to give you access to it. But, for now, ladies, I hope you will excuse me. Brenda, I believe I have an appointment."

Brenda immediately showed the guests out, and it took a few minutes for Charles to bring their cars around to the front of the house. Soon, Julia and Meredith were headed back to the office.

"Poor Jaden looked heartbroken," Meredith said.

"Not so much heartbroken as frustrated. I can't help wondering if that's more than just historical interest. Still, Alice Lockwood's diary after all these years. I'd love to know what's in it too."

"Wouldn't we all?" Meredith shook her head. "But I can understand Miss Charlotte wanting to look through it first. No matter how ladylike and discreet Alice was, her diary had to be full of things that were, if not actually scandalous, very personal."

Julia glanced at her with a slightly knowing smile. "I wonder how much of that diary her property manager looked over before he brought it to her."

"Richard? He's got to be in on all the family secrets, especially since he's the latest in a long line of family caretakers. It's really kind of amazing that someone in his direct line has looked after the Delorme Estate since Miss Alice's day. People just don't much do that anymore."

"Yeah," Julia said. "But look at the others who work for Miss Charlotte. She likes having good people around her, and she treats them so well they don't want to leave her. Look at Brenda. I understand her grandmother was the one who pretty much raised Miss Charlotte from the time she was a baby, and then Brenda's mother and now Brenda after her." She chuckled. "Miss Charlotte must have known Brenda from the time she was a baby. It's funny to think of that now that Brenda's looking after her."

"They're obviously very fond of each other. Brenda sure is protective of her."

"I'm glad someone is," Julia said as she turned the car onto the highway. "I guess Richard would be her closest relation at this point since she never had children."

"She doesn't seem to care for him too much," Meredith observed.

Julia grinned. "I don't think she appreciated him coming in with a toothpick hanging out of his mouth while she had company either."

Meredith snickered. "I'm sure that simply isn't done, and I can imagine she cringed when he left it on a plate on her elegant table. Brenda must have discreetly removed it."

"Was it removed?"

"Yeah. I noticed it was gone when we all got up to leave."

"You're probably right," Julia said. "It's probably part of Brenda's job to make sure Miss Charlotte's sensibilities aren't offended."

Meredith considered for a moment. "I wonder if Brenda would tell us more about Miss Charlotte's early life. I know you didn't find any evidence she was married, but I'd still like to know if there was anyone she considered marrying. Brenda won't likely say anything though. Not to us."

"I don't know. Maybe when we spend a little more time with Miss Charlotte we'll have some opportunities to find out more. I suppose Jaden will want to know things like that for her book, if nothing else. Do you suppose she'll keep asking us to come to lunch and everything? I mean, it is lovely, but I hate to think she has to make such a production of it every time."

"But she likes it," Meredith said. "The past and the old ways seem very important to her, and she has the money to hang on to them longer than most people. I can't say I'm not enjoying getting a taste of it myself too, though I wish she had let us see more of what's in that keepsake box of hers." She thought for a moment. "I wonder why Jaden lied to her about her contacts."

Julia glanced over at her and then back at the road ahead of her. "So that's what you were frowning about when Miss Charlotte asked her about glasses. Are you sure?"

"I saw the faint line of one in her right eye. I mean, there's nothing to be ashamed of about needing vision correction."

"I don't think so anyway," Julia said. "Are you sure that's what you saw? Could it have just been an odd way the light was hitting her eyes or anything?"

"Well, I couldn't swear to it. I mean I didn't want to be obviously staring or anything."

"We'll just have to both see if we can tell next time. She certainly lied with a straight face, if that's what she was doing."

"Now, don't get all cynical again," Meredith said. "Maybe I was wrong. We'll see what we can see at our next meeting."

"Fair enough," Julia said, and then the low-fuel indicator on her dashboard lit. "Oops, I'd better stop for gas. I know I still have fifty miles or so before I really run out, but I'd hate to get stuck anywhere, and Beau would probably never let me hear the end of it."

She pulled off the highway and into the nearest gas station, rolled down the windows and turned off the engine. Savannah was warm even in October, and she knew Meredith would be too warm in the car with the windows up and the air conditioner off.

It didn't take long to fill the tank and pay at the pump. She had just taken her receipt and was about to get back into the car, when she heard someone call her name. Smiling, she turned around and saw a stylishly dressed woman coming toward her, her navy felt cloche hat brightened with a rose made of cheerful red netting.

"Maggie Lu! Hi!"

"Julia. Meredith." Maggie Lu hurried over to them. "How are you both?"

"Doing all right," Meredith said, leaning closer to the driver's side window. "What about you?"

"Just seeing to some errands. Have you two been staying out of trouble?"

"We've just had tea at the Delorme Estate," Julia said.

"With Miss Charlotte," Meredith added significantly.

"That Miss Charlotte," Maggie Lu said with an indulgent smile. "Brenda has the hardest time getting her to do right and not wear herself out when she has company."

"Do you know Brenda?" Julia asked her.

"Sure I do. She comes to my church when she can, and she always sings in the choir when we have our Christmas and Easter music. I haven't really had a good talk with her for a while now, but we stop and chat all the time. Mostly she tells me about her two boys in Wyoming and their kids."

"And you never bring out your pictures," Meredith said dubiously.

"Maybe a time or two," Maggie Lu said with perfect innocence. "I can't really remember."

"I've got two boys and grandchildren too. You can't fool me."

Maggie Lu laughed low and warm. "You just wait until that great-grandbaby of mine comes. Then you're going to see pictures!"

"Hey," Julia said, "are you busy Saturday? We're all going to hear the free concert at Forsyth Park and have a picnic. The weather is supposed to be great, and we thought it'd be fun. We'd love to have you come with us."

"Who all is we?" Maggie Lu asked.

"Just Meredith and me and Beau and Quin. What do you think?"

"It sounds really nice, but I don't know if I could sit on the ground that long anymore." Maggie Lu gestured toward her hair. "I may not be completely gray yet, but sometimes my back reminds me I ought to be."

"Actually, we were going to bring lawn chairs for everybody," Julia said. "None of us is getting any younger."

"Please come," Meredith said, leaning closer to the window. "We're not doing anything fancy, but it'll be fun."

Maggie Lu looked from her to Julia. "Well, all right then. If you're sure. Can I bring something?"

"I think we're all set for food and something to drink," Julia said. "Just bring yourself and your knitting, if you want."

"What time are we meeting?"

"Have we decided?" Meredith asked Julia.

"Not specifically," Julia said. "Around lunchtime, but let me call you, Maggie Lu, so you'll know for sure."

Maggie Lu nodded, gave Julia a hug, and then squeezed Meredith's hand through the car window. "I'll wait to hear from you then. I haven't been to a concert in the park in I don't know how long. Maybe since before my Darwin passed. I'm looking forward to it."

"We'll call you," Julia said, and with a wave, she got into the car and drove away.

"I'm glad we saw her," Meredith said. "And I'm glad you invited her. I've been wanting to catch up with her."

"Me too," Julia said, "I'm glad she's free on Saturday."

"Isn't that the truth. I hope I still have that much going on when I'm her age."

"Me too."

Meredith sighed. "I guess that means we're going to have to finally decide on a menu."

"Well, it won't be as fancy as one of Miss Charlotte's luncheons, but I think we'll figure something out."

***

Saturday was warmer than Julia had expected, but there was a nice breeze, and the park was really very pleasant. Julia and Meredith had decided between them that they would have a classic picnic with fried chicken, corn on the cob, potato salad, lemonade, and strawberry cupcakes. Maggie Lu surprised them with her delectable addition of deviled eggs. They sat in the shade of the live oak trees, close enough to the orchestra to be able to enjoy the music, but far enough away so they could hear each other talk and not disturb anyone else.

After a while, Beau set his plate on the ground and slouched back in his chair. "That was delicious, ladies. Now I'm not sure I can stay awake for the rest of the concert."

"Nap if you want to," Julia told him.

"Before you drop off," Quin said, "how about we make actual plans to play a round of golf before long?"

"I'd like that," Beau said, sitting up a little. "When are you free?"

"Tomorrow?"

Beau chuckled. "It might be a little late to get a decent tee time at this point."

"How about I give it a try. If they don't have any times left for tomorrow, we can make it for next Sunday. What do you think?"

"That ought to be all right. Anytime in the afternoon would work."

"I'll see what I can get and call you, fair enough?"

"That's good. Let me know."

"How's your houseguest?" Quin asked.

"Jack? She's fine."

"Jack?" Meredith asked. "I thought her name was Bunny?"

Julia shook her head with a wry grin, and Beau chuckled.

"She doesn't seem to mind."

"Whoever ends up with her will probably name her something else anyway."

"Yeah, probably," Beau said, looking a little wistful.

He settled into his chair again, drowsy-eyed but not quite asleep as the orchestra began a low, lulling melody.

"So tell us about what happened at Miss Charlotte's tea," Quin said.

Maggie Lu took a sip of her lemonade and fanned herself with a paper plate. "I suppose it was elegant. Brenda tells me sometimes about what it's like when Miss Charlotte entertains."

"Elegant is the perfect word for it," Julia said. "Everything was so nicely done, and we got a chance to talk about her great-grandmother and the early part of her life. And Miss Charlotte brought out several of her things for us to see. And the most exciting thing of all is that, while we were there, Richard Sheldon, her property manager, came in to tell her he had found Alice's diary hidden behind a fireplace. We didn't get to really talk about it, but it looked like it must have been there for decades."

"I bet your writer friend was thrilled with that discovery," Quin said, sneaking a second cupcake.

"Writer friend?" Maggie Lu asked.

"Her name's Jaden Browning," Julia said, "and she wants to write a book about Alice Delorme and her foundation and what Miss Charlotte has done since Alice died."

Julia described the historical society meeting where they'd met Jaden and how interested she was in everything to do with the Lockwood family. "She wants to write this book for her thesis. She's still working on her master's degree."

"That young, is she?" Maggie Lu asked.

"Well, not a child, but still pretty young."

Maggie Lu chuckled and got out the beginnings of the yellow baby blanket she was knitting. "The older I get, the younger those young ones seem."

"She's very excited about what she's doing," Meredith said. "Miss Charlotte likes her, even if she's a little wary about her popping up the way she did. But she's fascinated by the family and is always asking questions."

"Even if she isn't very truthful about answering them," Julia said grumpily.

"Now, you don't know that for sure."

"Okay, okay, maybe not. But why would someone wear one contact if she didn't need to correct her vision?"

"Heterochromia," Quin said at once.

The soft click of Maggie Lu's knitting needles stopped. "Hetero-what?"

"Heterochromia," Quin repeated, giving her a good look at his eyes, one blue, one brown. "Many people with eyes that are different colors decide to wear one contact so they'll both look the same. I never felt like bothering with it, but some people do. It's a simple fix."

"Is it something you were born with?"

"I was," Quin said. "The way I understand it, eyes have pigment just like skin. And, like skin, the amount of melanin in them makes them darker or lighter. So brown eyes have a lot of melanin and blue eyes have very little. The trick with eye color, though, is that the melanin isn't produced in the eyes themselves. The cells that make it have to travel to the eyes during the pregnancy. If there is a problem and more of those cells get to one eye than the other, then one eye will get more melanin than the other and will be darker than the other."

"But it doesn't affect your vision, right?" Beau asked.

"Not at all," Quin said.

"So, if this is what's going on with Jaden," Meredith said, "then she wasn't lying when she said her vision was good."

"I suppose," Julia allowed. "If she did need a corrective lens, I don't know why she'd lie about it. A lot of people wear them, even at her age. But if it was heterochromia, I guess there's no reason she'd have to mention that if she didn't want to."

Maggie Lu started knitting again. "I suppose that's something that might be passed on to her children too."

"Actually, no," Quin told her. "My understanding is that, unless there's some kind of underlying syndrome, and those often cause severe medical problems, it's a result of a mild injury during pregnancy and not in the child's DNA. It is that way for some breeds of dog, but not humans except in very rare cases."

"So you think Jaden might have heterochromia?" Julia asked Meredith.

Meredith shrugged. "It's possible. Is there another answer if she was telling the truth about having good eyesight? That is, if she was actually wearing one contact and I wasn't just seeing something."

Quin shrugged. "I wouldn't have thought about it at all if I didn't have the condition myself. It's quite uncommon. Only about one percent of people in the world have it."

Meredith looked him over archly. "I knew you were special."

He gave her a wink.

They finished eating and then packed up the leftovers. The wind picked up a little, and it grew pleasantly cool under the trees.

"I'm still wondering about that diary," Julia said. "But I suppose if Miss Charlotte decides it's private, that will be that."

"She'll talk to Brenda about it," Maggie Lu said with a nod.

Chapter Nine

"Miss Charlotte might be the boss," Maggie Lu said as the breeze carried to them the orchestra's medley of songs from Puccini's *Tosca*, "but she and Brenda are more friends now than anything else." She smiled a little. "Brenda told me that when she was a little girl, her grandma Hannah told her she always had to be on her best behavior in front of Miss Charlotte. Miss Charlotte was always a stickler for proprieties, of course."

Meredith and Julia exchanged grins.

"But, from what Brenda says," Maggie Lu continued, "there's not much the two of them don't talk about."

"Probably because Miss Charlotte knows she can trust Brenda to keep a confidence," Meredith said.

Maggie Lu nodded. "Not that I'd ask, but I'm sure she wouldn't tell anything she thought Miss Charlotte wouldn't want told. Not Brenda."

Julia nodded. "I'm not surprised. Miss Charlotte obviously relies on her for a lot of things."

"Brenda keeps her schedule and looks out for her health and pretty much runs the household, from what I've heard," Maggie Lu said. "Of course, Miss Charlotte has plenty of staff, but Brenda outranks everybody but Miss Charlotte herself." She laughed softly. "And sometimes, if Miss Charlotte won't do right about getting the rest she needs or eating what she ought, Brenda pulls rank on her."

"I'm not surprised," Julia said, laughing too.

"This Brenda must be quite a woman," Quin said. "I'd love to meet her and Miss Charlotte sometime."

Julia looked over at Meredith, sure they were both thinking the same thing. Brenda had been very professional and capable when they had seen her, but she had mostly kept herself in the background. How were they ever going to have a talk with her about Miss Charlotte's life under those circumstances?

"If anyone knows about Miss Charlotte's life, it would have to be Brenda," Meredith said.

"It would," Maggie Lu agreed. "But she's not going to tell you anything personal. Not about Miss Charlotte."

"No," Julia said, "and we wouldn't expect her to. It would just be nice to know a little more about Miss Charlotte's life. But I guess that's what Jaden is trying to find out."

"And I suppose Miss Charlotte will tell her what she wants her to know," Meredith said, and then there was a slight, rueful smile on her face. "I guess we need to remind ourselves that we weren't hired to investigate Miss Charlotte."

Quin chuckled.

"I almost wish we were," Julia said. "At least then I'd have an excuse for my nosiness."

"Curiosity," Beau said sweetly, and she squeezed his hand.

Maggie Lu knitted thoughtfully for a moment longer and then paused again. "I can try to remember anything Brenda has said to me about Miss Charlotte. And tell you what I remember, about her and about Miss Alice too."

"Do you remember Miss Alice?" Julia asked, certain she looked as startled as everyone else.

"Not really," Maggie Lu admitted. "I was only five or six when she passed away, but I remember hearing people talk about her, how they were surprised, even at her age, that she had finally died, and how they felt sorry for poor Miss Charlotte being left alone, young as she was then, in that big old house. Did you know she was only eighteen? And all her family gone to their own rewards."

"I knew she was young," Julia said. "We were wondering if she had ever married. We couldn't find any record of it, at least not in Chatham County. I haven't had a chance to look into it any further, but it's awfully hard to prove a negative."

"What I always heard was that when Miss Alice died, Miss Charlotte broke off her engagement to her young man and didn't much socialize after that. Not for a long time."

"Really?" Meredith asked. "Did you ever hear why?"

"Not in particular," Maggie Lu said. "No."

"Do you know who she was seeing?" Julia asked.

Maggie Lu shook her head, knitting once again, the soft yellow yarn flying through her nimble fingers. "You'll have to let me think about that a minute. I'm sure I must have heard it sometime or another, but that was a long while back. It seems his father was big in industry, but I can't remember what it was. Shipping, I think. I'll remember the name in a minute. I know he went on to marry one of the Harris girls, their father had one of the big paper mills at the time." She pressed her lips together and shook her head. "I'll have to call you when it comes to me. Anyway, I never heard much more about it. Some folks said Miss Charlotte was so upset about losing her great-grandmother, she didn't want to go on."

"What do you think?" Julia asked.

"I don't really know. The way Brenda describes her, Miss Charlotte is a very strong-minded woman who's going to do what she needs to do no matter what else happens. Quitting just isn't something she does. But it could be it took her a while to grow into that. Eighteen is awfully young to be suddenly on your own, especially with the responsibility for the estate and the foundation too."

"But she was obviously up to the challenge," Beau said. "From all I've heard, the estate is thriving and the foundation has more than tripled in size since she took it over."

"That foundation was dear to Miss Alice's heart," Maggie Lu said. "That's one thing I remember folks talking about long after she died. She wanted to help those children find real families and get them out of orphanages and foster homes. And Miss Charlotte has made sure there's help for those new families while they're getting accustomed to each other. Sometimes people don't realize that there's more to it than just making the adoption legal. As fond as Miss Charlotte is of tradition, she makes sure the people who run the foundation for her are always looking for ways to improve what they do, to make it more efficient so they're able to help more and more people."

"I've always liked that about the Lockwood Foundation," Quin said. "And they have an excellent rating as far as how much of their donations actually go to helping the children and their adoptive families."

"No wonder Jaden wants to write about Miss Alice and Miss Charlotte both," Beau said. "But I wonder who'll take over for her when she's ready to retire."

"It sounds like that's not going to happen anytime soon," Julia said.

"But she'll pass away sometime," Quin observed. "And then what? She has to have someone designated to be next in line."

"I hadn't thought about that," Julia admitted, and she drank the last of her lemonade. "What do you think, Mere?"

Meredith shrugged. "I guess it would be that however-many-times-removed cousin of hers, Richard Sheldon, wouldn't it?"

"Maybe. Unless she put someone else in her will, and I don't know who that would be."

"If so, at least he'll know how to run the estate," Beau observed.

"But he might not be as likely to look after the foundation," Julia said. "At least not the same way he would the estate. I mean, he's been running the estate, not the foundation, and the estate brings in money, the foundation gives it out."

Quin shrugged. "Even if he wouldn't do it for philanthropic reasons, he could still use it as a tax write-off and to make himself look good publicly. He wouldn't be the first."

"True." Julia realized the music had stopped and looked over toward the orchestra. The musicians were packing up their instruments, and most of the picnickers were packing up their things. "It seems like the concert is over. This was so nice. We ought to do it again, concert or not, while the weather is still good."

Maggie Lu thought for a moment and then held up one finger. "Buckley. Timothy Buckley."

"Mm-kay," Julia said.

"That was the name of the man Miss Charlotte was going to marry back in 1949. I'm sure you can find out more about him on the internet somewhere. Nobody's safe anymore."

"Oh, great!" Meredith rummaged in her purse for a piece of paper and jotted down the name. "We'll definitely see if we can track down some information on him. Thanks, Maggie Lu."

"It was quite the talk when, about fifteen years later, Miss Charlotte started getting out again, mostly to raise money for Miss Alice's foundation and let people know about it."

"You mean she just disappeared all that time?" Julia asked.

"I don't know about *disappeared*, but I do remember people talking about it when she started going to some of the society parties and things like that again. You can probably find some mentions in the newspapers about it. But then, Miss Alice did about the same thing, Brenda's mother told me back then. After she came back from Chicago with her son. But you'll want to see if Miss Charlotte will tell you about that. I don't know anything more."

"If she'll tell us," Meredith said.

"She seems to like talking about Alice and her family," Julia said. "If she's going to cooperate with Jaden on that book, she's going to have to give at least some information about Alice that isn't common knowledge now. And, I would think, at least a basic account of her life. The biography on the foundation website is pretty sketchy on details. We'll have to see what we find out next time Miss Charlotte invites us."

"Maybe we ought to invite Miss Charlotte," Meredith said. "It's the only polite thing to do."

"But would she come? Besides the events she goes to, I'm not sure she goes out anywhere."

"She does like being the hostess," Maggie Lu said. "I don't remember Brenda ever mentioning that she went to someone's home. At least not lately."

"It could be that all her close friends have passed on by now," Beau said. "She's getting up there."

"Maybe," Julia told him. "But she can have new friends. I'd like to be her friend."

"Me too," said Meredith. "But somehow I can't see her dropping by for lunch or texting me for my crab salad recipe."

Quin grinned. "She is rather a personage."

"A lonely personage, if you ask me," Julia said. "I know she and Brenda are close, but Brenda has other friends. Miss Charlotte ought to too."

"Does Brenda ever mention her visiting anyone?" Meredith asked Maggie Lu.

Maggie Lu shook her head. "Not in some while. Miss Charlotte used to have ladies from her church visit her now and again, but the ones she was particular friends with passed on some years back. Brenda says she's too set in her ways to put up with anyone new."

"She seems to like Jaden," Julia said.

Meredith chuckled. "I think she hasn't really spent time with anyone that young in a long time. She seems more amused by her than anything."

"Maybe so, but I think it's good for both of them."

"I think so too," Maggie Lu said. "Ladies of a certain age, even ladies of *my* certain age, need to spend time with young folk now and then. Keeps us from thinking they don't know anything."

"I guess that's true," Beau said. "And lets them know we old folks know a little something too."

Maggie Lu smiled at him. "There's that."

Quin glanced at his watch and stood up. "I'm sorry to have to do this, but I'm supposed to meet with my client in a little while, and I probably should get going. Did you ladies learn anything about this man he wants to go into partnership with?"

Julia shook her head. "We followed every lead you gave us and tracked down everything we could about him. We didn't find anything that seems out of order."

"Not yet anyway," Meredith added. "But we don't think you ought to give him the green light just yet. There are several businesses he's been a partner in with the same woman, and we haven't been able to learn anything about her at all. Until we do one way or another, you probably shouldn't tell your client to go ahead."

"Thanks for the update," Quin said. "I'll tell him, but I'm afraid if you don't find something definite against the idea, he's going to go ahead anyway. That is if he hasn't already."

Meredith stood up too. "We'll keep trying."

He squeezed her hand. "Thanks. I'll be in touch. I'll call you about golf, Beau. Julia. Maggie Lu. It was good seeing you."

"We'll see you soon, Quin," Julia said as he walked away.

"I guess we ought to go too," Beau told her. "I want to make sure our patient is doing all right."

Julia shook her head and got out of her lawn chair. "She's got you wrapped around her little striped paw."

He slipped one arm around her. "Jealous?"

She laughed. "Terribly. Come on. Let's see how she is. Maggie Lu, we'll see you soon. We're planning on having Meredith over for dinner soon. Would you like to come?"

"I'd like that," Maggie Lu said as she packed up her knitting and then picked up the container that had once held the deviled eggs. "Have you decided when?"

"I'll call you. It won't be anything fancy, not like the dinners Miss Charlotte has, but we'd love to have you."

"Just something casual with friends is the best kind of dinner. And I want to see this Miss Bunny who's got Beau running."

"She may not be very sociable with strangers," Beau said. "She isn't quite sure of Julia yet."

Julia rolled her eyes. "That's not so. She just especially likes you because you let her sleep in your lap all the time."

Maggie Lu held up one hand. "I'll let the two of you work that out. Julia, you let me know about dinner and what I can bring." She hugged Julia and then Meredith. "I'll talk to you both soon. If I think of anything else I've heard about Miss Alice or Miss Charlotte, I'll let you know."

"Can we give you a ride home?" Beau asked. "Meredith rode with us, so we're taking her home too."

"That'd be nice, if it's not too much trouble. Thank you."

"No trouble at all."

Between the four of them, they gathered up the chairs and the leftovers. It didn't take long to drive Meredith and Maggie Lu home. A few minutes after Beau and Julia got back to their own home, Beau was sitting with Bunny in his lap.

"You're going to spoil her," Julia said with an indulgent smile.

"I'm just making sure she's healing up right and not in any pain."

She sobered. "You'd better not get too attached. You know we're not keeping her."

"Yeah." He stroked one hand down the wide black stripe that ran from the top of her head to the tip of her tail. "I just figure she deserves a little affection while she's healing up. Who knows how long it will be before she gets a real home."

"I know." Julia sat on the arm of his recliner and scratched under Bunny's chin, earning a rich, rumbling purr for her efforts. "But we don't need to make it harder on ourselves when it's time to let her go."

Bunny looked at her with her luminous green eyes and then ducked her head against Julia's hand, purring louder.

"You little flatterer," Julia said, shaking her head as she stood up. "Well, you two have fun. I'm going to see if I can find out anything else for Quin's client while I'm thinking about it."

"We'll be right here," Beau promised. "*Arsenic and Old Lace* is coming on, and I don't think Bunny's seen it before."

Bunny replied with a throaty meow, and Julia laughed.

"Well, I won't spoil it for her then. I'll be at my computer."

***

On Monday morning, Brenda James telephoned Julia again to ask if she and Meredith were available for another of Miss Charlotte's teas that afternoon at four.

"I realize it is short notice," she said, "but Miss Charlotte has been reading the diary Mr. Richard found, Miss Alice's diary, and she thought you and Miss Browning would care to hear some of it."

"Oh, we'd love that. Please tell Miss Charlotte thank you, and we'll be there. Four o'clock?"

"She thought you all might like to come at two. That will give all of you a little more time to talk."

Talk before what? Julia wondered. Perhaps another of Miss Charlotte's "appointments."

"Brenda," Julia said. "Please tell me something. Is it too tiring for Miss Charlotte to have us visit so often?"

Brenda laughed softly. "Oh, no. To tell you the truth, I haven't seen Miss Charlotte so pepped up about anything in twenty years. Why, after all of you left on Friday, she made sure I had Miss Alice's wedding things aired and laid out like she likes them, eager for you to see all of it." She paused a second. "Of course, she's been a little preoccupied since Mr. Richard found the diary, but I guess that's to be expected. It was as big a surprise to her as to anyone. Since she didn't find it when Miss Alice died, she thought it was gone. I'm wondering if Miss Alice didn't write that and hide it away so long ago that she had forgotten about it herself by the time she turned everything over to Miss Charlotte. She was ninety by then."

"I guess that's possible. Has Miss Charlotte said anything about what's in the diary?"

"No, she's been reading in it since Mr. Richard brought it to her, but she hasn't said anything even to me. That worries me a little, I have to admit. Between me and my mother and my grandmother, who raised Miss Charlotte, there's not much about her I don't know. And there's not much she doesn't tell me. But she hasn't told me anything about this diary. I know it's Miss Alice's, but what's in it or why she hid it that way, I can't say." Brenda hesitated again. "I'm sorry, Julia, I probably shouldn't be bothering you with this."

"Oh, no. Please. It's not a bother. I'm glad you said something. Is there anything we can do to help?"

"I don't know what it would be," Brenda admitted. "And it's not that Miss Charlotte is upset. She just seems…well, not actually worried. Maybe *preoccupied* is the best word. I don't quite know what to think of it."

"You know Miss Charlotte better than anyone," Julia said. "And please be honest with me. Would it be better if Meredith and I didn't come this afternoon? We wouldn't be lying if we said we had business matters we had to take care of. Maybe with everything she has on her mind, it would be better if she just rested."

"I appreciate your concern and your consideration, but I think Miss Charlotte would be very disappointed if you didn't come. It would be good for her, I think more than anything, to have some company and a little diversion. So please come. I think it would do her a world of good."

"All right, we will. And we'll trust you to let us know if Miss Charlotte has an appointment she needs to keep."

Brenda chuckled. "I'll do that. And thank you for understanding."

"Thank you. Please tell Miss Charlotte that Meredith and I will be very happy to come this afternoon at two. And let her know she doesn't need to send a formal invitation. We'll be there."

"Oh, no, that's one thing I can't do. Miss Charlotte has her ways, and she expects all of us to see things are done accordingly. Miss Alice wouldn't have allowed anything less."

"All right then. Let her know we'll be there today at two."

"Actually…." Brenda hesitated for a moment. "If you have any information you'd like to pass on to Miss Charlotte, I'm sure she'd be very happy to see you before two."

"We're still working on it," Julia told her. "Just let Miss Charlotte know that we'll report back to her as soon as we know something."

"Thank you," Brenda said. "Miss Charlotte will be looking forward to it."

Chapter Ten

Once she ended the call, Julia put up her phone and went into Meredith's office.

"That was Brenda," she said. "We're invited for tea again. This afternoon at two."

"Oh good." Meredith pushed back her chair. "I've been doing more research on this man Quin wants to know about. The man Quin's client wants to partner with, Hammett, has already made several business deals with a woman named Meyers. This Meyers is a real piece of work. Four different times, she's sold multifamily housing developments in small towns, greasing palms to get them to change zoning to allow it and, after turning a quick buck on barely standard construction, she sells out and moves on. I guess you can't necessarily blame Hammett for her end of it, and I can't see he's been involved in any of these particular deals, but if I were her, I wouldn't be able to sleep at night."

"Well, all we can do is let Quin know. He can give his client the best professional advice he has, but the client is the one who has to finally decide what he's going to do."

Meredith nodded. "Should I keep researching this guy?"

"Let's tell Quin what you found first. Then we can go from there. If his client is as bullheaded as Quin says he is, he's not going to listen anyway. No use wasting everybody's time and money if that's the case."

"True. So what did Brenda say?"

"Seems Miss Charlotte wants to tell us a little about what's in Alice's diary. I told her we'd be there."

"Of course we'll be there." Meredith stood up and stretched her arms and shoulders. "I'm already ready for a break. When are we supposed to go?"

"Not till two. She's having tea at four again, but we'll have time for a quick lunch before we go."

"And Jaden?"

Julia nodded. "Brenda said she'll be there too. She's got to be so eager to know what's in that book. And it seems that Miss Charlotte is eager to get some information on Jaden. I placed a few calls earlier this morning, but I haven't heard back from anyone."

"She hasn't given us much time yet," Meredith said, "especially since we just got some specifics from Jaden on Friday. I guess we'll have to really get moving on this one. Do you want me to go ahead and call Quin about his client now? Then I'll have that off my plate."

"Sounds good," Julia said. "And I'll have time to tie up a few loose ends I'm working on before we go."

***

As usual, Jaden was already with Miss Charlotte when Julia and Meredith were shown in. This time, instead of meeting in the dining room, they had tea in the East Parlor, a warm and decidedly feminine room with Louis XIV furnishings and velvet drapes and a glorious view of the estate grounds. There was even a vine-covered gazebo in the middle of a rose garden, the elegant columns that supported it smaller versions of the ones at the mansion's grand entrance.

"Grandmama always had this as her morning room," Miss Charlotte told them. "This is where she wrote her letters and received callers. All of this furniture is the same as before she passed on. I couldn't think of changing it."

Julia perched gingerly on the plush settee. It was perfectly preserved, but given its age, she didn't want to unknowingly cause any damage to it. It couldn't have been used much in the past ninety years and still be in such good condition. She had a feeling that having tea in the East Parlor was a distinct privilege.

After they chatted for a few minutes, Jaden leaned toward Miss Charlotte, her golden-brown eyes alight. "Now that everyone's here, can we see? Can we see the diary?"

"I thought we could start off with Grandmama's wedding dress and things," Miss Charlotte said serenely. "Brenda?"

Brenda came into the parlor and helped Miss Charlotte to her feet. "This way, ladies, if you will."

They went to the sweeping front stairs, and then, to Julia's surprise, they stopped.

"If you would," Miss Charlotte said, "please go up and wait for us at the top of the stairs. We will be there directly."

Julia and Meredith exchanged an inquisitive glance, but they did as they'd been asked, and Jaden came right behind them.

"Now what?" Jaden asked, looking down the long hallway.

Before anyone could answer her, a door behind them opened, and Miss Charlotte and Brenda stepped out.

"A few years ago, Brenda insisted I have an elevator put in," Miss Charlotte said. "I was opposed to it, of course." She looked over at Brenda, who had a knowing look on her face. "But when she convinced me they made them small enough to fit into a closet without destroying the look of the home and without being horribly noisy, I finally agreed."

"And you're glad of it, Miss Charlotte," Brenda said. "Don't even tell me."

"Yes," Miss Charlotte said, patting her arm. "I certainly am. Now shall we go on?"

They went down the wide hallway, past several rooms with their doors open. Most of them were bedrooms, and much like the rest of the house, they were elegantly decorated and perfectly preserved and seemed long unused.

At the end of the hallway, a set of paneled double doors were open just a crack, giving a tantalizing glimpse of the master suite inside. It was no doubt Miss Charlotte's private apartment. Most likely it had been Alice's until her death. Julia managed to keep her curiosity under control and followed the others through a less impressive door off to one side.

"This was Miss Alice's wardrobe room," Brenda explained.

It was a much larger room than Julia had expected, and tall windows at one end filled it with light. She caught her breath as they stepped inside. The room looked like a well-appointed vintage clothing shop. Most of the things looked to be from the 1920s, '30s, and '40s, but there were a few that looked much older. There was even some clothing for babies and small boys, likely things that had belonged to Alice's son and grandson.

Set up in the very middle, shielded from the sunlight by a folding screen, was a dressmaker's mannequin clad in the most gorgeous antique wedding dress Julia had ever seen. The photograph in no way did justice to the beauty of the design or the delicacy of the craftsmanship. It had a scoop neckline and lacy, bell-shaped short sleeves. The bodice was silk with heavy stays that pulled the waist into an incredibly small circle. From there, the frothy silk-and-lace skirt flared out, accented with cascades of tiny pearls that hadn't been noticeable in the picture.

Beside the dress was a brass stand that held the delicate lace-and-pearl wreath with the long lace train attached, and Julia remembered it once had orange blossoms in it. On the stand too was a pair of gloves with tiny pearl buttons running from the wrists and all the way up their long length. At the base of the stand was a pair of dainty high-top shoes, also with pearl buttons. Julia didn't dare touch them, but they looked like they were made of glove leather and very delicate.

"She never wore them except for that day," Miss Charlotte said. "None of these things were ever worn but once."

"They're amazing," Jaden breathed, her eyes still wide.

With the sun streaming in through the window, Julia could very clearly see the telltale circle that marked the edge of her contact lens. Meredith gave her a subtle nod. She had seen too.

Miss Charlotte told them all about her great-grandmother's wedding. "It was rather a quiet affair up in Chicago. She was nineteen then and hadn't been back to Savannah since the epidemic. She had no family there, and not much anywhere else. She had only her lady's maid, Beryl, and Beryl's son, Teddy, to look after her."

"She didn't have anyone to stand up with her?" Julia asked.

"My great-grandfather's sisters, Arabella and Martha Lockwood, were her maids of honor," Miss Charlotte said. "She wrote in her diary that she didn't know them well since they lived with their parents in a neighboring town, but despite her nervousness, not just about her in-laws but about the whole wedding, everything seems to have turned out well." There was a touch of fond amusement in her smile. "She didn't mention Grandpapa to me very often. I knew she had been fond of him, but reading her diary, I can tell she was quite smitten with him. It's very hard for me to think of her that young, about the same age I was when she left everything to me."

"Was there a lot about him in the diary?" Jaden asked.

"Oh, very much," Miss Charlotte said. "It is really very sweet. I wish they could have had more time together."

"I've heard he died while she was still in Chicago," Meredith said.

"He did. It was only their third Christmas together. She had her baby then, my grandfather, Matthew Lockwood, and Grandpapa had diphtheria. He died on December 22nd."

"How awful for her," Jaden said. "Does she talk about it in her diary?"

"Yes. She was heartbroken. I knew the story already, of course, but reading it in her own raw words made it more real to me than it had ever been. She was so young and had lost the love of her life."

There was sudden deep grief in the aged dark eyes, and Julia couldn't help think of the young man Miss Charlotte herself had broken from when she was a very young woman too. Perhaps that was what was in her mind now. But if she had loved that man so much, enough that even the thought of a vaguely similar loss could bring her pain, why had she ended things with him?

"I don't want to pry, Miss Charlotte," Jaden said, "but will you let us see it? The diary, I mean. It would be a wonderful resource for my book."

Miss Charlotte smiled, not quite meeting her eyes, and Julia couldn't help thinking of that one little glance she'd had of the diary. *"He accused her of terrible things, and now I can never explain—"* Who was "he" and who was "her," and what had he accused her of?

"Oh of course. Of course," Miss Charlotte said with an airy wave of her hand. "I'll have copies made for you of the pertinent pages. And we'll have a time where we can both look through it together. Please understand, though, it is very old and very precious to me. I wouldn't like to let it out of my custody."

"That makes sense. And I'd hate for you to let me borrow it and then for something to happen to it. I could never make it up to you." Jaden glanced around the wardrobe room and then bit her lip. "Um, excuse me, but is there a restroom I could use?"

She really looked mortified to be asking such a thing at such a moment, but Miss Charlotte merely nodded graciously.

"Brenda, will you direct Miss Browning to the powder room? It's only three doors down, my dear."

"Certainly," Brenda said. "Come with me, ma'am."

"I'll be right back," Jaden said. "Please don't tell any more juicy stories without me."

"We'll wait," Miss Charlotte assured her, and she sat on the gilt straight-backed chair near the window. "Forgive me for taking the only chair, but I don't stand as well as I used to."

"That's all right," Julia said, and she glanced at the door, making sure it was firmly shut now. "Since we have a moment alone, we wanted to let you know we haven't found out anything about Jaden yet."

"It's still very early," Meredith added, "but these things take time."

"I understand," Miss Charlotte said. "But do let me know if you find out anything I should be concerned about. I want to like Jaden. All right, I do like Jaden, but I want to know that I can trust her."

"That's certainly understandable," Julia said as Brenda quietly came back into the room. "And we'll be in touch, I promise."

Miss Charlotte replied with a gracious nod.

"You certainly have some fascinating things in here," Julia said when she didn't say anything more.

"Just things Grandmama kept. They were unremarkable at the time, but now that they're so old and in such good condition, they are of some interest."

"Would you mind if we looked around a little?" Meredith asked. "This is such an amazing array of vintage clothing."

"You're very welcome to look at anything you'd like," Miss Charlotte said.

Meredith started oohing and aahing over a number of antique hats, many of them quite dramatic even for their day, but Julia was looking at some baby clothes and shoes. She picked up one of the baby dresses.

"Were these your father's or your grandfather's, Miss Charlotte?"

"Those were made for my grandfather, Matthew Lockwood."

Julia went to one of the cupboards. "May I?"

"Certainly."

Julia opened a cupboard door, revealing a number of outfits there for a small boy, all of them carefully preserved.

"Those belonged to my father, Marcus Lockwood."

Julia looked through them and then, at the bottom, came across some items that must have belonged to a much younger child, a newborn perhaps. "It looks like there are two of some of these baby things. He was a lucky little boy."

Miss Charlotte immediately came to her side, and Brenda followed her, taking her arm.

"Grandmama raised him after his mother died," Miss Charlotte said, swiftly shutting the door again. "There was very little she didn't buy for him."

"That was when she started the foundation, wasn't it?" Meredith asked with a quick glance in Julia's direction.

"Not very long afterward," Miss Charlotte said, looking flustered as Brenda settled her back into her chair. "I think my father's birth made her consider those unfortunate children who had no families."

Julia realized she'd uncovered something that meant something to Miss Charlotte, something she had evidently forgotten was there.

No one said anything for a moment or two, and then Miss Charlotte looked toward the wardrobe room door and frowned. "Brenda, would you please go see if Miss Browning is all right?"

"Of course."

Brenda came back a few minutes later with Jaden in tow.

"I didn't mean to be so long," Jaden murmured, an extra touch of color in her cheeks, and then she gave Miss Charlotte an apologetic smile. "I'm sorry. I guess I'm so excited about seeing everything, my stomach is tied in knots. I think I probably ought to go home and lie down for a while."

"Is there something Brenda can get for you, my dear?" Miss Charlotte asked her.

"No, ma'am. I already took something to settle my stomach, but it doesn't seem to be helping, and if I'm coming down with something, I don't want anyone else to get it."

"That's very thoughtful of you. Brenda, please have Miss Browning's car brought up."

"Yes, ma'am." Frowning, Brenda took Jaden's arm and guided her toward the door. "Come right this way."

"That's too bad," Meredith said when they were gone. "She really wanted to have a look at that diary."

"Perhaps another time," Miss Charlotte said serenely.

"Could we still see it?" Julia asked her.

Miss Charlotte pursed her lips. "I don't know. Poor girl, she's been wanting so much to see it, I hate to not let her be the first to have a look. Would either of you mind waiting? I know it's rather selfish of me, but she's so terribly excited about it, I wouldn't want to disappoint her."

"That's not selfish at all," Julia assured her. "It's very thoughtful of you. We don't mind waiting, do we, Meredith?"

"Not at all," Meredith said. "I'm sorry she's not feeling well. Maybe we ought to cut this short until she's feeling better."

"Oh nonsense," Miss Charlotte said. "There are so many things we could talk about and look at until teatime. Is there anything in particular you'd like to know about?"

"I'm interested in seeing more photographs," Julia said. "I know Jaden is particularly interested in them too, but maybe if we have a look at some of them we can figure out why. I've seen the ones in your dining room, but do you have others? Maybe of your father and grandfather?"

"I'd love to see more of Miss Alice's husband," Meredith said.

"All right." Miss Charlotte looked toward the door. "Brenda will be after me for not using my cane when she isn't here to help—"

"May I help you?" Julia asked.

"If you will. Thank you. I had a fall two years ago, and Brenda gets quite upset if I take any chances now." Miss Charlotte turned to Meredith. "You're welcome to come along, if you like. Just to my bedroom. I have my family album there."

"I'd love to come."

Julia took Miss Charlotte's arm, and Meredith walked at her other side. Miss Charlotte's steps weren't quick, but she moved with all the genteel grace her carefully raised great-grandmother must have had. She made a dramatic pause when they reached the room at the end of the corridor.

"Of course, this room isn't open to the public, but for my friends—"

She pushed open the door, revealing a lush room with pale-teal walls and a canopied four-poster bed with silk hangings to match. The curtains and coverlet were a slightly darker shade of the same color, but the valances matched the canopy, and the lush rug that stretched almost from wall to wall in the large room was the same color interwoven with cream.

Opposite the foot of the bed was an ornate marble fireplace with brass fittings and two tall windows on either side. The fire that burned in it wasn't large. It was just enough to take the chill out of the room. Before it was a low, round table with a marble top and two plush chairs upholstered in cream-colored velvet.

One of the side walls was dominated by a wide, triple-door armoire. Like the bed and the edge of the round table, it was carved with swags of leaves and fruit and flowers, and the corners of it were carved just like the four bedposts.

"How beautiful," Julia breathed.

Meredith stared for a moment. "These posts are just like the ones in the front of the house."

Miss Charlotte gave a serene nod in answer. "It was made that way. All of the furniture was made for my great-great-grandmother when she accepted my great-great-grandfather's proposal and agreed to come here from England to marry him. It was designed by the finest furniture maker in Georgia, and built in this very room. As you can see, the armoire is far too large to ever be taken out in one piece."

All the wood was rich cherry, polished like glass, carefully preserved. Julia didn't dare touch it.

"How do you keep it so nice?"

"That's one of Richard's specialties." There was satisfaction in Miss Charlotte's expression. "His grandfather was a fine woodworker. He had a special sort of polish that he said would keep the wood from drying out. I couldn't tell you what's in it. It's really not my place to know. But as you can see, he knew his business." She sank wearily onto the end of the teal-velvet chaise longue that angled away from one of the windows. "I have been fortunate to find people to work for me who are excellent at what they do. I am happy to reward them, financially and otherwise, for that excellence, and I am pleased to say, they have rewarded me with their loyalty and hard work. They are why the Delorme Estate and the Lockwood Foundation have continued on as Grandmama left it."

"That's wonderful," Julia said, watching the older lady. Miss Charlotte's pleased expression had suddenly turned thoughtful, even wistful.

Miss Charlotte sighed. "I wish I knew what was to become of it after I've gone on."

"Maybe you could set up a trust of some kind," Meredith suggested.

"Oh, I've seen to that. I have people to look after things business wise. But I would feel better leaving it to someone in the family. Someone I could trust to love the estate as I do. To believe in the work the foundation is doing and not turn it into something that is merely a business."

"What about Richard?" Julia asked. "He's family."

Miss Charlotte gave her a look. "Yes, he is. And he does what he's asked to do. I can find no fault with his work. But money is the only thing that keeps him here. Not that he's said as much, but I can tell. I can tell when someone loves this place and when it's merely a job. His father loved the place. I'm sorry he's no longer with us. His grandfather as well. They loved this land. They loved this house. I might have trusted one of them to take my place. But Richard... The bloodline is so important, and I'm afraid he's all I have left now. He and his son and grandson."

"Wouldn't one of them be a good choice?" Meredith asked, seating herself in one of the chairs.

"Jeff, his grandson, is very young yet. Still in school. He works here part time, and I can tell he's like his great-grandfather in loving the place and wanting to stay here, but he may leave sometime to start his own life. He's a dear boy, a clever and hardworking boy, and I hate to stand in his way. If he stayed here, he would likely have to wait years before Richard is ready to retire. Tony, Richard's son, was never interested in this sort of work at all. He lives in town and works in an office." She sighed once more. "Perhaps, in this day and age, it's too much to ask anyone to work for the love of it. For the great tradition."

"I suppose people don't stay put the way they used to," Julia said, and she smiled. "Not like in Miss Alice's day."

"No," Miss Charlotte agreed. "Not like then."

"Do you ever wish you'd had children of your own?" Julia asked, sitting on the divan next to her.

She regretted it immediately, seeing the tears that filled Miss Charlotte's blue eyes. Was that what had pained her when Julia had uncovered those baby clothes?

She put her hand over the older woman's. "I'm so sorry—"

"No, no." Miss Charlotte smiled and pulled a delicate lawn handkerchief from her sleeve to dab her eyes. "Most days, I feel it was for the best. But then there are others, days when I wonder who's to love this place when I'm gone. Maybe it doesn't matter in the grand scheme of things. Only to me, and who am I? I've been granted long life and wealth and privilege. Perhaps I ought to think it enough and be thankful."

"There's Jaden's book," Meredith said. "If nothing else, it will be something that will tell your family's story long after you're gone."

"Our story," Miss Charlotte said thoughtfully. "Yes, that's true. She does seem to have a genuine interest in the family and in this place, though it's so hard to know whom one can trust."

"We should have some answers for you before long," Julia assured her. "Just give us a little time."

Chapter Eleven

"Miss Charlotte," Brenda scolded when she came back into the elegant bedroom. "I should have known you wouldn't stay put." Her hands were on her hips, and her lips were pursed. "And after what happened."

"That was two years ago," Miss Charlotte told her with a defiant lift of her chin. "And that was only because I tripped on the corner of the morning room rug."

Brenda huffed. "At least you're sitting down now."

"We came to look at my album. Was Miss Browning all right to drive?"

"She said she'd be fine in a while."

"Humph. Did you think she looked well enough?"

"She did seem a little washed out, Miss Charlotte. Maybe it's best she went on."

There was a telling look between the two women, and Julia narrowed her eyes slightly, wondering if there was more going on here than Brenda was saying. Brenda caught her glance and then looked back at Miss Charlotte.

"I didn't like to say anything in front of her, in front of Miss Browning," Brenda said, "but when I went to get her, she was coming out of this room."

Miss Charlotte stiffened.

Julia's mouth dropped open. "What?"

Brenda nodded, her mouth in a hard line. "Exactly what I said. I went down the hall to the powder room and saw her backing out of here, pulling the door to the way it had been when we came up that way earlier. I asked her if there was something she was looking for, and she said she was coming back to the wardrobe room, but she couldn't resist just a peek at the room Miss Alice used to have, it looked so pretty when she passed by it before."

"What do you think she was doing in here?"

Brenda frowned. "I don't know. I didn't notice anything was disturbed in any way. We don't really keep anything valuable here, so I don't know what she could have been looking for. It could be she was doing just what she said, just having a look around."

"She might simply have asked," Miss Charlotte said crisply. "I wouldn't have minded letting her see."

"It could be that Jaden couldn't help taking a peek while she was there," Meredith said. "I know I wanted to when we passed by."

"Me too," Julia admitted. "It really is a lovely room."

"And Jaden seems like the impulsive type to me," Meredith added. "As long as there wasn't anything missing, I don't know if there's anything to worry about."

"Maybe not," Miss Charlotte said, her eyes darting around the room. "Maybe not."

"Will there be anything else, Miss Charlotte?" Brenda asked finally.

"Make sure you telephone Miss Browning tomorrow, not too early now, and inquire as to her health and ask if there is anything we can do for her."

"Yes, ma'am."

"And when she's here," Miss Charlotte said, "keep an eye on her."

"I will, ma'am."

"Thank you. Will you be kind enough to bring another chair up to the table so we can look through my album now?"

Brenda brought over the chair that had been next to the bed and settled Miss Charlotte into it. "I'll go down and see to the tea things now, if there's nothing else."

"Actually," Miss Charlotte said, "if you would bring us some tea now, only the tea, I believe that would be just the thing to warm us up while we visit. What do you ladies think?"

"I'd love some," Julia said.

Meredith nodded. "Yes, please."

"I'll tell Ellen, ma'am," Brenda said. "Would you like your wrap?"

"Thank you, yes, I would."

Miss Charlotte patted Brenda's hand as she draped a black vicuña shawl around her shoulders. Then Brenda moved the photo album within Miss Charlotte's easy reach.

"I'll be back with the tea," she said, and she left the room.

"Now," Miss Charlotte said, "are you ready to see my photos? Or should we just have tea and save them for when Miss Browning can join us?"

"I definitely want to see them," Julia said, "but I am sorry Jaden isn't here to see them. She'd definitely want to. What do you think, Meredith?"

Meredith frowned. "I hate to think she's up to something if she's not. And really, we're here because of her. Maybe we ought to wait."

Miss Charlotte seemed pleased. "It would be the considerate thing. Perhaps we should just have our tea then. Let's go down and surprise Brenda."

Julia and Meredith exchanged an amused glance and helped her to her feet and over to the elevator.

***

"I'm not sure how much Brenda liked having her plans for tea turned on their head twice within the same few minutes," Julia said when she and Meredith were driving back to the office later that afternoon.

"You saw that little bit of mischief in Miss Charlotte's eyes when she explained to Brenda that we'd be having tea right then and in Miss Alice's bedroom. I think she enjoys keeping Brenda on her toes. And I think Brenda enjoys pretending Miss Charlotte has caused her a lot of trouble."

Julia laughed softly. "I think they're very fond of each other, despite all the old-fashioned formality. I wonder what Brenda thinks of Jaden now."

"I don't think she was very happy to find her snooping."

"I imagine she felt like she'd let Miss Charlotte down."

"Probably," Meredith said. "Though we still don't know whether it was just harmless curiosity or something more sinister."

"Brenda's been part of the family all her life, and she seems like a very perceptive woman even if she doesn't always say very much."

"I wonder if we could get her to open up a little. I mean, away from Miss Charlotte."

"Interesting idea," Julia said. "But I don't know how we'd do it." They drove in silence for another minute or two, and then she nodded. "What about dinner? Maggie Lu is supposed to come have dinner with us when you come next. Do you think she could get Brenda to come too?"

"I don't know. I don't want to make her feel like she's been set up or anything. She might wonder about it anyway, whether or not we ever actually ask her anything."

"Maybe we could invite her and not say anything about Jaden or Miss Charlotte at all." Julia sighed. "I don't know how best to handle it. Talking to Brenda casually is never going to happen at the estate. And I don't know how we can invite her without her knowing something's up."

"I guess we're just going to have to trust Maggie Lu to find out what she can. She and Brenda are already friends. We'll just have to resign ourselves to waiting a while to learn anything. That is, *if* we learn anything."

"I felt bad for Miss Charlotte today. She's put her whole life into that estate and into her great-grandmother's foundation, and now she doesn't know what will happen to it when she's gone. It makes me wonder even more if she regrets not marrying her young man way back when."

Meredith nodded. "Just one more thing Brenda could probably tell us all about, if only we could sit down and have a little chat with her."

"One thing at a time," Julia said. "We'll concentrate on Jaden for now. The usual things. We'll check on where she's lived and when. Who her family is. If she really is getting her master's in Dallas and what she's studying."

Meredith glanced at her watch. "It's getting late already. Carmen will probably have closed up by the time we get back to the office."

"That's all right. We've got plenty to think of for today. Tomorrow we'll really get busy checking up on Jaden. Maybe we ought to call and see how she is. We could get her number from Brenda."

"If she wasn't feeling well, she might have gone straight to bed. Maybe tomorrow would be better."

Julia nodded. "Tomorrow afternoon. After we've had a chance to do some investigating. Maybe we'll have some questions for her by then that we could work subtly into the conversation. And we'll have to check with Maggie Lu tomorrow too, to see if she talked to Brenda at church."

"And it could be that Brenda wasn't even there. From what Maggie Lu said, it doesn't seem like Brenda gets to come to services all the time. Miss Charlotte does seem to rely on her for everything." Meredith shook her head. "The conversations she must have overheard over all the years."

"And she wouldn't still be working for Miss Charlotte if she didn't know how to keep her mouth shut about them." Julia turned onto Whitaker Street and headed for the office. "I don't know if we're going to get much out of her anytime soon."

***

The next morning, Julia and Meredith ran into each other at the entrance to the Sentient Bean.

"How did I not see you drive up?" Meredith asked as they walked inside.

"You couldn't have missed me by much. It's a brisk morning, so I thought I'd get some specialty coffee after I stopped by the vet's office."

"Is Bunny okay?"

"Oh, she's fine. Beau seems to think she's sleeping too much. I told him that's what cats do most of the day and night, but I promised I'd stop by and talk to her doctor about it. She's got a regular appointment to see him in a few days anyway, to see how she's healing up, but I thought it'd be easier on all of us if I went ahead and asked now."

"You could have just asked me," Meredith asked. "And, yes, that's pretty usual behavior for a cat."

Julia chuckled. "You'd think Beau was a new father or something. He said he didn't care about what most cats did, just Bunny, especially since she's recovering. I'll have to call him and set his mind at ease."

"What do you think?" Meredith asked as they went up to the counter. "Should we bring an extra cup back to the office?"

Julia nodded enthusiastically.

***

When they got back to the office, Carmen came from the reception room. "Oh, I see my poor coffee isn't good enough today."

"I'm sure we'll drink yours too," Meredith assured her. "And this coffee wasn't planned. We both just happened to have the same idea at the same time."

"Sometimes it's nice to have a change," Julia said. "And I felt like a little treat this morning. After all, it's pumpkin spice weather, isn't it?"

"I'm sure it's very nice," Carmen said with a dramatic sigh.

"We didn't forget you." Julia took the extra cup from behind her back and presented it to Carmen. "Just to show you how much we love and appreciate you."

"Aww, how sweet," Carmen said. "*Mil gracias.*" She took a contented sip. "Oh, that's nice. So, do either of you have plans for today that I should know about? Or will you be in all day?"

Julia and Meredith glanced at each other, eyebrows raised.

"I expect to be here most of the day," Julia said. "I don't have any appointments, do I?"

"Not that you've told me about," Carmen said, taking another sip of her coffee.

"I don't either." Meredith went into her office to set down her purse and her coffee. "Are we planning to do anything else on that man Quin had us checking up on?"

"Not unless he asks for more." Julia turned to Carmen. "Any phone messages?"

"From yesterday," Carmen said. "Nothing urgent. I'll get them."

Julia went into her own office and sat down. Unless one of the messages was about something she had to see to first, she planned on getting right to work on getting information about Jaden Browning. Actually, she and Meredith needed to put their heads together and decide which of them was going to do what on this particular case. She had filled about half a page from her notepad when she heard the front door open and close. She recognized the voice asking for her and went into the reception room.

"Brenda. How nice to see you."

Meredith was right behind her. "Well, hello. Come in."

"Thank you," Brenda said, a troubled look on her face.

"Is everything all right?" Julia asked. "Miss Charlotte is okay, isn't she?"

"Oh yes," Brenda said with a faint smile of her own. "I hope it's all right. I know I don't have an appointment, but I was wondering if I could talk to you ladies about something."

"Certainly," Julia said.

"Come on into my office," Meredith told her. "Would you like some coffee?"

"Oh, no, thank you," Brenda said. "I'm seeing to a few things in town for Miss Charlotte, and I can't stay long."

She followed Meredith into her office and sat in one of the olive-green chairs in the corner. Julia and Meredith sat on either side of her.

"I'm guessing Miss Charlotte doesn't know you're here," Julia began.

"No, she doesn't. I'm not quite sure what to do about any of this, but I don't think Miss Charlotte would like me to say anything. Not about this."

Meredith's eyebrows went up. "Was there something Miss Charlotte didn't tell us when she asked us to do a background check on Jaden?"

"I can't say about that," Brenda admitted. "But there is something you don't know. I didn't want to say anything in front of you, and she said it wasn't something you ought to be bothered with. But I think you ought to know. And if you decide it doesn't matter, that's fine. At least you'll know."

"Any information you have would be helpful," Julia told her. "Even things that don't particularly impact the investigation help us get to know the subject a little better. And we promise that anything you say will be held in strict confidence."

"I wouldn't say anything to anyone about them if I wasn't worried about Miss Charlotte."

"Just tell us. We can look into whatever it is."

Brenda drew a deep, settling breath. "I always open Miss Charlotte's mail for her. Most of it, I handle myself. The estate bills go to Mr. Richard. And anything concerning the foundation goes to Mr. Bailey, who sees to things there. Miss Charlotte gets a lot of letters from people who need help, letters from people who want to adopt and from people who know of children who need homes, and she likes to read those herself so she can make specific recommendations to the foundation. She wants to know what's really happening and not just read reports, you know?"

Meredith nodded. "I think I'd feel the same way."

"Anyway, I was going through the mail this past Friday, after y'all left, and I opened an envelope that was addressed to Miss Charlotte and marked personal. Now, she told me a long while ago, right after my mother died and I took over looking after her, that I was to open those like any of the other letters that came for her, that she didn't have any secrets from me. So I opened this one. All that was in it was a slip of paper with just four words printed in block letters."

Julia leaned forward in her chair a little. "What did it say?"

"It said, 'I know about Emily.'"

Chapter Twelve

"'I know about Emily'?" Meredith asked. "That's all the note said? Who's Emily?"

"I don't know anyone called Emily," Brenda said.

"And I guess there wasn't a return address on the envelope," Julia said.

"No, there wasn't. No return address. Savannah postmark."

"Did you tell Miss Charlotte about this?"

"Oh yes."

"And she said?"

Brenda pressed her lips together once more. "She said it wasn't anything and tossed it on her fire. Just like that, she burned it up, the note and the envelope."

"And that was the end of it?" Meredith asked.

"Oh, no. Not very likely. I told her she ought to have shown it to the police, that she still ought to ask them to look into it. She said there was nothing they could do anyway, especially since there was no address or signature on it. I said they could have at least checked for fingerprints and that sort of thing. She said it was foolish to worry over such a silly thing. It wasn't a threat, it didn't mean anything, and she wasn't going to do anything but forget it. I just didn't know what to do. I know you're friends with Maggie Lu King, so I asked her if she'd talk to you about this. She said she'd be happy to, but there was no reason I couldn't come here myself."

"Of course," Julia said. "Anytime. And I agree with you. Miss Charlotte should have told someone about that note. If she didn't think it was worth taking to the police, she could have come to us about it."

"Well, that's what I thought. You know, now that I tell you about it, it doesn't seem like much of anything, but it still bothers me. Who would send something like that? And to Miss Charlotte? I can't recall her ever knowing someone named Emily. Now, there have been a lot of meetings she's gone to and organizations she's given talks to and I don't know how many parents and children the foundation has helped, so there's bound to have been an Emily in there somewhere. But as far as I know, she doesn't personally know anyone named Emily."

Meredith took a sip of her coffee and wrinkled her nose. It was not very hot by now, and she set it aside. "I wonder what there is 'about Emily' that this person knows and why he wanted Miss Charlotte to know he knows it."

"He or she," Julia said, and she considered for a moment. "Describe the envelope for me."

"It was just a plain white one," Brenda said.

"Legal or letter size?"

"Letter size. The note was folded in half inside it."

"And what was the envelope like? Good quality?"

Brenda shook her head. "Not at all. Very cheap. Something you could pick up at the supermarket or drugstore."

"What about the note itself?" Meredith asked. "Was it a full piece of paper?"

"No. Just a strip, but it was cut, not torn. The width of a regular piece of paper but about three inches high. The letters were black. It looked like they were written with a marker with a small tip. Not a very tiny fine tip, but not wide either."

Julia grabbed a notepad from Meredith's desk and started taking notes, quickly jotting down what Brenda had already said. "Were they upper- or lowercase?"

"All uppercase. Very straight and plain. Nothing telling about them at all."

"Somebody didn't want to be traced," Meredith said.

"Obviously." Julia tapped the notepad with her pen, thinking. "And it had only those four words? Nothing else?"

"That was all," Brenda said. "No threats. No demands. Nothing."

"Then it's likely just the beginning."

"Of what?" Brenda asked, looking from Julia to Meredith and back again to Julia. "Blackmail?"

"That would be my first guess," Julia said. "A blackmailer will often start with letting his victim know he knows a secret. He lets the victim worry for a while and then starts setting down terms."

"But I tell you Miss Charlotte doesn't know anyone called Emily," Brenda protested. "Even if it was years ago, I would probably have heard about it. There's not much Miss Charlotte and I haven't discussed over the years, and before that I heard a lot from my mother and grandmother."

"I don't know," Meredith said. "She's many years older than you are. There could be something that happened when she was young that she wouldn't want brought up. Your mother or grandmother might have not known about it."

"Or they might have promised to never say anything about it," Julia added. "You don't think it could be related to why Miss Charlotte suddenly broke her engagement, do you?"

"I don't think so. Not that I ever heard of anyway."

"We couldn't really find much information on that," Meredith said. "Maggie Lu said the man's name was Buckley. Do you know any details?"

Brenda nodded. "That's right. Miss Charlotte was going to marry a Mr. Timothy Buckley, whose father owned the Buckley & Madison shipping line. When Miss Alice died, Miss Charlotte told him she couldn't marry him. A couple of years later, he married Miss Ella Harris. Her father owned most of Coastal Savannah Paper, the big mill out south of us that burned down thirty years ago. Mama was about twelve when Miss Charlotte broke off with Mr. Buckley. She said that her mother, my grandma, was afraid Miss Charlotte's heart would break."

"Are you sure she was the one who broke off the engagement?" Julia asked. "He wasn't the one who left her?"

"Definitely not," Brenda said. "Grandma always said what a good man he was and how he loved Miss Charlotte like crazy. I asked her once why Miss Charlotte didn't marry him then. She told me not to talk about it."

"Why do you think she didn't marry him?" Meredith asked after a moment.

"Miss Charlotte doesn't talk about it. I think she was grieving for her great-grandmother and worried about if she was going to be able to do everything, for the estate and for the foundation, the way Miss Alice wanted it to be done."

"A good husband could have been a lot of help to her," Julia said.

"I know. It's sad, really, that she's done all of it alone for all these years."

Julia put her hand over Brenda's and gave it a comforting squeeze. "She hasn't been alone. You and your family have been a big part of it from what I can tell. I can't imagine how alone she would have felt without you."

Brenda smiled a little. "It's been our home too, you know. And Miss Charlotte was always good to us. I don't like to see her upset, especially not now. Whatever days she has left ought to be good ones, and I don't like this blackmailer, whoever he is, worrying her."

"We'll see what we can find out," Meredith assured her, "though we don't have much to go on."

Julia jotted a few more things on her notepad. "Is there someone you think would be likely to blackmail Miss Charlotte? Anyone she's had a disagreement with? Anyone who has a complaint? At the estate or at the foundation?"

"Those have both gone on a lot of years," Brenda said with a rueful chuckle. "There's nearly always somebody unhappy with whoever's running things. But I don't know of anything recent. And if it was something way back in the past, why would the blackmailer be bringing it up now?"

"Maybe some new information turned up," Meredith offered. "Maybe the blackmailer just found out whatever he knows about Emily. Has there been anything like that lately? News of some kind?"

Brenda thought for a moment, and then she bit her lip. "No. I can't think of anything like that that someone could blackmail

Miss Charlotte over. She hasn't wronged anybody, and if there's something in the past that somebody wants to hold over her head, I can't see that it would be something that's her fault." She clasped her hands together. "I really don't know. Maybe I should have just forgotten about that note like Miss Charlotte said. And maybe Jaden was just looking at that room like she said she was. It doesn't have to mean anything more than that." She stood up, clutching her purse in both hands. "I'm sure Miss Charlotte still wants you to do a background check on her, but that doesn't mean she suspects her of anything, all right?"

Meredith and Julia stood too.

"We'll see what we can find out," Julia said as they walked with Brenda to the front door. "Meanwhile, tell Miss Charlotte not to worry. We'll be in touch as soon as we have any news. And tell her that if she gets another note like that, we think she ought to tell the police or at least let us look into it."

Brenda stopped with her hand on the doorknob. "Oh, no. I mean, I'll tell her that would be a good idea, but I'm not going to tell her you said so. I probably stepped out of line coming here at all, and she won't be too pleased if she found out about it."

"We won't say anything. You don't have to worry about that. But, please, if she gets something else from this anonymous writer, urge her to do something about it. It could be nothing, but then again, it could be very serious. Please."

Brenda looked more than a little bit worried now, and she nodded rapidly. "I'll do that. Thank you for letting me come by."

With that, she tugged the collar of her jacket closer to her throat and stepped out into the windy street.

"She thought of something," Julia said as she shut the door after her. "When I asked her about there being anything new."

Julia followed Meredith back into her office, and they both looked out the window, watching Brenda get into a pearl-gray Cadillac and drive away.

"I thought so too," Meredith said finally. "She remembered and that's when she got flustered. I suppose there could be other recent discoveries too, but there's only one significant one I know of."

"Miss Alice's diary."

Julia nodded.

"But what could be in there that someone could blackmail Miss Charlotte over?" Meredith asked.

"'He accused her of terrible things, and now I can never explain—'"

Meredith wrinkled her forehead. "What are you talking about?"

"That's what I saw. I got only a glimpse of the diary before Miss Charlotte closed it, but that's what I saw on the page. 'He accused her of terrible things, and now I can never explain—' I don't have a clue what it means or who Miss Alice was writing about."

"You didn't see the date of the entry or anything?"

"Nothing but that. Now I'm wondering if the 'her' she wrote about could have been this Emily who was mentioned in the note."

Meredith thought for a moment. "Miss Charlotte doesn't get out a lot. As far as I can tell, she doesn't have a lot of friends. Maybe Emily was someone in her family."

"Could be, I guess. I don't remember there being an Emily on the family tree I made, but maybe I just didn't notice in particular. Let's go look."

They went to Julia's office, and she dug out the family tree she had roughed out for the Delormes and Lockwoods.

"James was married to Catherine," Julia said. "They had Jimmy, Alice, and Evan. Alice married Calvin. They had Matthew. He married Amelia. They had Marcus, who married Gladys, and they had Charlotte." She shook her head. "No Emilys."

"Funny they had only one child each. That's unusual for those times."

"Well, Alice's family died in the epidemic. Her husband died when her son, Matthew, was very young. Matthew's wife died when their son, Miss Charlotte's father, Marcus, was born. And then Marcus and his wife both died the same year, when Miss Charlotte was two." Julia shook her head. "I hadn't paid much attention before, but there's been a lot of tragedy in that family."

"There sure has. Maybe when she lost her great-grandmother, the only mother she'd really ever known, Miss Charlotte thought it would be better to not have kids and not risk them being left with no one." Meredith looked down at the family tree again. "What happened to her parents? Did you find anything on that?"

"I did find that they died on the same day. It must have been an accident of some kind. I didn't follow it up, but maybe that's something we could ask Brenda."

"Or Maggie Lu might have heard something about it too. Just curious about how whatever it was might have affected Miss Charlotte."

"I'm not quite sure what to make of this whole thing," Julia admitted. "But more than anything, I'd like to have a look at that diary."

"So would I. Miss Charlotte said we could see it."

"She did, but I'm sure she'll bring that up in her own good time. We could get the background check on Jaden finished up and then tell Miss Charlotte we want to come discuss the results with her. She'll be eager to hear about it, I'm sure, and then, when we're at her house, maybe she'll bring up the diary again."

Meredith lifted one eyebrow. "Were you this sneaky when you were still a judge?"

Julia grinned. "Definitely."

***

Julia and Meredith didn't have time to do much on Jaden's background check before lunch, and when they got back to the office after a quick trip out for Italian food, they found out they were invited back to the Delorme Estate.

"Lunch again," Carmen said, handing Julia the message. "Tomorrow at noon. You're supposed to call Brenda and confirm." She clicked her tongue as she walked away. "Tan elegante."

"Do you suppose she's invited Jaden again?" Meredith asked.

"I would think so, especially since we don't have any reason to advise her not to. That doesn't mean we can't see what we can dig up before then." Julia gave her a significant glance. "And it doesn't mean we can't keep a close eye on her while she's with Miss Charlotte."

"I'll call Brenda and tell her we'll be there."

"Tell her that, unless Miss Charlotte objects, we'll be there early. Earlier than Jaden usually comes. That'll give us a chance to tell Miss Charlotte what we find out."

Meredith frowned. "Too bad we can't ask her about the note too."

"She'd probably just tell us what she told Brenda, that it was nothing. But that doesn't mean we can't try to find out more. And maybe she'll actually let us see that diary too."

"I hope so." Meredith picked up the message with Brenda's phone number on it. "I'll call right now."

Chapter Thirteen

As they had arranged with Brenda, Julia and Meredith arrived at the Delorme Estate at eleven o'clock the next morning. Brenda immediately showed them into the morning room. Miss Charlotte was waiting for them with the photograph album they'd only glimpsed the last time they were there. She was immaculate in a petal-pink calf-length dress and a string of candlelight pearls. Her smile was gracious but wary.

"I suppose you have something to report to me," she said after they had gone through the usual niceties.

"A few things," Julia told her. "None of them are really important in and of themselves, but together they do make us wonder."

Miss Charlotte's mouth tightened. "About Miss Browning."

Julia nodded.

"Do you want to know what we did?" Meredith asked. "Or would you rather just have the results so far?"

"I think I would rather know what you found out," Miss Charlotte decided. "Then if I want to know anything more, I will ask."

"All right," Julia said, and Meredith took their notes out of her bag.

"But first," Miss Charlotte said, "I would prefer Brenda joined us."

"I'm right here, Miss Charlotte."

Brenda came into the room as Miss Charlotte had no doubt expected her to and sat down beside her. Miss Charlotte put a hand on her sleeve and then nodded at Meredith.

"Go on."

"We've really only started the investigation," Meredith said, "but we have found a few things that don't quite add up. Not all of it is troubling, of course." She glanced at the notes. "Jaden Marie Browning was born in Atlanta twenty-seven years ago, but her parents were born here in Savannah. On her mother's side, the family has been here for a while. We specifically researched the ones who lived in Savannah back up to Jaden's great-grandfather, Philip Masters. He was an adopted child, and we don't know who his birth parents were."

Miss Charlotte's hand tightened on Brenda's sleeve.

"We thought perhaps Miss Alice might have been involved in the adoption since it was right around that time that she started the foundation," Julia said, "but we haven't found much on that so far. It may have been too early for it to have been done through them."

"I wouldn't know," Miss Charlotte said. "There have been so many adoptions over the years, I'm certain Grandmama wouldn't have remembered all of them. I know I wouldn't remember many of them from my time as the head of the foundation. It did take a while to actually get it operational. The first year or two, I don't think there were many actual adoptions that we facilitated."

"We're still checking on it," Julia told her. "The foundation is being very helpful, especially since they know we're working for you."

"Yes." Miss Charlotte fixed her gaze on the small fire that flickered in the grate. "Yes, of course. What else have you found?"

Meredith looked at her list. "Jaden did go to the University of Texas at Dallas as she said, but she graduated three years ago. She's not currently taking classes there, but I guess that doesn't indicate she's not working on her thesis. And her degree is in chemistry, not journalism."

"Many people change directions after they've already graduated," Miss Charlotte said. "Perhaps she felt the sciences were more practical than the arts and then realized that writing is what made her happy."

"Could be," Meredith said. "And, again, we're very early in the investigation."

"And how does she support herself?"

"She works for a pharmaceutical company," Julia said. "We haven't found any indication that she's written for publication."

"But that isn't proof that she doesn't want to write," Miss Charlotte said with a quick glance at Brenda. "Perhaps she overstated her qualifications, but that doesn't mean she isn't sincere about wanting to write a book about my family's history."

"No, but she hasn't been entirely honest either. We just have to figure out why."

Miss Charlotte was silent for a long moment.

"I don't want you to say anything to her," she said finally. "Not yet."

Meredith glanced at Julia and then turned to Miss Charlotte. "Do you want us to stop the investigation?"

"No," Miss Charlotte said. "I want to know whatever you find out, but I'd rather you kept it between us for now."

"Miss Charlotte," Brenda began.

Miss Charlotte held up one pale hand. "No, I want to know. They haven't found any real harm in her. She hasn't asked for anything but to find out about Grandmama and the rest of the family and to write her book. I want to know if there's more to it than that, and we might never find out if we scare her away now."

Brenda pursed her lips and didn't say anything else.

"Now," Miss Charlotte said, "what else have you two found out?"

"That's all for now, at least the things that make us wonder what's going on," Julia said. "We didn't find anything criminal in her background. She's been employed since she graduated."

Miss Charlotte raised one delicately arched eyebrow. "If she is employed, how is it she's able to come here for an extended period? She's said nothing about having to leave here anytime soon."

"I called the company she works for," Meredith said. "All they would tell me was that she wasn't in the office. I suppose it could be as simple a thing as her taking vacation time. That's not unusual."

"No," Miss Charlotte said, staring again into the fire. "Not at all."

Before anyone could say more, there was a respectful tap on the open door.

"Miss Charlotte?" Richard Sheldon was standing in the door, a paper in his hand and his grandson, Jeff, with him. "Please excuse the interruption, but I was wondering if now would be a good time for me to do some work that needs doing in the upstairs bathrooms."

Miss Charlotte's mouth tightened. "I have guests now, Richard. And isn't this something you ought to discuss with Brenda?"

"Yes, Miss Charlotte, but I see you're both occupied, and I'm afraid if I don't get up there pretty quick, we're going to have a leak, and you don't want that. Not with all the nice things up there."

"Do you want me to see to it, Miss Charlotte?" Brenda asked quietly.

Miss Charlotte patted the arm she was still holding on to. "You can see to it on your own, can't you, Richard?"

"Certainly, Miss Charlotte. It shouldn't take but a few minutes."

Her expression softened. "And, Jeff, you see your grandfather does as good a job as you would."

The boy gave her an engaging smile. "I will, Miss Charlotte, but you know I'll be the one who ends up doing it anyway."

Richard scowled but didn't dispute the claim.

"Very well," Miss Charlotte said. "Go along, both of you, and thank you."

He nodded. "Miss Charlotte. Mrs. James. Pardon us disturbing you, ladies."

"Go along now," she said, and with another brief nod, he did.

"May I ask you something, Miss Charlotte?" Meredith asked after they'd had plenty of time to get out of earshot.

"Certainly, my dear."

"A few years ago, why did you have my husband do background checks on property managers for you? I thought you always liked to keep the same families working for you. And Richard is actually related to you, isn't he?"

Miss Charlotte's smile turned slightly brittle. "He's a direct descendent of Alice Lockwood's cousin, her father's nephew, Conrad Dumont. We spoke before of him coming to see to the estate when, after the epidemic, Alice went to Chicago for several years. His family has always looked after things for us. Why was I looking for someone to take his place? I told you already that Richard doesn't have the love of the place that his father and grandfather did. That all his family had, Grandmama told me. But perhaps it's something more. Something I haven't quite wanted to face."

She looked at Brenda and then significantly toward the door. Brenda got up and closed it and then sat down next to her again.

Miss Charlotte drew a deep breath. "I have thought," she said slowly, "ever since he was a child, he's felt wronged by my branch of the family."

"Wronged?" Julia asked.

"You know how it was back when Grandmama was a girl. It was generally expected for sons and grandsons and nephews to inherit the family estate. Grandmama was all that stopped Richard's branch of the family from inheriting everything, because she had the bad manners to stay alive. Richard has never said so, but I have often thought that he feels his family should have inherited this estate and all the family holdings when Grandmama's father and brothers died."

"He seems fairly well removed from the Delorme side of the family for that, if you ask me," Meredith said.

"Grandmama never mentioned her cousin or any of his descendants saying so. Richard has always seemed…dissatisfied with his lot in life. Needless to say, he has always been free to leave here and find something he feels himself more suited to, but he's never indicated he wished to go. After all these years, five generations now, I should think the matter well settled. Any question of ownership was settled long ago according to the law. If his ancestor had any sort of claim in 1876, the time for putting forth that claim is long past."

"I'd have to look into it," Julia said, "but I'm sure there's a period of time where people can challenge the title to property that's part of an inheritance, but I'd guess that time period is a lot less than one hundred fifty years or so."

"Probably," Meredith said with a chuckle.

"Has he ever brought up the subject?" Julia asked Miss Charlotte.

"Never. But he has from time to time made comments that lead me to believe this is what he thinks. When his son was a little boy, oh, perhaps ten years old, I heard him squabbling with another boy, the son of one of the gardeners, about how this whole place ought to belong to him and his family. Where else would a boy like that get such an idea if not from his own father? Especially with his father being in the particular situation he's in regarding my family."

"But none of them has ever asked you for anything?" Julia pressed. "He or his son? His grandson?"

"No. Nothing straightforward like that. It's like his work here. He does a good job. He does what I ask when I ask it, and he does it in a very competent manner. Those other men I had your husband check on for me, Mrs. Bellefontaine, two of them I already knew would not be suitable. The third, I very nearly hired him. He had a feeling for the land, for all that had gone on here before, but Richard is family, no matter what else. As long as he's here or his son or grandson, as long as he does his job properly and gives me no cause to turn him out, I'll keep him on."

Julia didn't like the man being around if Miss Charlotte had qualms about him, but she nodded. "Maybe he knows he or his family wouldn't have a legal claim after all these years anyway, and he doesn't want to risk everything he has here already."

"I don't know how old he is," Meredith said, "but it gets hard for a man of sixty or so to find a new job, especially a plum one like the one he already has. Miss Charlotte, I bet you spoil him like you do everyone else who works for you."

"A worker is worthy of his hire," Miss Charlotte said. "I always try to make anyone I employ happy to work for me. It was something Grandmama insisted on."

Brenda gave a hard look to the door the estate manager had just gone through. "Mr. Richard has nothing to complain about."

Miss Charlotte patted her arm. "Never mind him, now. I expect Jeff will see to things. For now, we're going to decide what to do about Miss Browning." With a startled intake of breath, she checked the watch brooch she wore. "It's nearly noon, Brenda. Miss Browning ought to be here."

Brenda got to her feet, her expression faintly disdainful. "I'm surprised she wasn't here at eight this morning. I'll go meet her when she comes."

"For now," Miss Charlotte said once Brenda was gone, "don't let on to Miss Browning that we've been discussing her."

"Of course not," Julia said. "Unless you decide it's time we said something because of something she says or does. We'll follow your lead."

Meredith nodded.

"Very good," Miss Charlotte said, glancing out the window at the sound of a car pulling up to the house. "I believe she has arrived."

A few minutes later, Brenda showed Jaden into the room.

"Hello, everyone." Jaden rushed over to their hostess, bubbly as usual. "Miss Charlotte, I'm so sorry. I realize I was nearly late, but I stopped to get you something."

She presented Miss Charlotte with a small box with a French name embossed on the top, which Julia recognized as the name of a premier and quite expensive Belgian chocolatier.

"How very sweet of you, my dear," Miss Charlotte said. "It wasn't at all necessary."

"No, ma'am, maybe not, but you've been so kind, and Charles said you liked those especially. They're dark chocolate buttercreams."

Miss Charlotte fought the tiniest of smiles as she opened the box to admire the rich contents. "I will have to speak to Charles about letting out my secrets." She handed the box to Brenda. "Will you kindly have Ellen put these in the icebox to cool? I believe we'll enjoy them after we've had lunch."

"Yes, ma'am," Brenda said, and she took the chocolates away.

Jaden was beaming. "I'm glad I'm not the only one who likes chocolate better when it's chilled."

"Much better that way," Miss Charlotte said with a serene nod. "Especially during Savannah's summers. I'm glad you've come, Miss Browning. I'm sorry you had to leave us prematurely last time. Brenda tells me you are quite recovered."

"Yes, ma'am. Thank you. I'm sorry I couldn't stay." She turned to Julia and Meredith. "What did I miss?"

"I started to show them my personal photo album." Miss Charlotte laid her hand on the large book on the table in front of her. "But we decided we would wait until you could come back and we could all look at it together."

"Oh, thank you! There's so much I'd like to see."

"It really is a privilege to see your personal collection," Meredith said. "Do you think you'll include some of these photos in the book, Jaden?"

"I'd love to. With Miss Charlotte's permission, of course."

Miss Charlotte frowned thoughtfully. "You know, I hadn't really given it any thought. Grandmama felt it was rather vulgar to have one's photograph in all the papers like some kind of advertisement. I'm sure she'd be horrified by what so many people put onto the internet for the whole world to see."

Meredith and Julia exchanged a smile.

"They certainly don't mind saying all kinds of personal things publicly," Julia said.

"But Grandmama has been gone a very long while now. Perhaps it's time people saw more of her and the rest of us." Miss Charlotte turned over a page in the album and then turned the book sideways. "This is the only photograph there is, to my knowledge, of Grandmama and her parents and her two brothers. It is certainly the last one."

The family was standing on the front porch of the Delorme mansion looking toward the camera, all of them wearing their Sunday best, the father and mother standing in the middle of the front step, the sons one on either side, and the daughter one step down in front of the parents, all of them solemn and decorous except for the younger of the sons. He was leaning against one of the porch's columns with his flat-brim straw hat pushed rakishly back on his head. The older one was at his mother's side, one hand supporting her elbow.

"This is my great-great-grandfather, James Delorme," Miss Charlotte said, indicating the heavy, dark-bearded man in the middle of the picture. "And my great-great-grandmother, Catherine."

The richly dressed woman was dainty and fair haired, her light-colored eyes hardly showing on the faded photograph.

"Miss Alice looked like her," Meredith said, reaching out but stopping short of actually touching the picture.

"Very much," Miss Charlotte said. "And so did her younger brother, Evan." She smiled a little at the boy with the rakish hat. "He was a scamp, Grandmama always said. She was fondest of him, I think, but she said Jimmy, the older one, was always good to her too."

Julia studied the man and woman in the background of the picture. The woman was middle aged, her gray-streaked hair mostly covered by a white cap and her dark dress covered by a white apron. The man next to her was young and fair haired, dressed in a dark suit that wasn't of the quality of the gentlemen of the house but was likely his best. He held some kind of cap in his hands and his head was turned to one side, but Julia could tell he had dark eyes.

"Who are they?" she asked Miss Charlotte.

"That's Beryl, the maid who came from England with Grandmama's mother, and her son, Teddy."

"You told us a little about them," Julia said.

"Grandmama always said she didn't know what she would have done without them after she lost her family."

"Did they stay with Miss Alice after that?" Jaden asked.

"All their lives. Grandmama wouldn't have it any other way. Beryl died around the turn of the century—1907, if I'm remembering correctly. And Teddy?" Miss Charlotte chuckled. "I remember him quite well. He died when I was eleven and he was eighty-five. I remember he always wanted to drive whatever was the latest thing in cars. Of course, he was Grandmama's driver when she still had horses and carriages. She'd buy whatever it was he thought she should have."

"He had a good long life then," Julia said.

"Oh yes. It's in our blood." Miss Charlotte stopped and smiled suddenly. "Even our employees live a long time."

Jaden studied Teddy for a moment. "Do you know when this picture was taken?" she asked.

"Not exactly," Miss Charlotte said. "The closest I can tell is about a month or so before the epidemic. Soon after that, they were all gone. Well, except for Grandmama of course."

"And Beryl and Teddy," Jaden added.

Julia studied Alice, comparing her to the not-so-much older young woman in the wedding portrait she had seen. "I suppose something like that changes people."

"Of course it does," Miss Charlotte said, and she turned to a different page in the album to a photograph of a solemn-looking toddler in a wool baby dress. "This is my grandfather, Matthew Lockwood. It was taken right after Grandmama brought him back here from Chicago. After his father died. Poor Grandmama, she was only twenty-one."

"It must have been hard for her to return to the estate after everything that had happened," Julia said.

Miss Charlotte nodded. "She was in mourning, of course, but she always said she knew it was time to come back home. Her life up north was gone, and she was eager to begin again here, to make the estate into something her son could one day oversee."

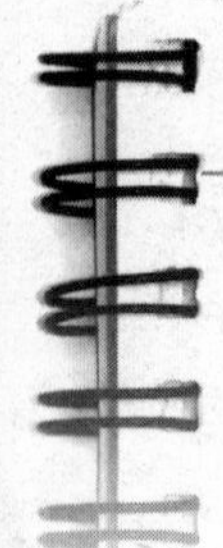

Savannah
May 1882

"He's here," Beryl said in an urgent whisper. "Let me put on your veil."

She draped the heavy black lace over me, letting it cascade from my head to down past my waist. I felt better being covered up like this, hiding myself away, never letting anyone see me. If only Calvin had lived—

"Come now," she said, taking my arm and guiding me to the door. "He's waiting. Once you get through this, the rest will be easy."

She was right. Of course she was right. But I didn't want to be here. I should never have come back here at all. I should have let him see to things as he had been doing ever since the epidemic. Coming here right now was a bad idea. It was too soon. What if he—

"It's time, Miss Alice," she said in the no-nonsense voice I was too familiar with.

I straightened my shoulders, lifted my chin, and followed her out into the parlor.

Conrad Dumont sprang to his feet and immediately took my hand, bowing over it. "Cousin Alice, how are you?"

"I am well," I said, keeping my voice low. "Please, do sit down."

"Allow me." He helped me to the settee, all solicitousness, and then he sat at my side. "I was most distressed to hear that you had been widowed, cousin. I would like to assure you that you can rely on me for any sort of assistance, great or small, that you may need in these trying times. But, despite the circumstances, I must tell you how pleased I am to know you have returned here. Your late father would be very pleased to know that his grandson will one day be master here."

"I came back here for his sake," I told him. "For my son's. Now that my husband is gone, we had no reason to stay up north."

"Young Mister Matthew ought to be raised in his family home," Beryl said, coming in with the tea tray and setting it down before us. "It would be unnatural if he wasn't, don't you think so, Mr. Dumont, sir?"

"Yes, indeed I do," he said, taking the cup she offered him. "Of course, I'm quite pleased, cousin, to continue managing things here for you as long as you like, but I know my uncle would have wanted you here. He would have wanted your child to know this as his home, and I am pleased to be of service to you and your son just as I would have been to your father."

I didn't take any tea. I would have had to raise my veil to drink it, and just now that wouldn't do. "Thank you," I said. "I hope you will continue what you've been doing. I need someone who can make sure things here are done as they ought to be, and I've been quite pleased with your work here since my father died. I'm sure I wouldn't know what to do without you."

"I am happy to do it, Cousin Alice. Your father meant a great deal to me, and if I can help you and your son, I think that would make him happy too. And my wife has asked me to let you know that she would be very pleased to do anything in her power to help you and your boy get settled in."

"You're both very kind, sir," I murmured. I hadn't met his wife before. There was no reason we couldn't become friends.

"She wanted me to ask most particularly about your servants."

"My servants?"

"I know you've brought your maid and your driver back from Chicago with you, but as you asked when I first came to look after the estate for you, I kept on only a few of your servants, just enough to maintain the house while you were away. Did you wish me to see which of them I might be able to bring back? Effie, my wife, thought it might be of some comfort to you to be tended to by the people who had looked after you and your family before your tragic loss."

"I— Surely, they have all found employment elsewhere after so long."

"Oh certainly, cousin, certainly. But if it would comfort you, I could try to bring them back."

I looked to Beryl, not knowing quite what to say, but she only gave him a gracious smile.

"Perhaps you'd rather start fresh now, Miss Alice," she said. "There is so much here to remind you of your dear mother and father and brothers, it might be rather difficult to surround yourself with so many people who would also remind you of the past. Why not start fresh? I would be happy to find the right ones for you and teach them their duties, and you won't have to think twice of it. Wouldn't that be best?"

"Yes. I think it would. I think for now I will let Beryl see to the servants, if you don't mind, Cousin Conrad, and you carry on doing what you have been since my father was taken and we'll go along that way for a time."

He was obliging as usual. "Certainly, ma'am."

He smiled, and I ducked my head, pulling my veil closer about me.

"You left many friends behind here, cousin, when you moved north. I needn't tell you how pleased they all are that you've returned. Several of them have told me they mean to come calling on you when you're recovered from your journey here."

"Oh no," I gasped before I thought.

Beryl was at once at my side, taking my hand in hers, patting it comfortingly.

"Shh, my lamb." She looked apologetically at our visitor. "You understand, of course, that Miss Alice is in mourning. Her husband's death was sudden and unexpected, and what lady of her breeding would not be prostrate with grief, not only to lose her husband, but to be left with a child to

raise alone. Would you rather wait a while to have callers, Miss Alice?"

I nodded gratefully, glad Beryl was always beside me, glad she always kept me from doing or saying the wrong thing. It was wearing to always have to be so careful every moment of every day.

"Wouldn't that be best?" I asked on a sigh.

My grief was still raw and fresh. I loved Cal. Even now I did, and he had loved me. Part of me was glad that he had died not knowing what I had done, but somehow I knew if he had known, he would have still loved me as faithfully and tenderly as before. He would have somehow made everything right, I know he would. How many times had I wanted to bury myself in his arms and tell him all?

Beryl had assured me that I would learn to go on without him, that he would want his son to have all the advantages the Delorme name and holdings could bring him. My poor little boy, he was a Lockwood. Only I had carried the name Delorme, and I had traded that for Lockwood too. At least that much was still mine even without my husband, without my Cal. I couldn't help it. I had to bring my lace handkerchief under my veil and dry my eyes.

"Please, Cousin Alice," Conrad said, taking possession of my other hand as he dropped to one knee. "I beg you to forgive me. I hadn't meant to trample upon your grief with my thoughtlessness. I will let your kind well-wishers know that you are not yet ready to receive them. Certainly, they will

understand the delicacy of your feelings at such a difficult time."

"Thank you," I said. "Please tell them I am grateful for their concern and will happily correspond with them until I feel ready to return to society. Many of them have written to me regularly these past few years. I would miss corresponding with them."

Conrad stood again, his expression all kindness. "Of course. I am certain they will want to do whatever is of the most comfort to you. And, as I said, anything my wife or I can do to ease your burden, Cousin Alice, you need only send word."

I nodded, unable to speak without betraying myself. I didn't deserve this good man's kindness. Perhaps, in truth, it was he who should have been in my place as owner of the estate, but I had to think of my son. Matthew would be heir to everything one day, and then all of this would be worth it. As long as I had Beryl to keep my feet steadily on the path, it would be worth it.

He kissed my hand in farewell, and Beryl rang for Teddy.

"Miss Alice wishes to have Mr. Beaumont's carriage brought around."

They exchanged a look, and there was a sly knowingness in Teddy's contrasting eyes.

He bowed his head very slightly, hooding those eyes halfway. "At once, Miss Alice. This way, sir."

Then he was gone and my visitor with him.

Beryl came to me once more and this time she sat at my side on the plush settee.

"You must be very careful, my lamb."

"I know," I whispered.

"But no one will expect a grieving widow to show herself in public." She smiled and patted my hand. "Not to worry now. I will be right beside you all along the way."

Chapter Fourteen

"Grandmama always remembered her cousin's kindness and his wife's as well through the years," Miss Charlotte told them. "And she was glad she could rely on him to see that everything on the estate was properly run."

"It must have been hard for her," Jaden said, "being in mourning when she was still so young."

"The rules were very strict back then about what a widow could wear and what she may and may not do, especially in public. But even though she kept to herself for a long while after she came back home, she was eager to be here in the place she was born, the only home she'd known until the yellow fever took her family."

Miss Charlotte turned the page again, this time to another wedding photograph. This one showed a young woman with very dark hair and large dark eyes seated in a plush chair with her arms full of flowers and her ruffled skirts covering all but the dainty tips of her satin slippers. Standing beside her with one hand on her shoulder was a nice-looking, fair-haired young man in a morning suit. With his free hand, he held a tall silk hat.

"This is my grandfather with his bride, Amelia Collins, in 1903."

"He favored his mother," Meredith observed. "At least he favors the way she looked in her wedding picture. Not as much in that picture of the whole family."

"Photography had improved between the time that family picture was taken and when Grandmama was married," Miss Charlotte said. "By the time Grandfather was married, pictures were much clearer still. But, yes, you can see the resemblance."

"What about his wife?" Julia asked. "Did Miss Alice talk about her much?"

"Grandmama always said she was very quiet, very gentle, and cried easily. Her father worked for the bank our family used, and Grandfather met her there. There was a lot of talk about it, because everyone expected him to marry someone from one of Savannah's leading families, but Grandmama said once he met Amelia, that was the end of it. They actually eloped three weeks later." Miss Charlotte laughed softly. "But Grandmama always said they were so happy together."

Savannah
September 1905

The howl of a thunderstorm and the wail of a newborn baby couldn't cover up the low fierceness in my son's voice on the other side of the door.

"Don't lie to me," he spat. "Don't try to deceive me when the proof is lying right there."

I heard only the low murmur of my daughter-in-law's response. I could make nothing of the words themselves, but I was sure I knew what she was saying. It was cruel, so cruel. Why hadn't I realized this could happen? Had I truly thought my sin would not find me out?

"And don't think I don't know who it was," Matthew grated. "Isn't it bad enough as it is without him being the one? He's old enough to be your father! And I trusted him. I trusted you both." His voice broke. "I loved you. With everything in me, I loved you. I thought you loved me."

Tears sprang to my eyes, and now I could hear Amelia's weak sobs as she pled with him.

"It's not true. Matthew, I love you. I would never betray you. I don't understand it, but it's not what you think. Not what you've said. Ask him! He'll tell you!"

"Ask him?" Matthew laughed bitterly. "And you think he'll tell the truth? Why should he when my own wife won't?"

He called her a vile name, and she began to weep again, softer now, tears of weary despair. I had to talk to my son. I had to tell him the truth. I couldn't let him destroy the woman who loved him so much.

I went to the bedroom door and reached to open it, but it flew away from my hand as Matthew stalked out. His eyes were half wild in the sudden boom and flash of thunder and lightning. His trembling lips were pressed hard together, and there were twin spots of heightened color in his wax-pale cheeks. He pulled the door closed behind him with deliberate care, not letting it make a sound.

"Matthew."

He clenched his jaw, daring me to speak to him. Too furious to listen.

"Please, honey, let me tell you something. You don't understand. She would never—"

"Don't talk to me, Mother." His voice shook. "Don't tell me it's a mistake or you don't know what could have happened. Don't say it. Just don't say it."

He stalked down the corridor and down the stairs and to his study. I followed right behind him, begging him to be reasonable. Begging him to listen, just listen.

He didn't answer me. He didn't look at me. He just went to his desk and yanked open his top drawer. I knew what he kept there.

"No. Matthew, what are you going to do?"

He took out his pearl-handled pistol and spun the chamber to make sure it was loaded.

"What are you going to do?" I demanded again.

"I'm going to kill him."

"You can't! He hasn't done anything!"

"He's betrayed me," Matthew said coldly. "He's betrayed you. How can you stand there and defend him?"

I grabbed the gun, trying to take it from him, praying it didn't accidentally discharge, but he wouldn't let go. Again the lightning flashed, and the rain beat at the windows like fine gravel.

"Matthew, please! Just listen to me! Listen!"

Somehow I wrenched it away from him, but he shoved me back against the wall, making the picture frames rattle.

Then, without another word, he ran down the stairs and out the front door into the storm. I dropped the gun and followed him onto the porch, calling his name, begging him to listen, but he didn't turn back. He didn't have a hat or coat, and with his shirt plastered to his back and the wind whipping through his hair, he strode down the muddy drive.

I watched him go, still calling him, my own face wet with tears. Then there was another strike of lightning, ripping through the sky and making it for an instant light as day. When I could see again, he was gone. Somehow at that moment I knew I would never see him again.

I clung for a moment to one of the beams that supported the porch, and then remembered he wasn't the only one who'd been hurt. I blotted my wet face with both hands and went back into the house. I took a moment to smooth back my windblown hair, and then I went upstairs. Beryl was coming through Amelia's door. She had soothed the crying baby to sleep, but there were tears on her lined cheeks, and her age-dimmed eyes were full of regret. Beyond her, I could see that Amelia lay quiet now. Her suffering had ended.

"I didn't think—" Beryl began, but I only swept past her into the room.

I wouldn't blame her for my weakness, for my sin, but I could not comfort her either. We had both reaped what we had sown.

"Sadly," Miss Charlotte said after she'd told them about her grandparents' happy life together, "she died when my father was born. So many women still died in childbirth in those days."

"But what happened to your grandfather?" Julia asked. "I couldn't find any more information on him."

"He left Savannah when Grandmother died. Grandmama always said he couldn't live with losing her. He simply walked away, leaving his son for Grandmama to raise. She hired people to search for him, to bring him home, but it was almost three years after that that she got a letter from a friend who had been traveling abroad. He'd found out that Grandfather had been killed in Moscow in some revolutionary skirmish. Grandmama could never talk about Grandfather without shedding tears. She said there were so many things she had wanted to tell him, things she wanted to explain, things that would have helped him in his grief, but she never had a chance. It was really quite sad."

"He accused her of terrible things, and now I can never explain—"

Julia had to force herself not to ask Miss Charlotte about what she had seen in her too-quick glimpse of Alice's diary. Had she been referring to her son then? Could it have been his wife he'd accused of terrible things? And had he left home out of grief or guilt? It had been over a hundred years since then, but somehow Julia felt there was something about it that Miss Charlotte wouldn't want to discuss.

"Do you think we'll have a chance to look at Miss Alice's diary today?" Jaden asked.

"Oh, yes," Julia said, "couldn't we?" Maybe she could find that page again and get a better look.

Miss Charlotte considered for a moment. "I think we could do that." There was a sudden twinkle in her blue eyes. "If you're certain you're genuinely interested."

Jaden blinked at her, and then she giggled. "You're teasing me, Miss Charlotte. Of course I am."

Miss Charlotte looked at her watch again. "Perhaps we should spend the time until we eat lunch looking at more of my photographs. And after lunch you can all see what's in Grandmama's diary. How would that be?"

"I would love that," Jaden said. "Thank you."

"Me too," Meredith added.

Julia smiled and nodded. "Until then, I'd love to see more pictures. Do you have any of your father, Miss Charlotte?"

"Oh goodness, do I! Grandmama would put any of today's grandmothers to shame with all the pictures she had taken of him when he was growing up."

Miss Charlotte closed the album and stood up just as the door to the morning room opened.

"Now where are you going?" Brenda asked, hands on hips. "And without your cane?"

Miss Charlotte looked like a naughty child. "I thought I'd let them see my father's photo album."

Brenda only looked at her until she sat down again. "I'll be happy to get it for you, Miss Charlotte."

"Did Richard and Jeff see to what they needed to do?"

"They're doing it now, ma'am. It shouldn't take long."

"Very good, Brenda. Thank you."

Brenda pursed her lips. "I'll get Mr. Marcus's album. Lunch will be ready in a few minutes."

Marcus Lockwood had dark eyes and hair like his mother, but his features had a decided resemblance to his father's and grandmother's. Miss Charlotte had been right about Alice Lockwood being a doting grandmother. In a time when having a photograph taken was a special event, she had apparently taken every opportunity to have them made.

"There are quite a few," Miss Charlotte said. "I'm sure you won't want to look at every one of them."

"But they're fascinating," Meredith said. "Not only seeing him grow up, but seeing the changes in the clothes and what's in the background and even the photography itself."

"Oh yes," Jaden said. "I would love to study all of these." She looked hopefully at Miss Charlotte. "I mean, maybe someday I can just look through them. I wouldn't want to bore you with sitting with me, but sometime when you wouldn't mind me coming by. I promise I wouldn't bother anybody while I was here."

Miss Charlotte glanced at the girl's face and then looked at a photograph of five- or six-year-old Marcus, front teeth missing and a sprinkling of freckles on his turned-up nose, as he sat on a black pony grinning. "They are telling, aren't they? We'll see what we can arrange. How would that be?"

Jaden beamed at her. "I'd like that."

Julia looked from Jaden to the child on the pony, not sure what puzzled her. And then she squinted at the fiftyish-looking man leading the pony. His head was turned as he looked back at the child.

"Is that Teddy?"

Miss Charlotte nodded.

"I wasn't sure if that was him. He looks dark eyed in the other pictures I've seen, but his eyes look light here."

Jaden leaned closer, studying the man.

"I think the light was at an odd angle in that one," Miss Charlotte said, "but that is definitely Teddy."

"And he came from England with Miss Alice's mother and her maid?" Jaden asked.

"No, he was born in Savannah after his mother came here."

"What about his own family?"

"He never had children," Miss Charlotte said. "Never married. He said it was his job to look after me and Grandmama, and that's what he did."

"That was very good of him," Jaden said, looking over the picture again.

"He was very loyal to our family his whole life. Grandmama said he and my father were inseparable. He taught my father to ride, and when Father was old enough, Teddy taught him to drive. Grandmama said they both drove too fast."

She turned a few pages ahead, to a photograph of a dark-haired young man with a wide grin sitting in the driver's seat of a light-colored 1927 Duesenberg. Beside him was a young woman with bobbed blond hair and a cloche hat and a jaunty scarf around her neck. They were leaning in for the picture, cheek to cheek, with their arms around each other.

"They were going on a picnic that day, and when they came back, they were engaged."

"So sweet," Meredith said, "and what a great car."

"It was bright yellow, Grandmama told me," Miss Charlotte said. "He always told people that besides my mother, it was the love of his life."

"When I was doing my research," Julia said gently, "I saw they both died the same year. What happened to them?"

Miss Charlotte patted her arm. "I never knew them, my dear. They died when I was only two, so it isn't painful to speak of them. I only remember how Grandmama carried her grief over their loss until the end of her life."

"I'm sorry. She had so much tragedy to deal with, I don't know how she carried on."

"I once asked her exactly that," Miss Charlotte said, and there was a touch of bittersweetness in her eyes. "She said that, as long as she had a child to care for, she had to go on. Now that I've grown nearly as old as she was, I can understand. But when I'm gone—" She patted Julia's arm again. "Well, you didn't ask about that. You wanted to know what happened to my parents. They were driving home from a party one evening, driving too fast, the police said, and hit another car head-on. My mother died at once. My father was brought home and the doctor came out right away, but Father died the next day. Poor Grandmama was left with another baby to raise."

"I don't know how she stood it," Meredith said. "So much loss."

"I think that's why she started the foundation. Couples losing their babies or unable to have any. Children losing their parents or being unwanted. By bringing them together, she could ease some of the pain in the world, and maybe some of her own too."

"Miss Charlotte?" Brenda said, coming into the room. "Ellen tells me lunch is ready."

"Very good." Miss Charlotte stood and reached one hand toward Jaden. "Take my arm, Miss Browning. If I fall and break my hip, I'm afraid you will have to wait even longer to see the longed-for diary."

Jaden did as she'd been told with a pert grin. "We wouldn't want that to happen, ma'am. I don't know if I could wait any longer."

They sat down to another of Miss Charlotte's lavish luncheons, still discussing the stories she had told them.

"I can't wait to start writing," Jaden said. "So much happened to Miss Alice, and we haven't really gotten to the foundation yet, or her war work or her involvement with educational causes." She took a quick bite of salmon brioche and a sip of water. "And you have so many wonderful pictures too. Not just of her. I hope you'll let me use some."

Miss Charlotte patted her hand. "Oh, I imagine I will. I just have to decide whether or not Grandmama would approve. And in this case, I think she might. I think—"

She drew a sharp breath and suddenly grasped Jaden's hand.

Jaden's eyes widened. "Miss Charlotte?"

Julia got up and went to her side. "Miss Charlotte, are you all right?"

Miss Charlotte looked pale, and she licked her lips. "I'm—I'm fine. Just a little dizzy for a moment there. I'm sure it's nothing."

Brenda hurried into the room, not waiting to be called. "Miss Charlotte? What is it?"

"It's nothing. Really. And we have guests."

"Well, right now you're scaring our guests." Brenda turned her so they were face-to-face, but a moment later, Miss Charlotte's head sank to her shoulder. "I think we'd better get you up to bed and give Dr. Kelly a call."

"Now, it's nothing, I'm sure." Miss Charlotte struggled to sit straight up again but couldn't quite manage it.

"Or do we need to call the ambulance?" Brenda asked her. "Because that's your other choice."

"All right. All right. I'll lie down for a while. I'm just the tiniest bit light-headed."

"No chest pains?" Brenda asked her.

"No, no, nothing like that."

"Do you feel sick?"

Miss Charlotte shook her head decisively. "Just a little dizzy."

"Has she had this sort of thing before?" Julia asked quietly.

"Not like this," Brenda said. "She gets a little weak when she overdoes, but mostly a little rest will fix her right up. You stay here a minute, Miss Charlotte. I'll get your medicine."

"Now, I don't—"

"That or the ambulance."

Miss Charlotte huffed, but she sat still until Brenda came back with a bottle of medicine and a spoon. Her patient swallowed it dutifully, but by her expression, Julia could tell it didn't have a pleasant taste.

"There now," Brenda said. "That ought to help."

"That's all I need," Miss Charlotte said, managing to sit up, and she gave her company a wan smile. "I feel terrible disappointing you all. Just when we were having such a nice lunch."

"It was a delicious lunch," Jaden assured her. "I'm so sorry you're not feeling very well. I think we've stayed too long, not just today but all the other times too."

"Nonsense, now." Miss Charlotte patted her again. "We'll get together again, all of us, and talk about your book and the pictures you can use for it. And the stories you'll want to put in it. As you said, we haven't even got to the part about the foundation and everything afterward."

Julia studied her. She didn't look exceptionally pale, but she was still having trouble sitting up. "Are you sure you shouldn't call the paramedics? They say, especially in women, the signs of heart attack can be very mild or even nonexistent."

"It's nothing so serious as that, my dear. Brenda will take me to lie down for a while, and she will call Dr. Kelly so he can scold me for overdoing it, and that will be that. Leave those paramedics for people with actual emergencies."

Julia grinned. Miss Charlotte had certainly not lost any of her spirit.

"Can we help you to the elevator?" Meredith asked.

"Oh, no." With Brenda's help, Miss Charlotte stood. "Brenda's used to looking after me. You three finish your lunch. After we can enjoy the Belgian chocolate Miss Browning brought us."

With that, she had Brenda help her out of the dining room.

"Shouldn't they call the paramedics anyway?" Jaden asked after a moment's silence. "Just in case?"

"I think so," Julia said, "but as you can see, Miss Charlotte has a mind of her own. I suppose, between Brenda and Dr. Kelly, she'll be taken care of. It's a shame though."

"I know. I don't think I can eat cake now."

Meredith gave Jaden's shoulder a comforting squeeze. "Come on, now. She didn't look too bad, and she has done a lot of visiting today. Brenda's taken care of her for years. I'm sure she'll get her help if she thinks it's necessary, whether or not Miss Charlotte protests. Why don't we finish our lunch and our talk and see what happens for the next few minutes? If we leave now and Miss Charlotte needs something, we won't be here to help, right?"

Jaden looked uncertain for a moment and then nodded. "I suppose so. I didn't mean to overstay."

"Of course not," Julia said, sitting down again. "You know, we don't know all that much about you. I understand your family was from Savannah."

"Yeah, but I was born in Atlanta. I moved to Dallas to go to school."

"And after that?"

"Oh, I got a job." Jaden stopped suddenly. "I mean, that was after I got my bachelor's degree. I still have to get my master's, like I said."

Meredith nodded. "That's hard to do, work full time and still go to school, especially when you're doing postgraduate work."

"A lot of people do it," Jaden said.

"How interesting that your family was from here," Julia said, seeing the questions were making Jaden nervous. "Do you know how far back that goes?"

"My grandmother was born here. And her father too. Before that, I'm not sure since he was adopted."

"Oh, that's interesting. One of the Lockwood Foundation adoptions?" Julia asked. Maybe someone in Jaden's family had known for certain.

"I'm not sure, though it's something I'd like to find out."

"It would be interesting to know," Meredith said. "When was he born?"

"April 10, 1905."

"Hmm, that might have been too early for the foundation to be involved. You don't have any records about him, do you? Or maybe someone in your family would know more?"

"I have some information. I came to Savannah, besides getting to find out more about Miss Alice and Miss Charlotte, to see what records I could find on the rest of my family. I was hoping to learn something about my great-grandfather. I'm having trouble finding any record of who his birth parents were. I guess they didn't want to be found."

"I'm sure many who gave up their children for adoption didn't want to be found," Julia said. "It was hard back then on a woman with a child and no husband. Of course, that's not the only reason a child was given up for adoption."

"No," Jaden said, "not always. It just makes it hard now to figure out your true ancestry, especially when it comes to medical conditions."

"Is there something specific you're tracing?"

Jaden shrugged. "Just curious, but you know what I mean. Just generally speaking, people should know what's in their background."

Ellen brought in the dessert just then, and they spent a few minutes oohing and aahing over it and then took their time enjoying it. Then Brenda came downstairs.

"How's she doing?" Jaden asked at once.

"She's asleep now. I checked her blood pressure and her pulse and her heart rate. She seems a little excited but otherwise all right. I'll keep an eye on her, but I think she was doing too much."

"That's good to hear," Julia said, and she stood up. "Maybe we ought to go now. If you're sure there's nothing we can do to help."

"No, thank you very much," Brenda said. "We'll be just fine. I talked to Dr. Kelly, and he said to take her to the hospital if she's not better soon. We've been through this before."

Jaden stood too, looking very dejected. "Maybe it would be better if we didn't come back. At least for a while."

Brenda looked wary for a moment, and then her expression softened. "I don't know if that will be necessary. You know, Miss Charlotte has enjoyed having you come talk to her. And she's about set on having that book written about Miss Alice. You go on home now but not for too long. I'm sure Miss Charlotte will be wanting to have another of her lunches soon."

"Do you think so?" Jaden asked, brightening. "I wouldn't want to do anything that's not good for her."

"I'll be in touch," Brenda said kindly. "For now, I'll have Charles bring around your cars."

"Goodbye, Jaden," Julia said, momentarily searching her face. "I'm sure we'll see you again soon."

Chapter Fifteen

"What did you think?" Meredith asked when they were headed back to the office.

"I think Jaden knows we're onto her." Julia turned onto the highway and picked up speed. "She was about to lie about something and then caught herself."

"About what?"

"When she was talking about getting a degree and then a job. It sounded to me like she was done with school already. I'm not exactly sure, but she stopped herself from saying something."

"Could be. I did notice her suddenly changing tracks." Meredith paused for a moment. "You know, it's interesting that her great-grandfather and Miss Charlotte's father were born in 1905."

"A lot of people were born in 1905."

"True."

"And if you think he was really Miss Alice's grandson given up for adoption, that won't work, because she raised him. He was Miss Charlotte's father."

"I know." Meredith sighed. "Just trying to make connections."

"And Miss Alice clearly doted on him, judging by the number of pictures she had taken of him and all the clothes and toys."

"Sometimes two of the same clothes. I know. I just sort of wondered, with his mother dead and his father missing, if it might have been easier for her to give the baby up, but you're right. She wanted him, and she wanted Miss Charlotte when she was left without parents too."

Julia nodded. "But it seems pretty obvious that her grandson was at least part of the reason, maybe the biggest part, why she started the foundation in the first place. And it could very well be that Jaden's great-grandfather was placed by the foundation."

"Or, if not by the foundation, by her personally. Perhaps to help out someone close to her." Meredith laughed suddenly. "Okay, you're going to think I'm crazy, but did it seem to you that Jaden was especially interested in Teddy?"

"I don't know if it was anything extreme, but she did seem interested. What are you getting at?"

"Well, you mentioned it yourself. Teddy's eyes looked light in that picture with the pony. All the other times, his eyes have looked dark."

Julia thought back, trying to remember another photograph where Teddy's eyes looked light. It could be very difficult to tell on those old pictures. Then she considered something else.

"Did you notice he always had his head turned in pictures?"

"Really?" Meredith asked. "I hadn't noticed. Now I want to go back and look at them again. I didn't pay all that much attention to him in the family photos. I was more interested in the Delormes and Lockwoods."

"Well, he did. And now that I think about it, his head was turned to the right in almost all of those pictures. All but that last one with the pony, the one where his eyes look light. Or I should say, where his *eye* looked light."

Meredith caught her breath. "You mean he might have had heterochromia?"

"I can't say for sure, but it's possible. It hadn't occurred to me till just now, and now I'd like to see those pictures again. If Jaden wears one contact because she has the same thing, it would explain a lot."

"As in, he could have fathered the child who was given up for adoption in 1905? He could be Jaden's great-great-grandfather?"

"It's possible, isn't it?" Julia asked. "It would certainly be an embarrassment for Miss Alice if one of her employees fathered a child out of wedlock. And, especially if he'd been with the family for so long, it seems like she'd want to help find the child a good home."

"But Quin said that heterochromia wasn't passed down genetically unless it was part of some rare disease."

"And Miss Charlotte said Jaden was asking about the family's medical history."

"But what would that have to do with Teddy then?"

"Oh." Julia exhaled. "That's true. Then I'm puzzled again. We'll have to do more research."

"Definitely." Meredith huffed. "It's too bad Miss Charlotte wasn't feeling well. We still haven't seen the diary, and I sure wish I'd gotten a better look at those pictures of Teddy."

"But if Jaden is related to Teddy," Julia said, thinking a little more, "why does she look like that picture of Miss Charlotte's father?"

Meredith sat up straighter in her seat. "What?"

Julia nodded. "I've been wondering what was bothering me when I saw Jaden looking at that picture of Miss Charlotte's father on the pony. I was wondering before that if she didn't look a little like Miss Alice herself, especially in her wedding picture. But then I saw Jaden looking at that picture of Marcus Lockwood on his pony. It's the nose. The nose and the freckles. The grin too. They're the same."

Meredith pushed her hair back with both hands. "This is crazy. I thought we were tracing her back to Teddy because of the heterochromia."

"I can't say I'm not really confused now, but we don't actually know if she has heterochromia. There could be another reason she wears one contact. I mean, it would be natural for Quin to mention that reason, because he has that condition. It doesn't mean that's the actual answer."

They drove on a while longer, both of them quiet until they got back to the office.

"I think I'd better call and see how Miss Charlotte is doing now," Julia said finally. "And maybe Brenda will answer a few more questions too. Now that I have a few more I'd like to ask."

"All of that would have been way before her time," Meredith protested.

"But people hear things. Brenda's mother worked for Miss Charlotte too. Her grandmother helped raise Miss Charlotte. I'd be surprised if her great-grandmother didn't work for Miss Alice too. Any of those women would have known a lot more about the family than almost anyone else. They may not say anything to anyone outside the family, but it's likely they talked among themselves."

"But would Brenda tell you if she knew anything about it anyway?"

Julia shrugged. "I can only try. And maybe I'll call and ask about Miss Charlotte tomorrow. That'll give me a chance to chat with Brenda again."

"Okay," Meredith said. "But I want to check something anyway."

"What?"

"Can we go into your office for a minute? I'm curious."

Julia raised her eyebrows and followed Meredith to the second office.

"Do you still have that family tree you made?" Meredith asked her.

"Right here." Julia got the page with the family tree she had jotted down and handed it to Meredith. "What is it?"

"When did Jaden say her great-grandfather was born?"

"April of 1905."

"What day?" Meredith pressed. "Do you remember?"

"The tenth."

"Uh-huh. Just what I thought."

Julia looked at what she had written down for Marcus Lockwood. *Born April 10, 1905.*

"Okay, I still don't get it. It is quite a coincidence, but—" Her eyes widened. "Twins?"

Meredith nodded rapidly. "It's possible, isn't it? And why did they have two of some of the baby things? It doesn't make sense."

Julia remembered that fragment she'd seen from the diary. *"He accused her of terrible things, and now I can never explain—"*

"But are you saying Teddy was the father of those twins?"

Meredith winced. "I don't know. Maybe. Whatever he had that may have caused Jaden to have heterochromia was maybe passed on to one of the babies. When Matthew Lockwood saw that child, he would have known it wasn't his. Maybe that's why he left the way he did, and why Miss Alice had to give the child away. It would have been a terrible scandal, and one they couldn't deny."

"Wait. Wait. As horrible as that is, let's say that's true. But that doesn't explain why Jaden looks like Miss Alice too. Teddy couldn't have been Alice's father. He couldn't have been more than two or three years older than she was. I guess he could have been the father of her son."

"Are you sure about that resemblance though?" Meredith asked. "Sometimes I can picture it, and sometimes not. In her wedding picture, I'd agree with you, but in that picture of the whole family, the one taken before the epidemic, I just don't see it at all. Maybe we should try to get another look at both pictures and see what we think."

"I think this case is getting crazier all the time, that's what I think. But maybe they don't look so much alike in the family picture because Miss Alice was only sixteen. Jaden's twenty-seven. If there's a family resemblance, it's seems logical that it would be more obvious when Miss Alice was in her twenties than when she was in her teens."

"Maybe." Meredith took a deep breath. "I think I'm going to have to get some coffee and think about all this for a while."

"That's a great idea."

They went into the hallway and realized there was no coffee.

"Are we out of coffee?" Julia asked when she and Meredith went to the reception area.

Carmen winced slightly. "Sorry."

"What happened?" Meredith asked.

"I was going to make some when you got back, but there's no more."

Meredith frowned. "There is more. I saw a whole case of it just a couple of days ago."

Carmen shook her head balefully.

Meredith huffed. "I'll show you where it is."

"I know where you're talking about, but it's no good. Instead of what we usually get, they sent us the wrong thing."

"Is that all?" Julia asked. "Why don't you make some anyway? Maybe we'll like it."

Again Carmen gave them that baleful shake of her head.

"Why not? What kind is it?"

"It's called Terminal Brew. It says it's the strongest coffee in the world. Three times the usual amount of caffeine."

Julia and Meredith looked at each other, eyes wide.

"How about," Julia said, taking Carmen's arm confidentially, "we manage the phones while you go to the store and get enough of our regular coffee to last a few days, and then you ship the strong stuff back and get them to send out our usual shipment?"

"I thought you might say that." Carmen nodded wisely and headed back to the reception area to get her purse and keys. "I'll be back."

"I thought we had a standing order that came well before we usually ran out."

"Oh, we do," Carmen said, "but the box is marked the same as we usually get, so I didn't open it until we were out. I guess I'll know to check it when it's delivered from now on."

"Well, no harm done," Julia assured her. "Take some money out of petty cash."

"I will."

Meredith sighed once Carmen was gone. "I almost wish we'd asked her to bring back something from the coffee shop. Those pumpkin spice lattes were sure good."

"Yeah," Julia said with a sigh of her own. "Probably not good for our waistlines or our wallets."

"So what about this supposed twin we have absolutely no proof of?"

"I don't know." Julia rubbed her temples. "Let's sit down and see what we come up with. Maybe Carmen will be back with the coffee before we go crazy trying to figure it out."

They hadn't figured it out by the time Carmen came back and made coffee. They hadn't figured it out by the time they left the office for the day, even though they had talked it all over with Carmen before they closed up. Beau couldn't come up with anything when Julia discussed it with him that evening. She finally decided to let it rest and see what she could find out from Brenda when she called to check on Miss Charlotte the next morning. Then she spent the rest of the evening with Beau and Bunny watching the old *Thin Man* movies. It was a great way to take her mind off the problem of Jaden Browning and Miss Charlotte's family.

She didn't sleep very well, unable to get her thoughts to slow down enough to really rest, and that made her late leaving the house.

Too late to take the time to eat anything for breakfast. By the time she got to the office, she was looking forward to an eye-opening cup of coffee.

"Maybe we should have kept a little bit of that Terminal Brew around," she said when Meredith came in a few minutes later. "It would either wake me up or kill me, and right now I don't care which."

Carmen had just finished making a pot of their regular blend.

"Did you figure out anything about Miss Charlotte's case?" she asked. "I sure don't know what to think about all of it."

"Not yet," Julia said. "I thought about it all night, and I can't think of anything that covers all the facts without some really crazy stretches of the imagination."

"*Que rompecabezas*," Carmen said, shaking her head as she walked away.

Julia wrinkled her forehead. "What?"

"What a puzzle," Carmen translated as she turned back to them. "*Rompecabezas* literally means 'breaks heads.' I always like that translation better. It's a real breaks-heads."

Meredith chuckled. "Our little head-breaker sure isn't doing a thing for me."

Julia took a deep drink of her coffee and let the soothing warmth seep into her. "Maybe a little chat with Brenda is the way to get today started off right."

She got out her notepad and wrote down a few things she wanted to make sure to ask about during the conversation. Just as she was about to call Brenda's number, her own phone rang.

"It's Brenda," she said, seeing the name on her screen.

"That's convenient," Meredith said halfway under her breath.

"Brenda," Julia said as soon as she answered. "I was about to call you."

"I'm sorry to bother you, Julia, but Miss Charlotte is in a bad way."

"She's not sick, is she? I thought she was only tired yesterday. Did she—"

"Miss Charlotte isn't sick. She's mad. She said, if there was any way possible, she would very much like you and Meredith to come to see her right away."

"Did something happen?" Julia asked, sure her expression was as baffled and alarmed as Meredith's was right now.

"Miss Charlotte said for me to let her tell you herself. But please, if you could, would you come? She said if you haven't eaten already, she'd be pleased to have you come to breakfast."

Julia's mouth watered at the thought of what breakfast at Miss Charlotte's must be like. "We'd be very happy to, but let me make sure we don't have any other commitments this morning."

She muted the phone and checked with Meredith. Meredith shook her head and then looked eagerly toward the phone.

"All right, Brenda," Julia said, after unmuting her phone and putting it back to her ear. "We're headed your way right now. Are you sure Miss Charlotte doesn't need to call her doctor or anything?"

"No, nothing like that. Not at all. She was just fine yesterday."

"Okay, tell Miss Charlotte that we're on our way."

"Thank you. We'll be expecting you."

Chapter Sixteen

Charles was waiting at the drive when Julia and Meredith pulled up to the mansion. Brenda must have been watching from the house, because before Charles could open the doors for them and take the car key, she was there to escort them inside. She looked more unsettled than Julia had ever seen her.

"Miss Charlotte is in the small dining room. Ellen is waiting to serve breakfast."

She hurried them to the table. Miss Charlotte was wearing a dressing gown that was a confection of lavender organza. As always, she was perfectly groomed, perfectly upright, but as Brenda had told them, right now instead of serene, she looked angry.

"Good morning," she said, her usually unlined brow creased and her lips pressed thin. "Please sit down."

Julia and Meredith took seats on either side of her.

"I'll tell Ellen—"

"No, I would rather you stay with us, Brenda, if you will. I told Ellen the ladies were here and to go ahead and serve."

"All right."

Brenda sat on Julia's other side, her face a mirror of Miss Charlotte's, except there was more concern than anger in her expression.

"What happened, Miss Charlotte?" Julia asked when no one said anything right away.

"I don't know how it could have happened." Miss Charlotte paused as Ellen came in and served them all coffee, and then she resumed. "It was very late last night, nearly three o'clock. Brenda will tell you I hadn't been sleeping well, but I had finally fallen asleep, perhaps an hour before. I'm not exactly sure why I woke again. I must have heard something. Looking back, I'm sure I did, but I couldn't tell you what. I just knew something was wrong. I knew someone was in the room with me."

Julia felt her own heartbeat become more rapid. "That had to be frightening for you."

Miss Charlotte lifted her chin as if she would deny it, but then she only nodded. "It was terrifying. I don't know how anyone could have gotten into the house, especially how anyone could have gotten as far as my bedroom. I wasn't sure if I should lie still and make the intruder think I was asleep or if I should call for help. Brenda's room is just next to mine."

Brenda nodded. "And I keep a gun in my nightstand."

"Charles lives on the property as well," Miss Charlotte added. "Though he wouldn't be near enough to hear anything. Ellen has a room off the kitchen, and there are quarters for several others of our housekeeping staff near her. But that's on the opposite side of the house from my room." Her hand shook slightly as she drank from her china cup. "I lay there a moment, and I heard someone moving from the door to my armoire. I heard a drawer slide open, very quietly, and then shut again. I could tell which drawer it was, and then I got angry. Angry that someone would dare to come into my home, into my very bedchamber, and take something that belonged to me."

"But what—" Julia began.

"I sat up then and demanded that whoever it was drop my property and leave at once." Miss Charlotte's lips were pursed, and she was breathing more quickly. "The thief didn't say a word, but he ran into the wardrobe room and out into the hallway. I got up, calling for Brenda, and went after him, turning on lights as I went."

"You say 'he,'" Meredith said. "You could tell it was a man?"

"No, no, I couldn't tell much of anything. It could have been anyone, but I refuse to call a single person 'they.' 'They' is plural."

Julia had to force herself not to smile. Whatever the circumstance, Miss Charlotte was always Miss Charlotte.

"Then what happened," she asked. "Did you call the police?"

Miss Charlotte huffed. "They wouldn't have arrived in time to do anything useful. I told Brenda to get her gun and follow me."

"That's very dangerous," Julia said. "The intruder could have been armed too."

"I saw no sign of that. But unfortunately, he was too fast for me. I really got no more than a glimpse of him when I was lying in my bed and the room was still dark. Once I started turning on lights, he dashed into the powder room and got out through that window. I looked out and I saw something go over the garden wall just beyond the patio down below and that's all."

Meredith frowned. "You're sure he went that way?"

"Very sure. I saw something dark go over that wall. It was just a glimpse in the shadows, but I saw it clearly."

"But what did he want?" Julia asked. "What did he take?"

Miss Charlotte clasped her hands together in front of herself. "He took Grandmama's diary."

Julia and Meredith looked at each other. The diary. The diary was gone.

"Why didn't you call the police?" Julia asked after a stunned moment. "You had an intruder in your bedroom. You had something stolen from your home."

Miss Charlotte sniffed. "I told you, they couldn't have caught whoever it was. They would have arrived much too late to do anything."

"But they could have investigated the scene," Meredith told her. "Maybe they could have found fingerprints or other physical evidence."

"They wouldn't have taken the trouble," Miss Charlotte said with certainty. "The diary has no value to anyone but me. They'd hardly use their time and resources on that."

"And nothing else was taken?" Julia asked.

Miss Charlotte shook her head. "And I never got the chance to show it to you or to Miss Browning. It's such a loss."

Ellen came in with breakfast, featherlight crepes with whipped cream and strawberries, sliced ham, crispy hash browns, and the fluffiest scrambled eggs Julia had ever seen, freshly squeezed orange juice, and more hot coffee.

"She's going to be very upset to hear about this," Meredith said once everything was served and Ellen was gone again.

Julia looked at her and then at Brenda. Jaden had always shown great interest in that diary. Did she have enough interest in it to break in and steal it? Who else would want it?

"Could we go up and see where the intruder was?" Julia asked once they had eaten.

"Certainly," Miss Charlotte said. "I didn't see that anything was missing but the diary, and I couldn't tell, except for the powder room window being open, that anything had been disturbed."

"Maybe we'll see something," Meredith said, taking her arm as she stood. "We know what to look for."

"That's what I hired you for," Miss Charlotte said. "Or, rather, it's what you're hired for now. I don't want the police involved, but I want Grandmama's diary back. I still haven't had a chance to read through the whole thing, and it's very important to me."

Julia walked at her other side with Brenda following watchfully behind. Miss Charlotte led them up to the powder room that wasn't far from her bedroom door. It wasn't a large room, but it was beautifully decorated in soft rose and cream colors to suit the age and history of the house.

"The intruder went through this window?" Julia asked, opening it up and leaning her head out to look down at the patio and garden wall beyond it. She wasn't sure she could have gotten her shoulders through the opening. "You're sure now? The person couldn't have left the house some other way?"

"No. Not and had a chance to get over that wall when I saw him."

Meredith came to the window and looked out too. "And that's the wall he went over?"

Miss Charlotte nodded. "I hardly saw anything, but it seemed like he just jumped up and caught the top of it and pulled himself over. It was so dark and he was so quick, I really didn't see very much at all."

"No," Julia said, considering. "It would be hard to tell in circumstances like that. May we see where the book was kept?"

"Of course." Miss Charlotte led them into her bedroom. "He came through the door and went over here." She went over to the armoire and opened one of the drawers. "The diary was in here."

There was nothing in the drawer now but a soft white towel, presumably to protect the book that had rested on it.

Julia closed the drawer and then opened it again. "That doesn't make much noise. Do you think this is what woke you?"

"I don't think so," Miss Charlotte said. "I think it must have been the door being opened before that, because I distinctly heard the drawer open after I was awake. Then again, I wonder if I just didn't feel that someone was in the room with me and that was what woke me. Actually, I'm not even sure I was actually asleep right then. I've had so much on my mind."

Julia glanced at Meredith, who gave her a subtle nod. Maybe Miss Charlotte would be willing to talk about the anonymous note now.

"Have you not been sleeping well?" Julia asked.

"Oh, about the same as usual, I suppose. We old people don't need as much sleep as we once did."

"I know I sometimes have trouble sleeping when I have a lot to think about," Julia said. "I hope there's nothing in particular bothering you."

Miss Charlotte looked down at the antique Persian carpet she stood on. "Oh, no. Not really. I do have some small concerns about Miss Browning, as you know, but nothing that would keep me awake nights, I don't think." Then she met Julia's eyes again, her expression serene. "Have you found out more about her, by the way?"

"Not yet, no. But we're still investigating. Tell me who you think would have had an opportunity to take the diary."

"No one I don't trust, people I've had working for me for a long while now. Who would want it anyway?"

"Jaden would."

"No," Miss Charlotte said immediately. "No, I don't think so."

"You know Brenda saw her coming out of your bedroom the other day."

"I know."

"That doesn't bother you?"

"She couldn't have taken it then. It was still in the drawer until last night."

"She might have just wanted to know where it was before she came back," Julia offered. "Whoever took it knew exactly where to look."

"Nonsense."

"What about the work that was being done up here?" Meredith asked.

"By Richard?" Miss Charlotte huffed. "What good would the diary do him? It's certainly not worth much, and he wouldn't be interested in my great-grandmother's thoughts. And again, the diary was here until last night. And Jeff would never do such a thing."

Julia wondered if Richard had made up a reason to work near Miss Charlotte's room. He might have had the same motive as Jaden for wanting to look there, to find out exactly where the diary was, but Miss Charlotte was right too. Why would he want it in the first place?

"Do you think we could go down to the patio and see the garden wall now?" she asked.

"If you like," Miss Charlotte said. "We can go through the wardrobe room, if you'd care to look there too. I didn't see anything."

Julia didn't see anything either. It looked fairly much the way it had when they had all been up here before, except the wedding dress and other accessories had been put away as had everything else they had examined that day.

Meredith examined the knob on the door that led to the hallway. "I suppose this has been touched since last night."

Brenda bit her lip. "Miss Charlotte said we ought not to worry about it."

"I wasn't planning to call the police, so what did it matter?" Miss Charlotte said.

"I see." Meredith shook her head slightly. "Should we go ahead and go downstairs?"

Miss Charlotte took Brenda's arm. "We will meet you down there, if you will go ahead."

Once they were together again, Brenda led them through the house and out onto the back lawn. Julia searched the ground for any obvious footprints or distinctive marks, but it had been a while since there had been rain, and she saw nothing that stood out. There were smudges here and there that might have been from someone's feet, but whether or not they were from last night, she couldn't be sure.

Then she looked at the wall itself. It was brick and went straight up. She didn't see anywhere that looked like it would have offered a good foot- or handhold. At five foot nine, she was relatively tall, but there was no way she would have been able to jump and reach the top of that wall even with a running start.

"Whoever got over that must have been in great shape."

"But as you see, there's no other way out of this part of the yard. If he, or she," Miss Charlotte added with a nod, "had known that, he would have gone out a different way."

"What's on the other side?" Meredith asked.

"There's a shed and then a garage for some of the equipment," Brenda said. "Then there's just fields."

Julia sighed. "I suppose if we couldn't make out anything here, we wouldn't be very likely to find anything out there."

Miss Charlotte took her arm. "Would you be so kind as to help me back inside, my dear? I'm feeling rather tired."

"Oh, of course."

Brenda looked a little alarmed, but she went ahead, opening the door and then guiding them to a nearby chair.

"You sit down now, Miss Charlotte. You shouldn't have been out there anyway."

"Oh, I'm fine now, Brenda. Would you kindly ask Ellen to bring us some tea?"

Clearly unhappy with being sent away, Brenda nodded. "Yes, ma'am."

Miss Charlotte stood when she was out of sight and took Julia's arm again. "Why don't we go back into the morning room? I think we'll be more comfortable there. Brenda will find us."

Chapter Seventeen

When they were settled in the other room, Miss Charlotte rubbed her eyes. "Is there anything you can do, ladies? I very much would like to have that diary back."

"It's a little harder now," Meredith admitted. "It would have helped for you to call the police last night."

"I told you why I didn't," Miss Charlotte said peevishly. "Besides, I don't want anyone to go to jail over it. I just want it returned to me."

"Jail or not, we don't have a lot to go on at this point." Julia propped one elbow on the arm of her chair and rested her chin on her fist. Then, remembering Miss Charlotte's always-perfect deportment, she straightened in her chair and folded her hands in her lap. "Who do you think might have taken it?"

Miss Charlotte looked faintly pained. "I couldn't say. It was so very dark, I couldn't see enough to tell."

"But who do you think would want that diary?"

"I don't know who would go to the trouble of breaking in and taking it. Miss Browning is the only one who showed much interest besides the two of you, and I was getting ready to show it to her. She had no need to steal it."

"Who else knew about it?" Meredith asked.

"It wasn't public knowledge. Brenda knew, of course, but there is nothing I would not trust her with. Besides, she was right behind me when I was following the thief."

"Miss Charlotte," Brenda said from the doorway, "Ellen will be right in with the tea."

"Come in and sit down now. Who all would have known about the diary?"

"Everybody who works here, I would imagine," Brenda said, taking the chair next to Miss Charlotte's. "Mr. Richard and Mr. Jeff and the men who were working there when the diary was found. Miss Browning. I wouldn't think there was anyone else."

"And none of them would have any reason to take it." Miss Charlotte pressed her palms together and leaned her fingertips against her lips. "Perhaps I should resign myself. It seems unlikely that the diary will ever be returned."

"We'll see what we can turn up," Meredith said.

"Thank you. Let me know the minute you learn anything. I still want you to uncover what you can about Miss Browning too. I know she will be disappointed about the diary, but there are still many things I can tell her about those days that will be perfect for her book."

"So you've decided to go ahead with that?" Julia asked. "We still haven't checked Jaden out completely, and you know she hasn't been entirely truthful with you."

Miss Charlotte's face was perfectly serene. "I realize that. I want you to keep on checking, and I want you to let me know what you find. For now, I will continue discussing the book with her. We'll see what comes of it."

Ellen brought in the tea, and they all drank it without saying much.

"We want to get to the bottom of this, Miss Charlotte," Julia said finally. "Is there anything else we ought to know? Anything at all that will help us figure out what's going on? Anything else that's troubling you? You mentioned not being able to sleep."

"Nothing," Miss Charlotte said coolly. "I would tell you if I needed your help with anything else."

"All right." Julia stood up. "Thank you for the tea and the breakfast."

"I don't know what we'll be able to find out about the diary," Meredith said, standing too, "but we'll give it a try. Do you mind if we look around some more? Would it be okay if we go around where that shed is on the other side of the wall?"

"It's mostly cement," Brenda said. "You won't likely find anything."

"But you're welcome to look," Miss Charlotte added. "You take your time, and let me know if you find anything helpful."

"If we do, we'll come back to the house and let you know," Julia assured her. "If we don't, we'll head on back to the office and see what else we can dig up."

"Very good."

Meredith stood up too, and put her tea on the tray Ellen had set on the low table in front of the settee. "I'm sorry you had something so unpleasant happen last night, Miss Charlotte. Does the house have a security system in place?"

"No. We've never had anything like this happen before, and I've always felt safe here. Richard usually has someone keeping watch at night to make sure everything is all right. I trust our people more than a machine that might malfunction, and even if it worked properly, it would take a while for help to come. But maybe I should reconsider."

"It would make sense, especially with all the valuables you have here. I'm surprised you have never had any trouble."

"It's always been a peaceful place," Miss Charlotte said.

"Did you have someone on guard last night?" Julia asked.

Miss Charlotte glanced at Brenda, her silver brows raised.

"I don't know," Brenda admitted. "Would you like me to ask Mr. Richard?"

"Have him come in, if you will, please," Miss Charlotte said. "Will you stay for just another moment, Mrs. Foley, Mrs. Bellefontaine?"

"Of course." Julia sat again while Brenda telephoned Richard and asked him to come to the morning room.

"Would you like one of us to tell Jaden about the diary being taken?" Meredith asked Miss Charlotte while they waited for Richard to make his appearance.

Miss Charlotte thought for a moment. "I think, for now, I would rather say nothing to her about it. I want to see how she seems the next time I see her. I will tell her about the diary when I find the proper time."

"When do you think that will be?" Julia asked. "I think we ought to be present, if that's all right with you."

"Oh, of course. I've enjoyed having both of you come visit. And there's so much more I'd like to tell you when Miss Browning is with us."

They talked for a few minutes more, and then Richard knocked on the open door. Jeff was there too, trying to peer around his grandfather so he could see who was in the room.

"Miss Charlotte?" Richard said, looking uncertain.

"Come in." Miss Charlotte gestured to the empty chairs to her left. "Jeff. I wasn't expecting to see you as well. Come in."

"Thank you, Miss Charlotte," Jeff said, ducking his head as he and Richard sat down.

"Richard," Miss Charlotte said, "I was wondering if you know anything about—"

"I told you," Jeff said in an undertone and then he turned serious dark eyes to Miss Charlotte. "I told Granddad he should come talk to you, ma'am. I told him you'd know before too long. It was such a foolish thing to do."

"Jeff," Richard said through gritted teeth. "Let me handle this."

Miss Charlotte looked him up and down, her demeanor perfectly cool. "Is there something you wished to tell me, Richard?"

He glared at his grandson and then turned to Miss Charlotte, the color coming up in his pale face. "I—I don't quite know how to start. I know you've always trusted me, and I'm sure you feel betrayed right about now. I just—Miss Charlotte—" He bit his lip helplessly.

"Just tell her," Jeff insisted.

"Miss Charlotte," Richard began again, and once more he faltered into silence.

"I told him he should tell you right out, ma'am," Jeff said. "I don't know what he was thinking in the first place after you've been so good to him all his life. Granddad, tell her."

Miss Charlotte turned to her property manager again, one fine eyebrow raised. "Are you trying to tell me that you were the one who stole my great-grandmother's diary?"

"What? No!" Richard swallowed hard. "The diary was stolen? When was this? No, ma'am, Miss Charlotte, I didn't take that diary. I didn't know it was gone. If I'd wanted it, I would have just kept it in the first place instead of bringing it to you, wouldn't I?"

"Perhaps," Miss Charlotte said.

"And what would I want with it? Miss Alice was your great-grandmother, not mine."

"Granddad," Jeff urged.

He turned on the kid, eyes blazing. "Either hush up or go back to the house."

Jeff hushed up.

Julia kept her own mouth shut, wondering what Miss Charlotte would say now. If it wasn't the theft of the diary, what had the man been confessing to?

Miss Charlotte let him stew for a few agonizing seconds.

"Jeff," she said finally, "what is it you wanted your grandfather to tell me?"

"Well," Jeff began, his voice a little unsteady, "I told him it was a bad idea. As soon as I found out, I told him—"

"I broke one of Miss Alice's chairs," Richard blurted out.

Jeff gaped at him, and Miss Charlotte pressed her lips together.

"You what?"

"Those chairs in the blue room where we were fixing the fireplace before, ma'am," Richard said, the words tumbling out of him seemingly all on their own. "The chairs Miss Alice's mother brought with her from England."

Miss Charlotte's mouth got tighter. "How did you manage that? You know how delicate those chairs are."

"Yes, ma'am, I do, and I wouldn't have done it on purpose for the world, but I was cleaning up in there after Steve and Amos had finished with the fireplace. I told them to let me do it because I know the things in that room are the oldest and most valuable in the house. I even made them leave the room, because I didn't want to take even a small risk of one of them damaging anything. And I was being careful, Miss Charlotte, I truly was. I had put everything back where it belonged, all but that one chair. I picked it up and was carrying it over to the corner where you like it to be, and I tripped on the edge of the rug. I went flying and landed across the chair legs. And one of them—" Richard ducked his head. "One of them came off."

"I see."

"I fixed it right away," Richard said quickly. "I don't think anyone would notice it had been broken. Actually, it wasn't broken as much as the leg came apart from the rest of the chair. I put it back together and used that good wood glue on it. Not a whole lot though, because I didn't want it showing when it dried. Maybe you ought to come look at it and tell me what you think. Jeff had a look this morning."

Jeff still gaped at him.

"He was the one who told me I ought to come tell you about it anyway," Richard continued. "He said it wouldn't be right for me to keep it from you. I just didn't want to upset you with it, knowing you have so much else on your mind."

"I appreciate your concern," Miss Charlotte told him with a tight smile. "Just what is it you think I have on my mind?"

"Well, I—I—"

"We heard you were sick yesterday, Miss Charlotte," Jeff said quickly. "That's why Granddad didn't want to bother you about the chair, but I thought he ought to tell you straight out so you wouldn't be upset if you found out later. We thought that's why you called him here. What happened to Miss Alice's diary? Was it really stolen?"

Miss Charlotte folded her hands. "It was. I asked your grandfather to come here because these ladies and I wanted to ask him some questions about last night."

"Was that when the diary was taken?" Richard asked.

Jeff frowned. "I'd like to know how somebody got on the grounds and how he got into the house."

"That's what we wanted to ask your grandfather," Miss Charlotte said.

"Did you have any of your people keeping watch last night?" Julia asked Richard. "Miss Charlotte says you usually do."

"Yes, ma'am," Richard said. "Baxter and Lopez. Do you want me to call them in here, Miss Charlotte?"

Miss Charlotte turned to Julia and Meredith, her eyebrows again raised.

"Will they be here all day?" Meredith asked Richard.

"Not until this evening, ma'am," he said. "They'll be on duty again tonight, eleven to seven."

"They would have reported to you if they'd seen something though, right?" Julia asked.

"Yes, they would."

"Do you have telephone numbers for them?"

"Of course. Would you like to speak to them?"

"If I could," Julia said. "If you don't mind."

Richard gave her the numbers for the two men, and Julia gave one to Meredith.

"Let's see what we can find out."

The calls were very brief.

"Mine didn't see or hear anything," Julia said.

Meredith shook her head. "Mine either. Have they worked for you for very long, Miss Charlotte?"

"We've known them both since they were born," Miss Charlotte said. "Ramon's mother and father both worked for me before he was born, and so did the Baxters. Whoever came into the house must have known their regular routine."

"But how did someone get into the house?" Meredith asked. "Did anyone check the outside doors for signs of forced entry?"

"He came through the kitchen," Miss Charlotte told her. "After I saw him go over the wall last night, I went around to check the doors. The one that opens out onto the garden from the kitchen was unlocked. I asked Ellen and all the girls who do the housekeeping about it. All of them assumed it was locked before they retired for the night, but obviously it was not."

"Whose responsibility is that?" Julia asked.

Miss Charlotte looked questioningly at Brenda.

"Ellen generally sees to that part of the house, ma'am," Brenda said. "I've never known her to forget to lock up at night."

"Perhaps someone came into the house who isn't part of our staff," Miss Charlotte offered.

"Were there any delivery people?" Julia asked. "Repairmen? Anyone like that?"

Brenda considered for a moment and then shook her head. "Not yesterday. No. Do you know of anyone, Mr. Richard?"

"We had some tractor parts delivered to the barn, but that was all. The driver hopped off the truck, slung the boxes down on the grass, and took off."

"Well, that's that," Miss Charlotte said. "I don't see how we can trace the diary now."

Julia patted her arm. "We're not giving up yet. We haven't had a chance to do much investigating yet. We'll see what we can find. There's almost always some clue the perpetrator leaves behind."

Jeff was sitting with his fingers laced together and his eyes on the floor. Richard pulled him to his feet.

"If there's nothing else," he said, "we both have work to do. Miss Charlotte, would you like me to bring that chair in here so you can look at it?"

"No, no," she said, looking as if she wanted to roll her eyes. "That would only risk damaging it further. When I have time, I will go and see for myself."

"I'm awfully sorry about it, ma'am, but I really don't think you'll be able to tell it was ever broken at all. But if you see something you don't like, you let me know and I'll take it into town and have the antique repairman see to it."

"I imagine it will be all right," Miss Charlotte told him, a touch of indulgence now in her expression. "But do come tell me if there are any incidents like that in the future, will you? Jeffrey, I'm trusting you to make sure he does right from now on."

Jeff nodded swiftly. "Yes, ma'am. If I can."

Julia caught Meredith's glance and gave her a subtle frown. There was something not quite right about all this. She and Meredith needed to talk.

She stood up once Richard and Jeff left. "I think Meredith and I ought to be going too, Miss Charlotte. We want to take a look at the other side of that garden wall and see if we find anything that might be helpful in tracking down your diary."

"I hope you can find something," Miss Charlotte said, "but I will admit I'm not very hopeful about that. The thief was too quick. Brenda, would you be so kind as to show the ladies around to the back of the garden wall and anywhere else they'd like to look?"

Brenda showed Julia and Meredith the back side of the wall and then the nearby shed and garage. There was nothing remarkable about them, and there was no sign of anyone having been in or around them recently.

"This time of year," Brenda said, "there's not much going on in this part of the grounds. Even if there were, it would be hard to trace someone going over this hard ground and then the cement."

Julia walked a few feet over to the edge of the nearby field. It had been plowed under a few days before and left to lie fallow until spring. There were prints from many different pairs of workboots and the gouges of heavy machinery, but none of them looked fresh enough to have been made last night. And who would steal Miss Alice's diary and then take off into an open field with nothing but more fields beyond?

"Dead end," Meredith said.

Julia nodded. "Did you see anything last night, Brenda?"

"I'm afraid whoever it was was gone before I caught up to Miss Charlotte," Brenda said, not quite meeting Julia's eyes. "I'm sorry."

"Do you think she might have been dreaming? Sleepwalking?"

"Not sleepwalking, no. She was wide awake when I saw her."

"But could she have been dreaming at first?" Julia asked, scanning the area and finding nothing to show that anyone out of the ordinary had been there. "Could she have dreamed something so vivid that it woke her and she thought it was real?"

"I suppose that's possible," Brenda said, "but I've never known her to do that before, and I've looked after her a very long time."

"It's just that her description of what she saw is very vague. She can't say whether or not she was actually sleeping or what woke her or whether the intruder was male or female or short or tall or much of anything."

"But the diary is missing," Brenda said, her dark brows drawn together. "She didn't dream that."

Meredith stood at the base of the wall, looking up at the very top. "I don't see how anyone could have scaled this without some kind of help. A rope or a ladder or something. Could Miss Charlotte have mislaid the diary? Or put it somewhere and forgot that she'd done it?"

"It would be very unlike her," Brenda said, the unease in her expression intensifying.

Julia put one hand on her arm. "You're our best resource in all this. You know Miss Charlotte better than anyone, so if we're going to help her, we're going to need you to help us. So thank you for telling us that and anything else you can."

"I'm doing my best." Brenda looked up at the gray autumn sky, shaking her head. "I wish there was more I could tell you. She's been very peculiar about that diary. She hasn't even let me see it. But maybe she's right and she should simply realize that it's gone and won't be coming back."

"Any more anonymous notes?" Meredith asked, putting her hands in her jacket pockets as the wind picked up a little.

"No. I would still like Miss Charlotte to talk to you about those, but she just won't do it. She doesn't think it's important."

"Maybe whoever it was decided that blackmail wasn't such a good idea," Julia said. "Still, we'd really like you to let someone know if something like this happens again, even if it doesn't seem like much."

Brenda nodded.

"What do you think, Mere?" Julia asked. "Are we done here?"

"Yeah," Meredith said. "We're spinning our wheels here, and it's getting cooler. Besides, we have some things to go over back at the office."

"We'd better get going then."

Julia followed Meredith and Brenda back to the house and through to the front entryway. Once there, Brenda took her cell phone from the pocket of her dress and asked Charles to bring Julia's car around.

"Things have been so unsettled this morning," she said once she'd ended her call. "I haven't even gone through the mail. Will you excuse me a moment? Charles will have your car for you right away."

"That's fine," Julia said, looking at the stack of letters sitting on the silver tray on the inlaid cherrywood sideboard in the entry. "Does Miss Charlotte always get that much mail?"

"Most days," Brenda said, rapidly sorting through the stack. "Mostly bills and requests for donations, of course. No one writes letters much anymore, and everyone Miss Charlotte used to correspond with has passed now."

"That's too bad," Meredith said. "It's almost a special occasion to get an actual letter anymore and not an ad."

"Or an ad disguised as a letter," Julia added.

Brenda's soft laugh abruptly stopped, and her mouth tightened. The envelope in her hand was addressed in very plain, very straight block letters. There was no return address. The postmark was Savannah. She put down the rest of the mail and slipped her finger under the back flap.

"No, wait," Julia said. "Wait. Let's not contaminate the evidence. You don't have any gloves, do you?"

Brenda thought for a moment. "I have some of those little plastic gloves that come in my box of hair coloring. Would those work?"

"Great idea. Could we use them?"

"Sure. I'll be right back."

While she was gone, Julia and Meredith examined the envelope, careful not to touch it.

"If our blackmailer, if he is one, is worth his salt, there won't be any fingerprints on it anyway," Meredith said.

"True, but we have to check."

"How?" Meredith put her hands on her hips. "Don't tell me you brought a fingerprinting kit."

"Of course not. I just want to be able to see what's in this one before I try to convince Miss Charlotte to call the police about it. And about the diary, if I can."

Brenda hurried back into the entryway, the flimsy little pink-tinted gloves clasped in one hand. "Do you think these will do?"

"Perfect." Julia took them from her and put them on. "Now, is it all right if I open this? I don't want you to get in trouble with Miss Charlotte."

"No, it's my job to open the mail. She didn't say I was to do anything different with these letters."

With the gloves in place, Julia picked up the suspect envelope, tore open the flap, and peered inside. There was nothing in it but a folded piece of what looked like cheap copy paper.

"That could have come from anywhere," she said as she carefully slid the paper out of the envelope.

She unfolded the page, touching it as little as possible, and laid it on the sideboard where they could all look at it. The note was written in the same very straight, very plain block letters as the address. This message was a little longer than the one Brenda had already told them about.

I Know About Emily. If You Don't Want Everyone Else to Know, You Will Have to Buy My Silence.

Chapter Eighteen

"Emily again," Meredith said, turning to Brenda. "Are you sure that name doesn't mean anything to you?"

"Not that I can think of. Not that Miss Charlotte's told me. And if she doesn't know who that is, why would she care what was said about her? Why in the world would she pay somebody to keep quiet about her?"

"I wouldn't."

All three of them turned at the steely voice from behind them.

Miss Charlotte.

None of them said anything, and finally Miss Charlotte came over to them, her expression cool and regal.

"I take it that letter is addressed to me."

"Yes, ma'am."

"I realize one of your duties is to sort through the mail and take care of the things that I don't need to see."

Brenda nodded.

"That one, I believe," Miss Charlotte added, "is something I *do* need to see."

"Yes, ma'am."

"Something no one else needs to see."

"It's my fault," Julia said, stripping off the pink gloves and guiltily handing them back to Brenda. "I realized what it must be and asked if I could open it."

"Oh really? You knew what it was before you opened it?"

Julia winced. "I didn't know for certain, but I thought it might be something to do with the investigation."

"And how would you have deduced that?"

"I thought—"

"I told them about the other one," Brenda said.

Miss Charlotte's mouth tightened slightly more. "I see."

"Anything we're told in the course of an investigation is confidential," Meredith said. "No one will ever hear about it from us without your permission."

"But this isn't part of the investigation." Miss Charlotte reached for the letter, crumpling it as she picked it up from the sideboard. "You were hired to do a background check on Miss Browning and, now, to see if you could find out what happened to my great-grandmother's diary. This nonsense," she said, making the letter crackle as she squeezed it into an even smaller ball, "has nothing to do with either of those things."

"Are you sure?" Julia asked her. "How can you know that if you don't know who it's from or what it's about?"

"Because it's an empty threat. Let this person say whatever he likes. It's nothing to do with me, and I'm certainly not going to be bullied into paying him for his brazenness."

"But, Miss Charlotte," Brenda said, her dark brows pulled together, "if someone's threatening you—"

"And what am I supposed to do? Even if I wanted to do what he says, I have no way of contacting him. He hasn't told me what he wants or when he wants it or how to get it to him." She tossed the paper ball into the wicker wastebasket that was placed discreetly beneath the sideboard. "If he writes anything that makes me change my mind about this, I will let you ladies know."

"I'm sorry, Miss Charlotte," Brenda said after a moment. "I would never have mentioned it to anybody else, but since they're working for you, I just thought they ought to know. I was worried about you."

Miss Charlotte's expression softened, and she took Brenda's arm. "I know, dear Brenda. I know, and I'm sure there's no harm done. I think Mrs. Foley and Mrs. Bellefontaine are as trustworthy as you are or I wouldn't have hired them in the first place. Now, I'm getting very tired of standing, so if you all would like, shall we go back into the morning room to finish our talk? Did you find anything behind the garden wall?"

"I think Charles probably has our car out front by now," Julia said, "and we really need to get back to work on your case, but no, we didn't find anything helpful. Whoever has that diary must be very clever."

"Perhaps," Miss Charlotte said, her eyes narrowing slightly. "Well, please let me know what you uncover. I still would like to have you and Miss Browning come back to hear more of what my great-grandmother did later in her life. I know Miss Browning is particularly interested in the start of the foundation."

"So are we," Meredith said. "Just let us know when you're ready for us to come back, and we'll be here."

Miss Charlotte's expression warmed. "We'll be in touch."

Julia watched as Brenda helped her back toward the morning room, and then she turned to Meredith. "Why don't you have a look and see if the car's out front," she said softly. "I'm going to take a quick peek at that chair."

"That chair?" Meredith asked, her voice low too.

"The one Richard said he broke. There was something not right about that whole story, and I want to know what it is."

"But you don't know what room it's in. You could be all day looking for it in this huge place."

"He said the blue room. I've looked at the layout of this place on their website before. The blue room is off the entryway, in the opposite hall from the morning room, just a little way down. It won't take me a minute. You keep watch. Make some noise or something if anybody comes."

"Julia—"

Julia gave her a little wave, mostly just a wiggle of her fingers, and then slipped into the hallway to the right of the entry. It didn't take long to find the blue room, the fourth door down. As it should have been, everything in it was blue, the soft blue of periwinkles and late afternoon. She saw indications that the fireplace had recently been worked on, and she couldn't help wondering just where Richard and his crew had found the diary.

She moved closer and ran one hand over the place that had been patched. If that was where the diary had been, it was sealed up now. She wasn't sure she would have really noticed the place at all if she hadn't already known it had been repaired just a few days ago. Maybe, as Miss Charlotte had said, Richard's heart wasn't in his work here, but he seemed to do a good job of it anyway.

There were several chairs in the room, but there was only one in the corner by the fireplace. It was a lovely thing, Queen Anne style, with the seat and back padded with blue brocade and the gracefully curved legs polished and gleaming. It certainly didn't look as if it had been damaged.

She got down on her knees and examined it more closely, especially where each leg was attached to the seat. Everything about it looked to be in pristine condition. Mindful of the age of the piece, she gave each leg a careful wiggle. Nothing budged. There wasn't even a telltale bubble of fresh glue to give away any sort of repair. Maybe Richard was better at his job than Miss Charlotte gave him credit for.

She got to her feet, careful to not put too much weight on the arm of the chair as she stood. Before she could take even a step toward the hallway, she heard the door to her right open, the one on the other side of the fireplace that led to the neighboring room. She froze where she was, knowing she didn't have permission to be in this room, knowing she'd been caught, but not knowing anything better to do than hope this was Brenda or even Ellen and that she would understand her curiosity and excuse her lack of propriety.

The newcomer came around the fireplace and right to where she was standing, and both of them caught a startled breath.

"Richard."

Richard blinked at her, another toothpick in the corner of his mouth and sudden sweat on his pale upper lip. "Mrs. Foley." He fumbled with the furniture polish and cloth in one hand and the tube of glue in the other. "I—I thought I'd better come make sure that repair was done right. I mean, if Miss Charlotte comes to look at the chair, I want her to be happy with it."

She smiled tentatively. "I hope nobody will mind, but I was curious about it. Well, I was curious about the room too. The pictures on the website don't do it justice. It really is lovely."

"Yes, ma'am, it is."

"And so is the chair. My goodness, it looks like it was never broken at all."

"Yes, ma'am, I'm happy to say it does. I was worried that it might not look right anymore, but I suppose I don't need any of this stuff after all." Still holding the glue, he swiped the back of his hand across his mouth. "Guess I'll leave well enough alone."

"And I'd better get going," she said, hurrying toward the door. "Charles will wonder where I've gotten to since he's probably had my car out front for the past few minutes."

Richard nodded. "May I show you out, ma'am?"

"Oh, that's all right." She was practically at the door now. "I know my way. Thank you."

She turned into the hall and then quickened her steps. Meredith was standing where she had been and looking more than a little bit uncomfortable.

"Thank goodness. I was sure you were going to get caught."

"I did," Julia admitted, trying her best not to giggle. "Come on, let's get going. We've got a lot to talk about."

***

"I'm sure of it," Julia said as they drove through the estate gates and out to the main road. "That chair was never broken."

"Then why was he in there with glue and polish?" Meredith asked.

"My theory is that he was going to add a few drops of glue to where one of the legs is attached so it looks like it was repaired and then he was going to polish it up so Miss Charlotte would think he did that afterward. I don't think that chair had had anything done to it since the last time everything in there was polished up as part of the regular routine."

"I see. So the whole chair story was made up to cover whatever he was about to confess to."

Julia nodded. "That's what I think anyway. But it wasn't the theft of the diary. If he came to admit that to Miss Charlotte, he would have said so when she brought it up. If you ask me, he's done something that his grandson found out about, and the grandson got him to go tell Miss Charlotte. And when Richard realized what she was accusing him of wasn't what he'd done, he needed something minor to be blamed for right then. The chair was a perfect substitute, because if he'd done the repair as perfectly as he claimed he had, then how could anyone dispute it by examining the chair? Especially if he went back and left some very small signs that the chair really had been fixed."

"Then he's not the one who took the diary," Meredith said. "And what he said makes sense. Why would he steal the diary when he could have just kept it when he found it and not said anything?"

"I suppose the workers in the room with him would have known about it."

"Yeah, maybe. We could ask, but you're not telling me he was the one who climbed through that little window in the powder room and dropped down to the patio below and then scaled that high wall. He looks a little too fond of southern fried chicken for that."

"True," Julia said. "His grandson looks a little more athletic, but he's still a big boy. It would be quite a feat even for him. And then again, why would he try to get Richard to confess to the theft if he was behind it in the first place? Why wouldn't he just keep his mouth shut?"

"And what did Richard do that Jeff found out about?"

"Good question. And I have to say they both looked pretty surprised to hear the diary is missing. Either that was genuine, or great acting runs in the family."

"Well, that could be the case too."

Meredith raised her eyebrows.

"Like Miss Charlotte," Julia said. "Brenda didn't see anything last night. There's no sign of forced entry. There's nothing in the garden or behind the wall, or even past there that would indicate someone ran away from the house. All we have is Miss Charlotte's very vague feeling that someone was in her bedroom and her thinking she saw someone going over the top of the wall."

"And she wouldn't say for sure if she thought it was a man or a woman. It was almost like she didn't want to point the finger at anyone specific."

"Right."

They drove in silence a while longer while Julia tried to figure out who else might have a motive to take the diary. Maybe someone who was not trying to hurt Miss Charlotte but protect her. If there was some embarrassing family secret Miss Charlotte didn't want getting out and someone was blackmailing her about it, maybe there was someone who would take the diary just to safeguard its confessions.

"Maybe Miss Charlotte did think she saw someone," Julia said eventually. "Maybe there really wasn't anyone out there but somebody convinced her there was."

"But there wasn't anyone there but..."

Meredith stared at her, and Julia nodded.

"Brenda. You know she was upset about the blackmail notes. Maybe she thought it would be safer if the diary was gone. Maybe then she figured the blackmailer wouldn't have anything he could prove about this Emily, whoever she was."

"But would she do that?" Meredith asked. "She had to know how much that would upset Miss Charlotte."

"I don't know," Julia admitted, "but maybe Maggie Lu can give us an idea about that. She and Brenda have been friends a long while now."

Maggie Lu picked up Julia's call on the second ring.

"Hi, Julia."

"Hey, Maggie Lu. Meredith and I are in the car coming back from Miss Charlotte's. We've got you on speakerphone, if that's all right with you."

"Sure. Hi, Meredith."

"Hi, Maggie Lu," Meredith said. "We were hoping you had a minute to give us your opinion."

"Oh, I always have one of those. What's up?"

Between the two of them, Julia and Meredith told Maggie Lu what had been going on at the estate.

"So, knowing Brenda and knowing how protective she is of Miss Charlotte," Julia said, "do you think she could have, not *stolen* the diary, but hidden it away? More to keep it safe than anything else."

"I guess anything is possible," Maggie Lu said slowly, "but I really can't imagine Brenda doing that. She'd see it as a betrayal of Miss Charlotte's trust."

"But thinking about who Miss Charlotte might actually be related to and how that ties into what Jaden may or may not suspect about her own ancestry," Meredith said. "Maybe she thinks it's worth it."

"I can't see that. I can't see Brenda doing anything she thinks will hurt Miss Charlotte. She's taken care of her too long."

"And maybe she's taking care of her now," Julia said thoughtfully.

"What do you mean?"

"Miss Charlotte's whole story doesn't really hang together. If she had an intruder in the house, why wouldn't she call the police? How was the thief small enough to get through the powder room window and big enough to get over that wall?"

"And why would Miss Charlotte try to go after a thief when she has trouble just getting around without her cane?" Meredith added. "Why in the world wouldn't Brenda object to her rushing around like that?"

"Well," Maggie Lu said, "that blackmailer wouldn't have anything to blackmail her about if the diary was gone. Maybe Miss Charlotte realized that herself."

"Yeah," Meredith said. "Maybe so."

"And Brenda backed her up." Julia shook her head. "No wonder she looked so uneasy. And that little fainting episode that Miss Charlotte so conveniently came up with right before she was going to show everyone the diary? What a great way to not let anyone see anything."

"That would work," Maggie Lu said. "I always heard Miss Charlotte was a wily old girl."

Julia's hands tightened on the steering wheel. "That must be it. I just wish we could figure out what is really going on. Or, I should say what *did* go on back in Miss Alice's lifetime, whatever it is Miss Charlotte is hiding. Something's just not making sense in all this."

"I'll tell you what you need to do," Maggie Lu said. "You need to talk to Jaden. Find out where she fits into all this."

"If she'll talk to us," Meredith said. "I mean, do you think she'll come right out and tell us what she's really after?"

"We can only talk to her and see," Julia said. "Maybe if we tell her what we've found out about her, and how that doesn't quite match what she's told Miss Charlotte, she'll confess. What do you think, Maggie Lu?"

"No harm in trying. Anything else I can do?"

"No," Meredith said, "but we appreciate you so much. Sometimes just talking these things over can make things clearer."

"I'm happy to help anytime," Maggie Lu said. "You let me know what you find out."

"We'll do that," Julia assured her. "Thank you. Talk to you soon."

Maggie Lu hung up, and Julia glanced at Meredith.

"Do you have Jaden's number?"

"It's in my phone. I'll call her." Meredith pulled her phone out of her purse. "She's busy until tomorrow afternoon," she said when the brief call was over, "but she said she'd be happy to come talk to us then."

"At least she's not reluctant to talk, which means one of two things."

Meredith nodded. "Either she wants to come clean or she wants to feed us more misinformation to keep us from finding out what she's really up to. Or maybe she's going to blow town."

"Right. I guess we'll see. Meanwhile, we'll have to see what else we can find out."

"I'll just check my text messages while I have my phone out," Meredith said, and then she laughed. "I have one from Quin. He says that, despite his advice, his client was about to sign the partnership agreement when the police came and arrested the other guy for real estate fraud."

Julia grinned. "I guess he was saved from a bad decision in spite of himself."

"And Quin wants to know what you're going to do about the cat."

"Really?" Julia gave her a wary look. "Do you think he wants to know, or is he asking 'for a friend'?"

Meredith chuckled. "The friend being Beau?"

"When I left home this morning, he and Bunny were still in bed together. He said he was just trying to check on her cast and the bandage on her other leg, but I think it was more of a cuddle than an examination."

"I'm telling you, you're going to have an awfully hard time letting her go when it's time. And it's only going to be worse a few weeks from now when she's out of that cast and all well."

Julia shook her head emphatically. "She's a sweet thing, but Beau and I already discussed it. And, if need be, we'll discuss it again tonight. We're not keeping her."

She scowled when Meredith only smiled to herself and went back to her messages.

***

By the time Julia and Meredith got back from lunch the next day, Jaden was waiting for them in the reception area. She was drinking coffee, and she and Carmen were chatting away about a book they had both read.

Jaden stood up as soon as she saw them. "Hi."

She was smiling and upbeat as usual, but there was also something else in her expression, something daunting and determined, something Julia had never seen there before.

"I'm glad you could come at such short notice," Julia told her. "Why don't we go to my office and have a talk?"

She picked up her coffee. "Sure."

Carmen gave her a nod and a smile, and then she looked over at Meredith and Julia. "And yes, I'll hold your calls."

Meredith stopped to get coffee before they went into Julia's office. "Want me to bring you some?"

"Yes, please," Julia said. "As long as it's not that terminal stuff."

Jaden's eyes widened. "You drink Terminal Blend?"

"Not if we can help it," Julia said, guiding her to her office door. "Come on in and sit down."

Jaden took the chair across from Julia's desk. Meredith came in with the coffee right afterward.

"I guess I know why you asked me to come," Jaden said before Julia could say anything.

"What do you think is the reason?" Meredith asked her.

"You're investigators, right? It only makes sense that Miss Charlotte would have me checked out before she'd let me get too close. I mean, she may not have thought of it if you hadn't already been around, but I just had to pick you two to introduce us in the first place, didn't I?" Jaden sighed. "So what now?"

"What do you think we've found out?" Julia asked.

Jaden shook her head. "You're both very nice, but I really think it's time I just told you the truth. I haven't been totally honest with you, I suppose you know that already, but it's not what you think." She laughed softly. "And don't ask me to tell you what you think."

"Why don't you just tell us what you want us to know," Julia said, "and we'll go from there."

"All right. For one thing—and you know this already because a friend of mine at work said you were asking about me—I'm not a writer. I mean, I write well, but I'm not a real writer. I'm a chemist. I work for a drug company. And I got my degree from UTD four years ago, and I'm not working on my master's."

"But you wanted to find out about Miss Charlotte's family history, right?" Julia asked, not surprised.

"Right. There's so little real information available about her or Miss Alice, I was hoping offering to write a book would convince her to tell me more and let me look at letters and things. Diaries. Whatever."

"What about Miss Alice's diary?" Meredith asked.

"I'm dying to see it. Miss Charlotte's been so coy about giving anybody a look, but I think she's softening up about it. If she hadn't started feeling bad yesterday, I think she would have shown it to us.

Have you heard how she is, by the way? I suppose I ought to call Brenda and ask."

"We saw her yesterday," Julia said, watching Jaden's eyes, the light coming through her window making the edge of her one contact very easy to see. "She's fine."

"Good. Maybe she'll invite us back over in the next day or two so we can really see the diary."

"She asked us to come over there yesterday to tell us that the diary was stolen night before last."

"What?" Tears sprang to Jaden's eyes. "No. No, it can't be gone. I wanted to see it. I *had* to see it."

"Because?"

"Because I'm related to Miss Charlotte."

Chapter Nineteen

Julia glanced at Meredith and then looked at Jaden. "Do you believe that or do you know it?"

"I know it." Jaden dug in her purse and brought out some papers. "A friend of mine does DNA testing. I had him check mine against Miss Charlotte's, and we're definitely related."

"That was quick," Meredith said, glancing over the report Jaden gave her, and then she handed it over to Julia.

"He did it as quickly as he could as a favor to me," Jaden said. "But that's why I couldn't come talk to you yesterday. I had to wait to get the results."

"From something you took from Miss Charlotte's room, am I right?"

"Her toothbrush. I had to do something so I could have a few minutes without anybody watching me, so I pretended I needed the powder room. Then I needed to get out of there before anybody realized what I had done. I— Do you know what heterochromia is?"

"Yes, as a matter of fact."

"We have a friend who has it," Meredith said.

Jaden nodded. "I have it too."

She leaned forward a little, closer to them, and removed her contact. Beneath it, her eye was pale blue.

"I have something called Waardenburg syndrome," she said as she put the contact into the container in her purse. "It can be a really terrible disease, but fortunately, it doesn't affect me much, but that's what caused me to have different-colored eyes. It was passed down from my great-grandfather, but I don't know the rest of his family history."

"How did you decide that you were related to Miss Charlotte?" Meredith asked. "As far as I know, she doesn't suffer from that."

"Evidently not, based on the DNA testing. I've been trying to piece this together for a very long time. I have some letters and other things that were my grandmother's and some things one of her aunts told her about when her father was adopted into the family. Nothing specifically mentions Miss Alice, but they said a very wealthy lady would sometimes come by the house. She wouldn't stay long and she never played with the baby or picked him up, but she would leave things for him and leave money. Their mother always said she was a Mrs. Smith. I decided I would try to figure out who she was and what she had to do with my great-grandfather. After narrowing it all down, I realized she had to have some connection to the Lockwoods."

Julia scanned the DNA report. "This does show a family relationship. Why didn't you just come right out and tell her?"

Jaden winced. "It's so hard. She's a very traditional lady, and my great-grandfather wasn't an acknowledged member of the family. I don't know why he was given up for adoption. That's part of what I want to find out, but I couldn't bring myself to just ask her outright. Not until I at least had more information. And now—" She faltered a little. "I really like her a lot. I don't want to hurt her or embarrass her. And maybe I ought to write that book. The more I've gotten to know her, the more I don't want her to be disappointed in me. I don't want her to think I've betrayed her."

"But you have, haven't you?" Meredith asked softly.

Jaden lowered her eyes to her lap. "Yes. I don't know what to say, except I know I have to go talk to her. I have to tell her what I found out and ask her to tell me what she knows. I don't know what I'm going to do now that the diary is gone. Do you think you can get it back?"

"I don't know. With the information we have, no. But maybe you can help us."

Jaden frowned. "How can I— Oh, wait a minute. No. You don't think I took it."

"Actually," Julia said, "I don't. I don't think that at all. The way Miss Charlotte described the intruder and what happened at her house that night is too contradictory. Even if you were in her bedroom without permission the other day."

"But I told Brenda I only wanted to see the room! That's all! I know I'm not going to be very credible at this point, but I really am interested in the family's history, not just how it relates to me, but because it *is* history. It fascinates me. And talking to Miss Charlotte is incredibly rewarding. She won't believe me once all this gets out, but it's true."

"Maybe she would."

"But there's something else," Jaden said. "Something I don't understand. Something that might really hurt her or make her mad."

Julia and Meredith both looked at her expectantly.

"I had Richard Sheldon's DNA tested too. There was so much excitement about the diary when he brought it in, I knew nobody would notice that I took that toothpick he'd been chewing on. I needed some DNA from Miss Alice's father's side of the family just to see if I could tell if the Waardenburg syndrome was passed from Miss Alice's mother or her father."

"I wondered where that toothpick went," Meredith said half under her breath.

"And?" Julia urged. "What did you find out?"

Jaden shook her head. "He doesn't have it. But I'm also not related to him."

"What?"

"It's true."

Jaden gave Julia another DNA report, and the findings were clear. There was no relationship between Jaden and Richard Sheldon. Julia's thoughts whirled inside her head. What did that mean?

"If you're related to Miss Charlotte and not Richard," Julia said, "that means Miss Charlotte isn't related to Richard either. Does that mean Miss Alice's father wasn't really her father? That her mother had an affair or something?"

"Maybe the disconnect was somewhere else in the family line?" Meredith suggested. "Maybe Miss Charlotte's father and Jaden's great-grandfather, the twins, were both fathered or even grandfathered by Teddy. Is there any way to find out for sure? Maybe the missing diary is the only possible answer, but where is it?"

"Maybe you should just tell Miss Charlotte straight out who you are and what you want to know," Julia said. "She might be angry, and I think that's understandable, but I think she genuinely likes you. She likes that you really want to know about Miss Alice and all of the family. She likes that you and she share a strong interest in history. If I were going to place a bet on it, I'd bet that she would appreciate your honesty about the situation, especially since you're trying to find out more about the condition you have. I think you ought to at least give her a chance."

Meredith nodded. "I agree. She can be very rigid at times about what she expects, but she can also be very forgiving. You saw how she was with Richard, Julia."

"Yes," Julia said, "even though she's not so sure about what he's up to."

Jaden bit her lip. "Do you think I should come right out and tell her?"

"It's your best bet. Would you like us to come with you?"

Jaden nodded.

***

On Jaden's behalf, Julia called Brenda to find out when they could come talk to Miss Charlotte. Brenda called her back only a few seconds later to tell her that Miss Charlotte would be happy to receive them anytime that afternoon.

Little more than an hour later, they were all seated in Miss Alice's morning room. There was no coffee or tea this time. There were no gourmet refreshments or other luxuries. There was just Miss Charlotte sitting on the plush settee with her ebony cane clutched in her fine-boned hand and Brenda seated close beside her.

"You had something you wished to tell me?" she asked Jaden without prologue.

Jaden swallowed hard. "Yes, ma'am. I wanted to say I'm sorry."

She lifted her head, looking straight at Miss Charlotte, and the difference in the colors of her eyes was strikingly obvious. "I haven't been totally honest with you. I think you already know that."

Miss Charlotte's mouth tightened. "Why don't you tell me about it?"

"I have something called Waardenburg syndrome. That's why my eyes aren't both the same color. That's why I usually wear one colored contact to cover it up. It was the same thing my great-grandfather had. He was an adopted child, and I've been trying to find out who his real family was for some time now. I found out I'm related to you, ma'am, and I wanted to find out how. That's why I told you I was a journalist and a graduate student. Neither of those is true. But I meant it when I said I wanted to know about your family. Our family. And I really do think there should be a book about Miss Alice and everything she's done, especially about finding homes for children who needed them. But I never meant you any harm. I want you to believe that."

"And just how do you know we're related?"

"I had the DNA tested." Jaden glanced helplessly at Brenda. "It showed a match."

"And how did you manage that?" Miss Charlotte asked. "I didn't give you any kind of sample."

"I took your toothbrush. I took it when I said I had to go to the powder room."

"I don't see how your medical condition connects you to my family," Miss Charlotte said tautly.

"I don't know exactly," Jaden admitted, "but I thought it was true even before I got the DNA report back. Especially after I saw pictures of your father." She reached in her purse and pulled out a photograph. "This is my great-grandfather, Philip Masters."

Miss Charlotte studied it for a moment, and her eyes filled with tears. Julia peered over her shoulder. The little boy in the picture was standing beside an iron fence in front of a small, neat house. A small black dog was looking up at him, his tongue out in a panting, doggy smile. The boy was maybe a year or two older by then, but he was the spitting image of Miss Charlotte's father, except even in the sepia-toned photograph, it was clear that one of his eyes was light and one was dark.

"Where did you get this?" she asked, her voice hardly audible.

"My grandmother gave it to me with some other family pictures and papers before she died a few years ago. They were twins, weren't they? And Miss Alice had to give this one away because of his eyes. Because then people would know."

"Know what?"

"My grandmother said that her aunt, Philip's sister, said there was a rich lady who came to visit sometimes after he came into the family. She said that lady's driver had the same kind of eyes my great-grandfather had. And I just knew that lady wouldn't come visit if that child didn't have something to do with her family, something closer than just being the child of someone who worked for her. Now I just want to know what that connection was."

Miss Charlotte looked at her for a long moment, and Julia couldn't tell if there was sorrow or anger or longing or something else mixed in her expression.

"Why do you think I would know?" she asked finally. "That was well before my time."

"But I was hoping that Miss Alice may have said something to you about it. I suppose it's something that would have been a scandal back in her day, and I wouldn't want to bring up anything that would hurt you, Miss Charlotte, but I want to know." Jaden winced faintly. "I was hoping there would be something in Miss Alice's diary that would explain everything."

Miss Charlotte raised one eyebrow. "I presume Mrs. Foley and Mrs. Bellefontaine have told you that the diary was stolen from me two nights ago. Whatever is in there is lost now."

Jaden exhaled heavily. "Are you sure? Maybe Julia and Meredith can find whoever took it."

"I think," Julia said quietly, "that it's still in the house."

Jaden and Miss Charlotte both stared at her.

"In the house?" Jaden asked.

"Nonsense," Miss Charlotte said. "I told you I saw someone—"

"You saw someone small enough to get out through the powder room window and big enough to spring up to the top of your garden wall. Someone who left no footprints anywhere and who didn't break in."

"Poppycock."

"Was there something in that diary you didn't want anyone to know, Miss Charlotte?"

Miss Charlotte huffed. "You are impertinent, Mrs. Foley. I think it's time you left. I think it's time all of you left."

"Is it because Miss Alice's father wasn't really her father?" Jaden blurted out.

Miss Charlotte's face went white.

"I found out I'm related to you, ma'am, but not to your cousin Richard. He was the nephew of Miss Alice's father. Why wouldn't we both be related to him?"

"Don't be silly, Miss Browning," Miss Charlotte sputtered. "There could be any number of reasons. Someone on that side of the family—"

"Is that what Richard was trying to blackmail you about?" Julia asked suddenly. "Why he's always thought his family should have inherited the Delorme holdings rather than Miss Alice? I don't think it was the chair being broken that he came to tell you about earlier. I don't think that chair was broken at all."

"I know that," Miss Charlotte said. "I knew those foolish notes came from him in the first place. That's why I wanted you to leave the whole matter alone. Since he couldn't have the estate, he was just hoping to scare me into giving him some money. I never gave him two thoughts over it. He didn't have any proof of anything."

"You mean he didn't have proof of anything without the diary, isn't that right?" Julia asked. "He found it and looked at it enough to find out something about your family you didn't want getting out. So you said the diary had been stolen so he wouldn't have anything to blackmail you with."

"You are impertinent," Miss Charlotte repeated, but this time her voice shook. "There is nothing in my family that won't bear the most intense scrutiny. I don't know anything about these DNA tests or what they mean. Miss Browning's great-grandfather does bear a resemblance to my father, it's true, but that doesn't mean they are related. And for you to imply that my great-great-grandmother was somehow false to her husband is highly offensive. I won't hear of it.

Not in my own home. Her memory, Grandmama's memory, I won't have them tarnished by your wild accusations. I won't—"

"Miss Charlotte," Brenda interrupted quietly. "Don't you think it's time?"

Miss Charlotte lifted her chin defiantly but then said nothing.

"It doesn't matter now," Brenda continued. "They know most of it. Are you going to let them think that Miss Alice's mother wasn't a good woman? A good, faithful wife? Isn't that worse than the truth? Especially now?"

"Brenda, I can't—"

Brenda took Miss Charlotte's frail hand, rubbing it soothingly between her own. "Do you know what my grandma told me about when Miss Alice died?" She looked over at the other three in the room, Julia, Meredith, and Jaden, and then back at Miss Charlotte. "She told me that, just before she died, after she had her little talk with you, that she was more at peace than anytime Grandma could remember before then. Grandma helped raise you and loved you like her own, Miss Charlotte. You know that. She couldn't bear to see the burden you carried after Miss Alice told you the truth. Whatever it was, don't you think it's time you let it go too?"

"Don't you know?"

"It's the only thing about you I don't know," Brenda said, "but it's not something you should have to carry anymore, Miss Charlotte. It should never have been your burden in the first place."

Miss Charlotte sat for several seconds with her eyes locked on Brenda's, saying nothing. Then she put her free hand over her eyes and dropped her head. Brenda still held on to her hand, still gently soothing it.

"Miss Charlotte," she murmured. "Let it go. Please, let it go."

"Miss Charlotte?" Jaden said softly. "There's one other thing you ought to see. Along with the photos and other things my grandmother gave me, she also gave me this."

She handed Miss Charlotte a yellowed piece of paper that crackled with age. Miss Charlotte opened it and held it with both hands. She took so long reading it, Julia was sure she must have read over it twice or more. Finally, she handed it to Julia, and with Meredith scanning it over her shoulder, Julia read it too.

Chapter Twenty

My precious grandson,

You cannot know, perhaps you can never understand, why I must give you to someone else, why I must never acknowledge you, why I can never see you or hold you again. It does not matter why, only that this is the way it must be. It is for the sake of your brother, the brother who will never know you, the brother you will never know, and for the sake of your poor, broken father from whom I might also be separated forever. Your mother, may God bring her His rest, surely knows all now. I pray she understands and that you will one day do the same.

I have made provision for you, dear child, so that you need never suffer want because of what I am forced to do. And I have made sure that the family I have given you to will love you as their own, as your own mother and father would have done if I had not made such foolish choices in my own unfortunate youth. I will always keep watch over you. You

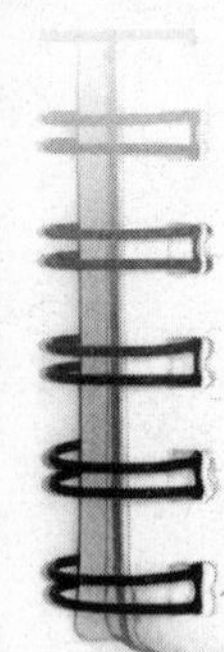

will not know it, but I will hear of your every success and your every achievement, and I will rejoice over them.

I cannot give you our name, but I can give you my love and pray that God will bless and keep you and that, somehow, you will forgive me.

Grandmama

Julia looked at Meredith, more puzzled than ever now.

"I don't understand."

"That was Grandmama's," Miss Charlotte said, a catch in her voice. "I know it is, the handwriting and the words. It was Grandmama's. My grandmama's."

"Then it's true," Jaden said. "My great-grandfather and your father were twins."

Briefly closing her eyes, Miss Charlotte nodded.

"But I don't understand why she had to give up one of her grandsons," Jaden said. "Was it only because he looked different? If it was something her mother did, why does Miss Alice say it's her fault?"

"And what about Teddy?" Meredith asked.

"Teddy?" Miss Charlotte caught a hard breath and looked up. "What do you know about Teddy?"

"We noticed that he always turned his head for photographs, and his eyes looked dark," Julia told her, "but in that picture with the pony, his head is turned the other way. His eye on that side is light. He had heterochromia, didn't he?"

Again, Miss Charlotte nodded.

"He couldn't have been Miss Alice's father," Meredith said, "but they could have had the same father, and that's how that trait was passed down to him and, eventually, to Miss Alice's grandson."

"Yes," Miss Charlotte said. "They had the same father, but it's not what you think. It's not what you think."

"Miss Charlotte," Brenda soothed. "Let me get you some tea."

"No." Miss Charlotte drew herself up straight and clutched her cane again. "No, Brenda. Bring me the diary. It's in—"

"I know where it is. I'll get it."

"You knew where it was all the time?" Julia asked, dumbfounded.

"Not all the time. No, ma'am. But after I thought about things for a while, I did a little looking around on my own. Miss Charlotte, you don't think that, after all these years, I don't know your hiding places? But I didn't read the diary. I would never do that without your permission."

For a moment, Miss Charlotte looked as if she were going to be angry, but she only sighed. "I didn't realize you knew where I—"

"Miss Charlotte," Brenda said quickly, "just because I know where it was hidden doesn't mean everyone else needs to."

There was a touch of a wry smile on Miss Charlotte's face. "Very well. If you will, please bring it down."

When Brenda returned and put the diary in her hands, Miss Charlotte sat holding it, looking at the cover as if she were able to read it without opening it.

"Grandmama wrote about it all in here. Some of it I knew about, some of it I didn't. Some of it she told me when we had our last talk."

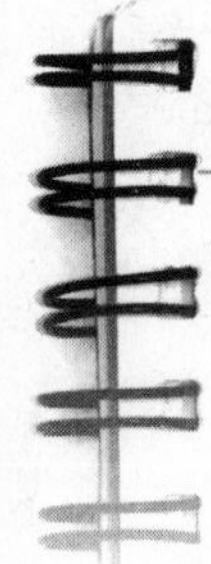

Savannah
May 1949

Charlotte looked at me, her young, innocent eyes full of confusion and disbelief.

"But, Grandmama—"

"It's the truth," I told her, my hands gripping her slender shoulders.

Somehow, after all these years of hiding, of covering things up, of lying, I had finally said it. I had finally told the truth. Maybe it was more than I should have burdened her with, but I knew I could trust her with my secrets.

"For your own sake now, I want you to go on, to honor the Delormes and the Lockwoods in the only way we have left." I put my arms around her and pulled her as close as I was able. "I know what I did was wrong, but it seemed so easy at the time. When my mother and brother said it was what we should do, I wasn't strong enough to tell them no. I'd been so very ill and I was so tired. And, after all, everyone in the family was dead. They wouldn't know. They wouldn't care."

"But you couldn't. You couldn't do such a terrible thing," she said, pushing away from me. "You had no right. Oh, Grandmama."

"I know." I felt the familiar wrenching of my heart, a pain that hadn't lessened even with the passage of more than seventy years. "I know. I've wanted to confess my wrong from the very first, but my mother was there, urging me along, telling me it didn't matter now that it was done, and what would we

do if anyone found out? And what if they put me in jail for my brazen lies? And my brother...oh, sometimes he made me afraid. It was just little things here and there, but I knew he wouldn't be happy if anyone found out. I wasn't sure what he might do."

"But when they were gone," Charlotte said, the tears welling up in her eyes now. "When they were gone, couldn't you have—"

"By then, after all I had done, I convinced myself it was too late to do any good. The harm was done and couldn't be reversed. My son and his wife were dead, and so was my grandson—your father—and your mother. All I had left is the legacy I had in the estate and the foundation, the good it had done, and the honor I had brought to the family name. And I had you. I had given away one precious child, but I still had you. I couldn't leave you with nothing. I can't leave you with nothing. All I can do is leave you what I've built in the past seventy-three years, what I hope has somehow done some good to outweigh the wrong I've done."

"Grandmama—"

I pulled her close again. "Promise me. Promise me you'll carry on what I've started. What I did was wrong, but think how many people have benefitted since then. All the children that wouldn't otherwise have had parents. All the couples who never would have had children. Everything else that the Lockwood Foundation and the Delorme Estate has become. All of it would be ruined by a scandal like this. All the good that's been done will be forgotten, and only the shame will be left behind me. Please, Charlotte, my darling girl, you're all I have. Don't shame me. When I am gone, there will be nothing left of me but the good name of Alice Delorme Lockwood. Promise me you will honor it and protect it. Promise me."

"I promise," she sobbed, clinging to me now, brokenly weeping. "I promise, Grandmama."

As I held her, I couldn't help remembering how I had clung to my mother so long ago, promising her I would try to do what she had asked of me, fearing I could never be strong enough. But I had carried it all this time, the weight of these years, and my Charlotte, she would be strong enough to bear it too. She would make me proud.

"She didn't tell me all of it that last day," Miss Charlotte said, her voice serene as the tears flowed down her lined cheeks and her withered hands clutching the diary even more tightly. "But she told me what she had been hiding since that terrible epidemic in 1876. Her name was Emily Watson. Her mother was Mrs. Delorme's maid, Beryl. Her brother was Teddy, who looked after her all those years. Alice Delorme died of yellow fever with the rest of her family. Beryl and Teddy convinced Grandmama to take Alice's place. That's why she went to Chicago as soon as she was well enough to go and why she didn't dare come back to the estate for several years afterward. Why she never went out unless she was heavily veiled. Her husband's death gave her an excuse to wear mourning, and when she finally stopped, she was old enough that no one ever realized she wasn't the girl they had known." She took the handkerchief Brenda pressed into her hand but did not use it. "I suppose after all 'Miss Alice' had been through, no one expected her to look the way she had."

"And her son didn't know?" Julia asked, her voice barely above a whisper.

Miss Charlotte shook her head. "She never told him, not even when his twin sons were born and one of them had eyes of different colors. With Teddy having the same condition, Matthew assumed the child was proof of his wife's unfaithfulness. He left before Grandmama could tell him the truth."

Julia remembered the snippet she'd glimpsed from the diary. "*He accused her of terrible things, and now I can never explain—*"

She nodded at the confirmation. "And she couldn't keep the child because it would be evidence of her real identity."

Miss Charlotte looked weary now.

"And I knew then that I had to break my engagement. I could never marry. I couldn't risk having a child or a grandchild whose eyes would give the secret away. Grandmama found the child a home and swore the parents to secrecy. She supported him financially and sent him to the best schools, but she always carried that guilt."

"She chose all this," Jaden said, her chin quivering. "The house and the land and all the rest, all of this over him."

Miss Charlotte reached over and took Jaden's hand. "Please don't think harshly of her. She did wrong, I know that. She knew that. But by then she was so deeply enmeshed in her stolen identity, she couldn't see her way out." Her lips trembled into a smile. "I know how she felt. I want to make it right, but how can I? How can I really? After a century and a half, it has all been long settled. I inherited this place and the foundation legally. What good would publicly shaming myself and Grandmama's memory do now?"

"But you would be free of it, Miss Charlotte," Brenda said quietly. "Miss Alice, the good Lord rest her, pushed her burden onto you before she went on to her reward, but you shouldn't have to carry it anymore. You shouldn't have to worry anymore about someone finding out your secret. It doesn't matter now."

"But what about the scandal? Who would donate to the foundation knowing it was all based on a lie? All those children—"

"What Miss Alice did doesn't change the good the foundation has done," Meredith said. "Surely they would understand."

"I don't know." Miss Charlotte finally brought the handkerchief to her wet eyes. "I thought if I said the diary had been stolen, Richard would give up his silly blackmail idea. And how could I confront him with what he'd done when I'd been living a lie all this time? When he could ruin everything by speaking out? Oh, I wish I could leave everything to him. His branch of the family would have inherited all this if Grandmama hadn't done what she did. He ought to have it now, but I know I can't trust him with it. He doesn't love the estate. He doesn't love the work the foundation does. If only Jeff were old enough..."

She trailed off, and then her expression brightened. She was still holding on to Jaden's hand, and she leaned a little closer.

"Miss Browning. I suppose I may call Jaden you since I am your first cousin twice removed."

Jaden smiled a little.

"What did you expect from me, Jaden, when you came here?"

"I wanted to know about my family. I wanted to know why my grandfather was disowned. I know how it is when people stare because my eyes aren't the same color. I suppose it was worse in my great-grandfather's day. I guess I wanted to find out if he had been given up for adoption because of how he looked. It made me mad, I guess. It makes me mad to find out that was true, but at least the reason for it wasn't only because he would have been unacceptable to the family."

"And you weren't expecting any kind of inheritance?" Miss Charlotte asked. "Because, as you can see now, there is nothing you're entitled to."

"No, ma'am, I know that. I meant it when I said I didn't want anything. But I would like to write your story. Miss Alice's story."

Miss Charlotte looked at her for a very long moment, and then she cupped Jaden's cheek in her frail hand. "I want you to write that book, my dear. I want you to read this diary and look at my photographs and all my mementoes and write the story of Alice Delorme and of Emily Watson Lockwood. Grandmama made a foolish decision all those years ago, a weak one, and I took on her burden because I didn't want to shame her."

"You tried to do the right thing with what you knew."

"And so did she." Miss Charlotte patted Jaden's cheek and then picked up the diary in both hands. "I'm going to give this to you. Read it and try to understand who she was and why she did what she did, and write that book. And when I am gone, you publish it. I will pay you to write, and I will be very generous with you in my will, all provided that you keep your silence until the Delorme inheritance is returned to those who should have had it all along."

Julia and Meredith looked at each other and then smiled. Had Meredith come to the same conclusion?

"Jeff," they said simultaneously.

Miss Charlotte nodded, a new light in her faded eyes. "He's young yet. I can't leave everything to him right now, but he'll be old enough soon. He was raised here and has worked here for the past few years already. I could trust him with all of it. I could trust him to make me and Grandmama and even Miss Alice, the real Miss Alice, proud." This time she took both of Jaden's hands in her own, looking earnestly into her differently colored eyes. "What do you think, my dear? Will you wait?"

Tears brimming, Jaden nodded. "Yes, ma'am. I'll wait. And I promise that I'll do my best to tell Emily and Alice's story in way that will please you. And yours." She squeezed Miss Charlotte's hands. "I'm sure I'll have a lot of questions to ask you while I'm writing, and you can help me get it all just right."

"I'm sure I'll enjoy that very much." Miss Charlotte reached over to clasp Brenda's hand with hers and Jaden's. "And my dear Brenda, my very dear Brenda, will help us along the way."

***

"I never expected that," Meredith said as they drove back to the office. "I thought we had it all worked out about Miss Alice's mother having an affair or Teddy being the father of the twins or something. But Miss Alice not being Miss Alice at all? I don't think I'd have ever guessed that one."

"Me neither," Julia said with a shake of her head. "But that does explain what Richard was trying to blackmail Miss Charlotte over and why she pretended the diary had been stolen. She sure went through a lot all this time trying to cover up for what her great-grandmother did."

"Yeah," Meredith said, "and she looked so happy when she was talking to Jaden about what she's going to do. With the money and the property and everything. Jeff's the perfect choice. Sometimes it takes a while to see what's right in front of you."

Just then, Julia got a phone call through the hands-free setup in her car.

"Beau," she said once she'd answered. "What's up?"

"Carmen said you'd gone to see Miss Charlotte again. Did you get everything straightened out?"

"Oh boy, do I have a story to tell you, but only if you can keep a secret for a very long time."

Beau chuckled. "Sure. Are you coming home anytime soon?"

Julia glanced at Meredith. "What do you think? Have we had enough for one day?"

Meredith nodded wearily. "I'm still trying to get my mind around everything we just found out."

"Okay," Julia told Beau. "I am definitely coming home soon. All I have to do is drop Meredith at her car. Why? Is something going on?"

"Not much. I just thought you ought to pick up more cat food and maybe some food and water bowls that would be Bunny's especially. What do you think?"

Julia couldn't hold back a smile. "Sure. I'll get everything on the way home. What about that bed you were talking about?"

"Yeah, that too. Jack probably won't use it since she always seems to be in ours, but you might as well get her one anyway. I'll see you in a little bit."

"All right, honey. I won't be long."

Meredith frowned at her when she ended the call. "Wait a minute. What's all that for? Did you find a home for Bunny? I guess they'd appreciate starting out with all the stuff she needs."

"Yeah, we found her a home. Like you said, sometimes it takes time to see what's right in front of you. Beau and I talked about it for some time last night. He gave me all these reasons why it was better if we didn't keep Bunny, and when he was done, I just shook my head at him and told him neither of us was fooling anybody. We're keeping her."

Julia thought about how happy Beau had been when they finally made their decision. Beau had already been smitten with little Bunny, and Julia had come to really enjoy the cat's gentle presence.

"Funny how much better you feel," she said, unable to keep from smiling, "when you finally admit the truth."

Dear Reader,

I was so happy to be able to let Julia and Beau adopt little Bunny. At first, Bunny was just going to stay at Julia's until she was well enough to be adopted. But as the story went on, Beau got very attached to her, and I really couldn't bring myself to separate them.

November is National Adopt a Senior Pet Month, and as Julia finds out, there are many advantages to bringing an older dog or cat into your life. Sure, the puppies and kittens are precious, but they can be a handful to train. Older pets are usually already trained and, in general, are much calmer than their juvenile counterparts.

My heart always breaks for the older pets I see in shelters. They were often the beloved companion of many years to someone who has passed away. Not only does the animal suddenly lose its best friend, it loses the comfort and security of its home as well. It trades that love and that home for a cage in a shelter, a cage that might be its whole world for the rest of its life.

Next time you're looking for a new pet, I hope you'll consider one of the older ones. Senior pets are among the most grateful of adoptees, returning many times the love shown to them by someone willing to look past their age and into their eager hearts. You'll be a blessing and be blessed as well.

Love,
DeAnna

About the Author

The author of twenty-three traditionally published books and with more to come, DeAnna Julie Dodson has always been an avid reader and a lover of storytelling, whether on the page, the screen, or the stage. This, along with her keen interest in history and her Christian faith, shows in her tales of love, forgiveness, and triumph over adversity. A fifth-generation Texan, she makes her home north of Dallas with three spoiled cats and, when not writing, spends her free time quilting, cross-stitching, and watching NHL hockey. Her first novels were a trilogy of medieval romances (*In Honor Bound, By Love Redeemed,* and *To Grace Surrendered*) for Crossway Books, and she has since written a number of contemporary mysteries for Annie's Fiction and for Guideposts and has more in the works. Also, as Julianna Deering, she writes the Drew Farthering mysteries set in 1930s England. The series debuted from Bethany House with *Rules of Murder* and is followed by *Death by the Book, Murder at the Mikado, Dressed for Death, Murder on the Moor,* and *Death at Thorburn Hall*. She is represented by Wendy Lawton of the Books & Such Literary Agency.

The Truth Behind the Fiction

One of the most terrifying threats for residents of Savannah in the eighteenth and nineteenth centuries was yellow fever, a hemorrhagic illness that causes sudden death in victims. There was a mystery surrounding the disease. Was it caused by swamp vapors or brought in by immigrants from Savannah's port? Or were poor sanitary conditions to blame? The unsanitary conditions, especially in the poorer parts of town, were certainly a contributing factor, especially since the sewage system left much to be desired, but unknown at that time, the disease itself was carried by the mosquitoes that multiplied during Savannah's hot, humid summer months.

Savannah suffered epidemics in 1820 and in 1854, but the worst was in 1876. Within a period of about two weeks in August that year, 1,065 deaths were attributed to yellow fever, but it is suspected that there may have been many more since some doctors listed the symptoms of the fever as the cause of death in their patients instead of listing the actual disease. Or they called it "intermittent fever," a term that was also used for malaria and other fevers. It was customary for those who were able to do so to leave the city during the height of the summer, but the poorer classes seldom had that luxury.

They were, as a result, more likely to be infected and less likely to have the medical care they needed to survive the disease.

It wasn't until 1900 that it was proven that mosquitoes caused the spread of yellow fever, and in 1905, New Orleans suffered the last yellow fever epidemic in the United States. Two vaccines for yellow fever were developed in the 1930s.

Miss Charlotte's Strawberry Mousse

This is a super easy dessert that will make even a simple meal seem as special as one of Miss Charlotte's teas.

You'll need:

- ¾ pound strawberries
- ½ cup sugar
- 1 cup cold whipping cream
- A few perfect strawberries and more whipped cream for decorative topping

Directions:

Put clean, sliced strawberries and sugar into a blender or food processor and puree.

Pour cream into a cold bowl and whip until stiff peaks form. Gently fold in all but ½ cup puree.

Divide reserved puree into 4 sundae glasses and top with whipped cream/strawberry mixture.

Chill for at least an hour. Add an extra dollop of whipped cream and fresh strawberries on top of that and you have a treat that's as good to look at as it is to eat.

Quick and easy and so delicious!

Read on for a sneak peek of another exciting book in the Savannah Secrets series!

Willful Transgressions

BY KATHLEEN Y'BARBO

MEREDITH BELLEFONTAINE SHIFTED IN HER seat and glanced back to see that Julia Foley, her best friend and partner at Magnolia Investigations, was hurrying up the aisle. It wasn't like Julia to be late, especially to a funeral.

"I'm sorry," she said as she settled down on the church pew and tucked a strand of silver hair behind her ear. "I had car trouble. Beau's car is at the airport, so I had to call a ride share. Anyway, I'm glad you saved me a seat. This place is packed."

"Of course it is. Everyone in Savannah knew Tommy Two."

Tommy Two, whose real name was Thomas Daniel Worthington Jr., was the grandson of Daniel Worthington, a man who owned half of Savannah when he died under mysterious circumstances in 1971. Not literally half, of course, but practically, given the vastness of his real estate holdings and the wealth he had accumulated. Thomas Sr. and his younger brother, Simon, took over the business interests of the Worthington family, but they could never quite manage to control their mother, Wilhelmina.

Now, some sixty years after Wilhelmina Styles Worthington penned her infamous will disinheriting her children and grandchildren from her estate, the clause governing the distribution of the family's millions held in trust and untouchable by any living Worthington had been satisfied. With the death of Tommy Two, the last known surviving grandchild was dead.

Meredith had known Tommy Two as a rather kind man who lived nearby. She'd been shocked when Trey, or Thomas the Third, Tommy's only son and a University of Georgia graduate, had been indicted in a high-profile case involving organized crime's influence in the New York banking industry. Trey agreed to testify, and that was the last anyone heard of him.

Literally.

Around Savannah, the consensus was that Trey Worthington had disappeared into the witness protection program. Some, however, believed the Mob had the final say in his destination—or rather, resting place. Meredith thought of Thomas III on occasion, especially when Georgia played football, and said a prayer that he was alive and safe, wherever he might be.

She leaned to her right to get a better view of the family pew on the front row. Tommy Two's wife, Katherine, died last year, an event that some say sent Tommy Two careening in the same direction at light speed. He lasted seven months once she was gone, a testament to their long and lasting love.

Tommy Two's younger brother, Spencer, lost his life in a boating accident, leaving behind a young widow, Sunny, and twins Kate and Kenneth. Sunny Worthington Conrad, now married to investment banker Chip Conrad IV, sat between her husband and her pretty blond daughter.

Now married with young children, Kate Worthington Collins was a well-loved weather forecaster for the local television station, WSVG. More than once since Meredith sat down Kate had glanced around the room as if she hoped someone was coming.

Likely her brother, since he was absent from the family pew, Meredith decided. Kenneth, also known as Skate—whose profession was skateboarding, according to the scuttlebutt going around at the beauty shop yesterday. Since the two ladies were the only ones other than Chip Conrad to be seated in the family pew, it appeared Kenneth had decided not to attend today.

Trey was missing as well, but then it would have been a bigger surprise to find him here today.

When the service was over, a who's who of Savannah society exited the church and made their way down the white marble steps of the venerable First Baptist Church to await the slow drive to the Bonaventure Cemetery. The Worthington family had kept a mausoleum under the moss-covered oaks since the turn of the last century.

The first Worthington plopped down a few coins for a substantial piece of land in what became downtown Savannah, but unfortunately he didn't stay alive long enough to enjoy it. With the Worthington family, that was apparently a common thing to do.

After weaving her way around the conversations being held on the steps despite the unseasonably warm and humid November morning, Meredith stopped at the sidewalk to wait for Julia. Why was it that her best friend's hair never danced to the tune of Savannah humidity? While Meredith had spent a full half hour trying to keep her curls from turning to frizz, Julia's silky silver tresses were absolutely unaffected.

Meredith didn't dare take a peek at the mirror in her compact. She knew without looking that the latest round of pricy hair products had been bested by the morning air.

"I'm assuming you'll be riding with me," Meredith said when Julia joined her, reminding herself this was a funeral and not a fashion show.

"That's the plan," Julia replied. "Beau will pick me up from the office later." She paused. "You are going back to the office after the graveside service, aren't you? I know some are invited back to the Worthington home for a reception after, but since I'm not in the inner circle of Savannah society, I wasn't included. Were you?"

Meredith had been but probably because of her proximity as a neighbor rather than any sort of social standing she might have. "I hadn't planned on going," was the answer she chose.

It was the truth. She hadn't.

"Julia, Meredith!"

A glance in the direction of whoever called her name showed a somewhat familiar face coming toward her, Attorney Theophilus Tiberius Lucas III. "Theo Lucas," she said when the young lawyer drew near. "Is that you?"

"It is," he called. "Could I have a word with you two?"

"Of course," Julia said.

"It's good to see you," Meredith added. "I was so sorry to hear of your grandfather's passing. I didn't get to speak to you personally at the funeral."

Meredith had certainly attended more than her fair share of funerals in recent days. Just six weeks ago, Theophilus Tiberius Lucas Sr. had opened the back door of Lucas, Wilson, Kyler & Strong, the law office where he had been the senior partner since 1960, as he habitually did every weekday morning at precisely seven thirty-five. Theo Sr. had taken a seat behind the massive desk in his grand office, spreading out his morning reading material of an array of local newspapers in front of him, and then—according to the coroner's report—promptly went home to Jesus while leaving his earthly body dead in his chair.

Despite the fact Theo Sr. had been ninety-seven when he passed, it was a shock to know that he was mortal like everyone else. It was an even bigger shock when the shaggy, bearded grandson, who'd barely made a cameo at his grandfather's funeral, turned up in Savannah as the new Lucas on the office letterhead.

Julia had heard from scuttlebutt around the courthouse that Theo III had slipped right into his grandfather's position as senior partner at the firm despite the fact that he'd barely been out of law school long enough to qualify as a junior partner at any other firm in town. It hadn't taken an insider to know that the more senior attorneys, Kyler, Wilson, and Strong, were not pleased that a kid from Atlanta Legal Aid was occupying the office they had all aspired to. Such was the influence of Theo Sr. that, even from the grave, he was dictating who ran the law office in his absence.

At least the kid from Atlanta Legal Aid had seen the good sense in getting a haircut and having his beard groomed to a more socially acceptable length. Meredith predicted that in six months, when the summer heat hit Savannah, the beard would be gone altogether.

"My grandfather was fond of both of you," Theo said, interrupting her musings about his grooming. "Though he did profess a slight fear when he came before you on any sort of court matter," he added to Julia.

"I cannot imagine why," Julia said.

"According to him, you were the only judge who could see right through his blustering and tell him to get to the point."

"He did tend to be rather long-winded on occasion," Julia admitted with a wry smile. "But always entertaining. And he had a sharp legal mind."

"How can we help you?" Meredith asked, thinking she'd like this Theo to get to the point as well. At this rate, the funeral procession would leave without them and she and Julia would be forced to hike through Bonaventure Cemetery from the back of the parking lot in their heels.

"As I was saying, my grandfather held you both in high regard, so based on that recommendation of your character, I would like to talk to you about a case I am working on." He glanced around then back at them. "Not right here and now, of course. It wouldn't be appropriate, considering the circumstances. But perhaps later today? Or tomorrow?"

"My, you are in a hurry." Meredith exchanged a look with Julia. "Perhaps after the graveside service?" At her partner's nod, she returned her attention to Theo. "Do you know where we're located?"

"I do, and I'll be there after the graveside. Thank you, ladies."

Theo hurried off, leaving Meredith to watch him weave through the remaining stragglers on the sidewalk like a running back heading for the goal line. "Oh my, how he does hurry. What do you want to bet we get back from the graveside and find Theo waiting for us?"

"You think?" Julia said with a grin. "He seems anxious, so you might be right."

After making the hike Meredith had dreaded and listening to the pastor intone his words so softly that mosquitos might have buzzed louder, she and Julia headed back toward their office. Meredith parked in her spot behind the building, and Julia used her key to open the back door and let them both in.

Cool air hit Meredith like a blessing from above, and she smiled. "Oh, that feels so good. Why in the world is it so warm and humid in November? Weren't we all wearing coats just last week?"

"Another cold front is coming, and we'll be back in our coats soon, or so Kate Collins, the weather lady on TV, says." Julia moved through the kitchen and headed toward the front of the building. "Meanwhile, we'll simply deal with the fact that it feels more like summer than fall today."

Meredith kicked off her shoes and reached into the fridge for a bottle of water. "I don't mind either. I would just like to know which season I'm going to get when I wake up in the morning."

"Kate would tell you, if you bothered to watch WSVG in the morning like I do," Julia called.

"The last thing I want to do in the morning is watch the news," Meredith responded as she followed her friend. "Although I do like Kate. And as long as we're stating facts, Kate wasn't on the show this morning, was she, smarty-pants?"

Julia laughed. "You've got me there. No, she wasn't. She was at the funeral."

Their assistant, Carmen Lopez, looked up from her desk and grinned. "Welcome back, ladies. There's a cute guy sitting on the steps. He hasn't buzzed to come in yet, though."

Julia walked to the door and looked out. "Carmen, go out and tell Theo we'll meet with him in the conference room, then grab waters for him and me, please."

"Theo? That's his name?" Her smile broadened. "I wonder if he's single. I've got a friend he'd be perfect for."

"Carmen," Julia said, her tone light as she shook her head. "He's here on business, but he cannot conduct that business out on the steps."

Carmen shrugged. "You two are no fun. I'll go get him, but he is cute and obviously employed, so I'm thinking they'd be perfect for each other."

"Please don't lead with that when you talk to him," Meredith said.

"Which part?" Carmen shrugged. "The 'my bosses are no fun' part or the 'you're a cutie and need to meet my friend' part?"

"How about the part where Carmen is looking for a new job?" Meredith asked with a grin.

Carmen giggled. "Oh please. I can't be gone five minutes without you calling to ask me where something is or how to do something."

Julia laughed. "Sad but true. Still, behave with Theo, okay?"

Carmen crossed her heart with her finger as if making a promise and then headed toward the door.

Meredith, still smiling at their assistant's antics, followed Julia down the hall. They could have hired someone more professional to work the front desk, but where would be the fun in that? Carmen was not only a great assistant, she also brightened the office with her youth and her effervescent personality, knew how to handle people, and was bilingual to boot.

Plus, she was right. Carmen did know where everything was. And when you worked for investigators who were busy handling other things, that job skill was priceless.

"You go on in," Julia said. "I'll be right there. I need to check something on my computer first."

Meredith nodded and stepped inside the conference room. Situated in the back of the first floor opposite Julia's office, for more than two decades the conference room had been her husband Ron's office. All of that changed a few days ago when the remodel of the room was completed.

The walls had been repapered in a pale yellow silk that was true to the era of the home. Ron's old walnut desk had been moved to Meredith's office, and the rest of his office furniture was relegated to the attic at her house until the boys decided if they wanted any of it. In the center of the room, an elegant rosewood table, purchased at auction and rumored to once have been in the dining room at the governor's mansion, stood beneath a crystal chandelier.

Whether or not the story was true, Meredith loved the beautiful classic lines of the table and the six chairs that had come with the set. The armchairs, meant to go at the ends of the table, were now placed on either side of the fireplace and accessorized with tapestry pillows she'd found at a local antique store. The remaining four chairs were in pairs opposite each other at the table.

Lush Boston ferns on antique iron plant stands stood in front of each of the windows, softening the old shutters that had been repainted with the same warm ivory paint Meredith used on the woodwork in her office at home. Meredith had vetoed the plants as too much work, but Carmen had promised to tend the ferns, so they stayed.

While the room was lovely, a cozy haven and a sunny space where they could meet with clients, it was also the place that held the most memories of Ron. This was a good thing, she reminded herself as she let out a long breath. Good memories were the best way of remembering.

If only the good memories didn't still hurt just a little.

And on some days, maybe more than just a little.

Meredith settled at the table, facing the wall where Ron's plat map of historical Savannah now hung over the fireplace. Lots of good work had been done in this room. By her and by Ron.

"Thank You, Lord," she whispered, "that the work continues. May it be done to Your glory."